FIXED *up* EVER *after*

A NEW BEGINNINGS ROMANCE NOVEL

ANASTASIA DEAN

For my younger self who needed to see a romance story with a plus size queen

Author's Note

This book contains elements of:

- Death of a loved one (off page)
- Fatphobic comments toward the FMC
- Struggles multiracial people face (specifically identity)
- Panic / anxiety attack
- Explicit sexual scenes

Please make sure you are protecting your mental health. If you need more information, send me a message on any of my socials. Otherwise, happy reading!

CHAPTER 1

Lola

Lola Roberts managed a feeble smile at her sister's engagement news, even when Marisol announced she would be marrying Archie, Lola's ex-boyfriend. It was fine. Totally and completely fine. In fact, Marisol did her a favor. No woman in their right mind would voluntarily agree to marry a guy with the first name of Archibald, as if they were living in their own little version of Bridgerton.

Sir Archibald of Douche Baggery and Lady Marisol of Back Stabbery.

Honestly, they were a match made in hell. A business exchange disguised as two people happily engaged. Or as happy as Marisol could be. She rarely saw her sister smile and for most of her life, Lola didn't think Marisol was capable. Except someone turned up the wattage inside her brain and her radiant smile lit up the room. She clung to Archie like pet hair to black clothing.

Their manufactured happiness disgusted her.

Not as much as her mother's over-the-top reaction though. Her stone-hearted mother openly wept over the news and expressed how proud she was of Marisol. Their mother, Luciana, thrived on material goods and a well-rounded image. Lola, her youngest daughter, had never been able to fit into the box crafted for her.

Her hair was too unkempt. She was too fat. Her clothes weren't by the right designer. Her job didn't scream luxury. She didn't befriend the right people. The list went on, but thinking anymore about all the ways she came up short in her family would make her spiral. And she couldn't do that without a strong drink in her hand.

No one noticed as she left the table, too consumed with admiring the giant rock on Marisol's left hand. It was a miracle her petite sister could even carry it on her slender finger without breaking a bone. She wondered if the ring had originally been made for her when she believed Archie would propose, but like everything else in Lola's life, the ring and the man went to Marisol.

"They sure are good-looking, aren't they?" the bartender asked. Unconsciously, she had made her way over to the open bar, the one positive thing her family did at special dinners.

"Sure. If you can look past their superficial facade, then I guess they look good together." So she was feeling petty, but her sister marrying her ex would do that to a person. She deserved to be a little bit of a bitch.

The poor bartender fumbled for something to say, but clearly, his classes on mixology had not prepared him for Lola's particular brand of sulking. She spared the man by requesting whatever beer he had on tap. He fluttered away, all too happy to get away from her.

The gray cloud in the room.

As far as Lola was concerned, she had two options right

now: she could sulk and drink away her sadness, or she could do something brave to wipe her mind of the last hour.

Sulking was always a safe option. She could throw herself a literal pity party back in her hotel room—complete with ice cream, pizza, those little street tacos she liked so much, and cake because every party deserved cake. Basically she wanted all the foods her mother would normally chastise her about while never letting her forget how many carbs and calories she was consuming.

"Dolores, do you think you'll magically lose the baby fat if you keep eating like a high school boy?" Her mother would constantly nag, no matter how many times Lola asked her not to. The "baby fat" was just fat at this point. She was twenty-four, but her mother still treated her like a teenager who lived under her roof.

Thank goodness she didn't. Lola had been put through enough fad diets under her mother's watchful eye to last a lifetime. Her mother couldn't fathom how Lola liked her body. As if bigger bodies weren't worthy or desirable.

Lola was far from cocky, but she knew she looked good, even with her thick thighs, soft belly, and heart-shaped face. It took her a long time to appreciate the body she had, but when she stopped hating herself for simply existing in a bigger body, her life got tremendously better. She found clothes that showed off her curves. Learned how to style her thick curls and watched countless YouTube videos of plus-size beauty influencers doing their makeup until she found a routine that worked for her face structure.

She was thriving. Until she'd met Archie and lost the woman she was in order to become the woman best suited to be on the arm of a future CEO of a multimillion-dollar company.

If she were a character from one of those superhero movies her father enjoyed so much, this would be her villain origin story.

A cold, pale beer was placed in front of her, giving Lola a reprieve from her wayward thoughts. The bartender disappeared, as if afraid she'd rope him into another off-putting conversation. "Coward," she mumbled under her breath, bringing the beer to her lips and taking a sip. The rich coldness of the beer sent a jolt of electricity through her, stiffening her spine.

It was exactly the shock her body needed to get out of the funk this whole engagement dinner put her in. She still couldn't believe she voluntarily got on a plane from Florida to fly to where her sister lived in California, only to walk into this messy disaster. No one seemed to care how she felt, so why should she give these people power over her? It was time to pull up her big girl panties and take matters into her own hands.

She needed a way to leave this crappy family function because there was no way she could spend another second watching Archie and Marisol pretend to be in love. What she needed was a good, old-fashioned hookup. And thanks to the wonderful world of dating apps, Lola did not have to search far.

With newfound vigor, she swiped up on her phone, letting face recognition unlock it. Her finger hovered for a second until she remembered what folder she put the dating app in. "Dating app" was probably not the best name because she doubted anyone had found love amongst a pack of horny people. Its purpose was hookups and that was what she needed.

The app opened under her manicured finger. It had been months since she last used it. The last two times had been a week after Archie broke up with her and again when she learned he had started dating her sister. So she had a few security questions she needed to answer before it restored her profile.

The red dot at the bottom of the screen indicated she had unread messages in her inbox. After a quick scan, she determined they were all over two months old and promptly deleted them. They served her no purpose now. Instead, she fell down the rabbit hole of endlessly swiping left on countless men.

There was a whole damn sea of them. She didn't consider herself picky, but she could only handle so many profile pics of men holding fish. Most of these men were as white as her father and definitely didn't want a plus-size half-Mexican woman.

No, she needed a man who could handle all of her for one night.

Out of the legion of men, only one caught her eye. His name was Javier and his dark eyes held a certain warmth that drew her in. His golden-brown skin stood out against the white of his shirt, pulled taut at the chest. He sat alone in his photo, smiling wide at whoever took the picture.

Scrolling through his brief bio, Lola discovered he was adventurous, enjoyed video games, and loved horror movies. Next to the job box, he stated he worked in construction. That was evident in his well-toned biceps, which were covered from wrist to shoulder with tattoos.

Lola was a sucker for a man with tattoos. It was one of her weaknesses. Which made her relationship with Archie so odd. He was as vanilla as they came, and yet she had bent over backward for him, lost in her weird, out-of-character obsession.

A boisterous laugh from the table brought her attention back toward her family. Her father's pale cheeks were a bright tomato red from laughing at something Archie said. Marisol laughed politely, still hanging on his shoulder. Next to her father stood her mother, fussing over Marisol's hair. Lola tried not to make eye contact, but Luciana was a damn lioness, sensing prey from miles away. Their eyes met briefly and then Luciana bent over to whisper something in her father's ear before making a beeline for Lola.

Before her mom got too close, Lola sent off a quick message to the stranger on the app. She cut straight to the point, not wanting to waste their time, and mentioned she was only here for one night. Once the message went through, she clicked her screen off.

"Dolores, what are you doing all the way over here? You should be with your family, congratulating your sister. This is a very important day for her." Her mother's posh voice grated on her nerves.

Luckily, Lola had a wonderful poker face. She plastered on the same fake smile she wore in most of her staged family photos. She did a decent job at convincing people she was happy because no one ever questioned her. "They're getting quite enough attention without me, Mom."

"Oh, please, don't be like that," her mother chided. "Don't start a scene or ruin this night for your sister. If not for her, do it for me."

Now she really had to hold her tongue. Did no one remember that Archie had been Lola's boyfriend first? How they were together for almost two years before he cut her out of his life like an expired coupon, only to immediately get into a relationship with her perfect sister not even a month later?

But of course, *she* was the one causing a scene. Typical. Fortunately, she was used to being the black sheep of the family.

Lola opened her mouth to say something that would only dig her into a deeper hole when her phone chimed. She looked down and read the notification that popped up. A smile crept over her features.

> You don't have to ask me twice. I'll be there in an hour.

"Dolores, are you listening to me?" Her mother's patience ran thin, but for once she didn't care.

"No, sorry. I have to go. A friend is waiting for me."

"A friend?" Her shrill voice suggested she didn't believe Lola was capable of making friends. Which, ouch. "This is your sister's engagement dinner! What friend could be more important than this?"

"A new friend. Goodbye, Mom. Give Marisol my best."

Luciana sputtered incoherent nonsense as she left the overly priced private dining room. Not once did she look back.

She had a hookup to meet.

CHAPTER 2

Javi

There were times in Javi's life where he had done questionable things, like the time he set a dumpster on fire to see if it truly did smell as bad as his friends said it did. Spoiler alert, it smelled worse.

Teenage Javi was a terror and had no reason to be so feral. But since becoming a father who worked full time to provide for his six-year-old daughter—who was only getting more expensive as she aged—he thought he had become a more mature, well-rounded person.

Certainly not the type of person that downloaded hookup apps, dropped his daughter off at his sister's house, and drove forty-five minutes to a fancy hotel in the rich part of town to get some action.

Except that was exactly what he was doing.

How the hell had he become so desperate? Well, he knew the answer to that, though he hated to think about his time with Estella. He had fallen so head over heels in love with her, he planned on making Estella his wife.

That was five years ago, but the grief never fully left him. In many ways, Javi felt responsible for Estella's death, no matter how many times his sister or father told him there wasn't anything he could have done. He didn't believe their lies, but appreciated the comfort they attempted to give him.

Since Estella, he hadn't pursued another relationship. He had many excuses as to why, most notably his lack of free time. He juggled being the best father he could be to Camilia and the rest of the time was spent at his job.

As if working hard, long days would allow him to escape any emotions still lingering after Estella's death. The minuscule amount of free time he had was spent with Camilia, who was growing so fast. Javi didn't want to be an absent father like his own father had been. He wanted Camilia to have memories of him at all her important life events and never doubt how much he loved her.

Going out tonight was a big fucking deal. He wrestled between guilt and acceptance. He deserved a night of fun without feeling like he was a bad dad for leaving his daughter behind. He wanted—no, *needed*—physical touch from a woman who desired him on a simply superficial level.

So all of that to say, he might have been feeling lonely. He hadn't been celibate since Estella's passing—he was no monk —but the last time he took a woman to bed had been over a year ago. The urge for sex had been easy to ignore, but suddenly it was getting harder to block out those urges. Seeing how happy his sister was with her husband and their new son made him miss the touch and comfort of another person.

That was the only reason he pulled into the labyrinthine parking garage. He shoveled out an exuberant amount of money just to leave his car behind so he could meet a woman named Dolores.

Actually, he was going to do a hell of a lot more than meet with her, and that unnerved him.

Javi was not a one-night stand sort of man. He was not sure what kind of man he was, but it was not this. Maybe teenage Javi, but that had changed after Estella. Then changed again once Estella died. He was an anomaly.

A fucking horny anomaly.

The hotel looked like something he'd only ever seen in spy movies, where the millionaire criminals hid amongst the unsuspecting wealthy. The building had to be at least twenty stories high, and from that vantage point, probably overlooked the entire city. He always wanted to see what downtown San Francisco looked like from a bird's-eye view. At night it would be lit up, twinkling beneath him like millions of tiny stars.

Javi knew this place was fancy when a literal doorman greeted him on the way. His job was rather unnecessary considering the doors were automatic, but he smiled at the man nonetheless.

"Where is the bar?" Javi asked, stepping inside.

The blond man smiled and pointed his finger to the right. "If you see the restaurant, you've gone too far."

"Thank you." Javi made his way through the lobby and off to the right like the man indicated. Nerves began to set in, but so did an undercurrent of excitement. He was about to taste a forbidden fruit. He shouldn't indulge, but why pass up the fruit when both parties consented and wanted to feel good for one night?

His phone buzzed in his pocket and he pulled it out to see a message from Dolores. He clicked on the notification, quickly scanning the message.

At the bar. I'm in pink.

Another text popped up, but this time from his sister who was watching Camilia. It was a photo of Camilia and her two-year-old cousin Arturo wrapped up in a *Paw Patrol* blanket. The corners of Javi's lips pulled up into a smile and he saved the photo before pocketing his phone.

The bar was hard to miss. A giant horse fountain indicated he had found their arranged meeting spot.

Not many people occupied the stools: an elderly couple sipping champagne, a man in a full tuxedo with his tie askew, a middle-aged woman with twin boys running around her feet, and finally his eyes landed on the woman dead center.

She wore a blush-pink eyelet dress that went down to her mid-thighs. He only knew the term "eyelet" because his mother had been into sewing and mended plenty of clothes. The woman's beautiful golden-brown skin shined under the chandelier. She was giving him a sneak peek at her legs, and Javi couldn't tear his gaze away from her thighs. He drifted closer to get a better look.

After what was probably an inappropriate amount of time staring, his gaze slowly traveled up the dress, to where the thin fabric strained against her hips and chest. When he finally reached her face, she was staring back at him. Her muddy-brown eyes challenged him as if to say, *"Can you handle me?"*

God, he hoped so.

If she wanted to honor him by suffocating him between her thighs or working him past his breaking point, then Javi would say he'd experienced a life well lived. He couldn't envision a better way to go than with this goddess sitting on his face.

"Have you decided if you are staying or leaving yet?" a sultry voice spoke, going through him like molten-hot lava as it settled in his core. She said the words so carelessly, but her searching gaze told him she wasn't nearly as confident or relaxed as she pretended to be.

Because he was an idiot, he still didn't respond nor made any attempts at moving forward. *Good fucking job, Javi. She's going to think you're a virgin who is about to see tits for the first time.*

Her gaze darkened as she took another sip of her cocktail. "You're Javier, right?" she asked.

When his voice decided to come back to him, he nodded once. "Javi. Are you Dolores?" She obviously was, but his brain decided now was the time to do a full system reboot.

"Lola," she corrected, "I just go by Lola." She gestured to the spot next to her, repeating the question from earlier. "Now that you've seen me, are you staying or leaving?"

His brow furrowed. What did she mean by that? He saw her in her photos and she caught his attention on a purely superficial level. He read her bio and she seemed like an amazing woman, but he knew this arrangement was only for tonight. He didn't want to invest in a woman he would no longer see.

She was so fucking beautiful. His treacherous body was already reacting to her. "Why would I leave?" He took the spot next to her and called the bartender over to order himself a whiskey. He needed some liquid courage to give him the confidence he was lacking when faced with a sexy woman.

Dolores—no, Lola—looked surprised by his answer, but shrugged. "No reason," she said and took another long sip of her cocktail. It was already half gone; he would need to drink his own quickly because he didn't want to keep her waiting.

A long moment of awkward silence stretched out between them. When he found his voice, Lola opened her mouth to speak and Javi's words turned into a weird, whistled groan.

Lola at least had the decency to pretend that she didn't notice his nerves. "So, you should probably know that I don't normally do things like this."

The tension in his shoulder subsided and he sighed in relief. Of course, he would not judge her if she hooked up with strangers often, but it felt like solidarity to know he was not alone in this. "Neither do I."

"And I'm not going to ask you the reason you agreed to…"

She made a weird gesture with her hands that made Javi raise a brow. "Sex?" he supplied.

The faintest blush heated her cheeks, but was gone a second later. "Yes, sex. So I think we should set some ground rules before I take you back to my hotel room."

The conversation came to a natural pause as the bartender placed Javi's drink in front of him. He picked it up, just as a flash from a camera went off. Lola unabashedly had her phone out and was pointing it right at him.

"Did you take my picture?"

"I did," she said, typing out something on her phone before placing it down on the bar counter. "And I sent it to my best friend so if you are planning on murdering me, she'll send your ass to jail so quickly that my body will still be warm when she finds me."

At that, Javi nodded. "Your friend's a cop?"

"No, baker. Why?"

"No reason." It was his turn to smile, hiding it behind his crystal glass. He probably should have asked the price of this whiskey, but it was too late now.

"Anyway, I needed to threaten you. Do you feel threatened, Javi?"

"Oh, most thoroughly. Go on, what is your next rule?"

"This is a one-night thing. After tonight, I'm deleting the

app. It will be easier if we both agree on this to alleviate a messy situation for after."

That was easy enough to agree with. It was the reason he was here. Javi was still not in a place where he could handle a relationship and from the looks of it, neither was Lola. They both had an itch to scratch and they were each other's backscratchers. That was it.

"I'm pretty much open to anything, but I don't like being blindfolded or called derogatory names in bed," she added. "Tied up is fine though, but I doubt it will come to that."

Just then a vision of Lola, lips slightly parted, chest heaving, and tied spread eagle to the bed, emerged in his brain. He imagined her panting and begging for him, demanding him to fuck her until both of them passed out from sheer exhaustion.

The thoughts went straight to his dick and he cursed. The last thing he needed was to be walking around with a boner, announcing to the entire hotel what they were about to do. He tried to readjust himself covertly, but Lola's eyes trailed down his body, straight to his crotch. His cock stiffened as if to say, *"Hello."*

Fucking hell.

With a sly smile on her lip, Lola brought her attention back up. "Is anything off the table for you?"

He racked his brain hard—pun intended—to come up with some sort of answer to her very reasonable question, but not even five minutes ago, he was prepared to die by thigh suffocation. There wasn't a whole lot off the table for him.

He settled on, "Nothing comes to mind, but if it does, I'll be sure to tell you."

Lola nodded. "Wait, did you bring a condom?"

"I brought several, actually." He said, ignoring the glare from the elderly couple who heard Lola say the word condom.

They were young once. They should know how it felt. And honestly, they should be happy that they were being safe. Safe sex was never a reproachful topic.

Taking the final sip of her cocktail, Lola placed her glass on the table before pushing off her high chair. Her dress rode up to dangerous territory and Javi didn't know he was staring until he caught her smirk.

"Well let's go. The night isn't getting any younger and I need a good distraction after my hellish day."

Javi did not get the opportunity to ask what she meant, because Lola was already walking toward the elevator. "Are you coming?" she called over her shoulder.

He wasn't coming yet, but he intended to by the end of the night.

Javi downed the last of his whiskey, ignoring the burn down his throat. He threw money on the table, hoping it would cover the cost, before racing after Lola.

CHAPTER 3

Lola

Faking confidence was a skill Lola learned at a young age. Chubby chicks always had to exude extra confidence for simply existing. The moment she let her guard down, someone always had to remind her that she was fat. As if that was a secret and not the reality of Lola's everyday life.

Over the years, her feigned self-assurance morphed into acceptance. No, she was not conventionally skinny, nor did she fit societal beauty standards like her mother and sister, but her body was a damn temple and she was a goddess. Even Aphrodite had rolls and she was considered to be the most beautiful goddess of them all.

It did not matter what her parents, sister, or anyone at that damn engagement party thought of her. Right now the only important opinion was her own and Javi's, since she was taking the very hot and muscular man back to her room. Teenage Lola was freaking out because Javi looked like a member from one of the countless boy band photos she hung up on her wall like a religious shrine.

He was wearing a skintight, black, long-sleeved shirt, rolled up to his elbows. Decorating both arms were beautiful and intricate tattoos that she wanted to study. His hair was cropped short and styled with more product than she probably used in her own hair. He had a beard and whispers of a mustache trimmed close to his face. Lola's dirty thoughts conjured up the feeling of those fine hairs brushing her between her thighs. It sent a delicious jolt down her spine.

Even if the sex sucked she would forever summon the image of him for her spank bank for months to come.

Her overpriced hotel room was a gift from her father for flying from Florida to California in order to attend her sister's engagement party. She had not known that at the time, and wouldn't have agreed to come if she did. No doubt her mother made her father keep it a secret since she was certain they had known.

Opening the door to her room, they were greeted by an extended hallway leading toward another area in the suite. Off to the left was the bathroom with a large walk-in shower and a claw-foot tub, adding a vintage element to the space. She reached back for Javi's hand, leading him down the hallway and into her bedroom.

Floor-to-ceiling windows took up most of the wall. The view was pretty, though not as nice as the view from the main room, and Lola did not bother with the curtains because they were too far up for anyone to see them. The moonlight shining in through the windows provided enough light for them to see each other without having to turn on the harsh, unnatural lights of the room. It seemed less intimate this way.

That was the kind of vibe Lola was going for. She wanted no confusion over what this was and what they would be doing. Javi did not seem like the stalkerish type or a man that overstayed his welcome, but she had been wrong before when it came to making assumptions about a beautiful man.

Lola reached down to unclasp her heels before kicking them off and turning to Javi who was still taking in the extravagant room. Sometimes she forgot that not everyone was in her father's tax bracket and she appreciated when people humbled her. She never wanted to lose touch with reality like her parents.

Or her sister.

"Do you want a tour, or do you want to take my clothes off and rail me?"

Her crude words made Javi blink, swiveling his head back toward her. A small smile creased the sides of his lips and Lola felt an invisible pull toward him. She wondered how many panties dropped for this man when he smiled at a girl like that. Did he know what power he possessed with those lips and that smile?

"Nah, I've seen enough. I choose the second option," he said and stepped closer to Lola. She took an involuntary deep breath at his proximity. She probably should feel embarrassed about it, but there was a certain freedom in knowing she would never see this man again. She did not have to put on an act and that alone was refreshing.

Lola leaned in, but then stopped once her plump breasts grazed his pecs. "You don't have a wife and baby at home, do you? Or a girlfriend?" She didn't know what possessed her to ask, but she couldn't go through with this if she would be Javi's dirty little secret.

She watched his face, waiting for the lie, but it never came. His eyes remained kind, albeit lustful, and his voice never wavered. "No wife. No girlfriend."

He did not say anything about a baby, but that was the

least of her worries. If she was screwing a dad, then so be it. Even fathers needed to let loose once in a while. Or so she assumed. She had no children or nieces or nephews herself, but she imagined parents had a lot of pent-up frustrations and sex was the perfect outlet.

"Well, lucky me." How no one had snatched this sexy man up was beyond her, but Lola was going to take full advantage of this situation. She pressed against Javi, feeling his hard muscles underneath his clothes. He felt like the type of guy that could handle every inch of her, every curve, and not think twice about throwing her around.

That was exactly what she needed right now. To be thrown around and told what to do. She was usually the dominant one in the bedroom, but after her day she did not want to think. She wanted to be told what to do and be called a good girl when she obeyed. She wanted pleasure for the sake of pleasure and judging by the hungry gleam in his eyes, she guessed Javi wanted the same thing. Or why else would he be here right now?

Lola opened her mouth to say something else, anything to break the increasing tension between them, but her words were swallowed up in Javi's kiss. Thank God. She was prepared to make the first move to get Javi to loosen up, but she was glad she didn't have to. His mouth was warm and wet, tasting of spearmint and whiskey.

A needy moan left her as his arms wrapped around her hips, hands resting on her ass. His large hands engulfed her cheeks, kneading them. If he was determined to drive her wild within five minutes of getting to her hotel room, he succeeded.

"Turn around." Gone was his light, teasing demeanor from the bar; in its place was the deep baritone of a man who knew what he wanted and took it. If he asked her to get on her knees,

Lola would have shattered both kneecaps with eager compliance.

She did as she was told, turning away from him. Javi ran his hand up her back, finding the zipper to her pink dress. He was careful of her hair, which Lola appreciated, making sure it was twisted out of his way before he pulled the zipper down to the top of her ass.

Her puffy sleeves slipped off her arms, exposing more of her brown skin. Unlike Javi, her skin was free of tattoos, mostly because she was too afraid of needles and far too impatient to sit and wait for the tattoo artist to finish.

Lola let the sleeves fall completely before pulling her arms out. The dress was too low cut to wear a bra underneath it, so her large tits were on display. The room was cold, causing her brown nipples to perk up in response.

Javi made an appreciative sound from behind her. She expected him to reach up and cup her breast, but he no longer touched her. She could feel the heat radiating off his body and sense his eyes all over her, but his hands were nowhere to be found.

"Take off your dress, Lola." His hot breath hit the back of her neck. Her panties flooded with moisture at his command and she shimmied out of her dress leaving on her lacy pink panties—ones that left little to the imagination.

Finally, she turned around to face him. Javi bit his bottom lip and the need to tease him grew strong. She was a flirt by nature and appreciated it when people enjoyed her body. It made her want to put on a show.

She cupped her own breasts and then pinched her nipples between her thumb and forefinger. Javi groaned and stood still, his gaze piercing her as if he were afraid to miss even a second of her show.

"You have far too many clothes on, big guy. Why don't you change that?" she purred. She could tell her voice went straight to his cock, because of the bulge forming in his jeans. It gave her a confidence boost and Lola backed up to the bed, easing her body down gracefully.

Still, Javi did not move. It was as if he were in a trance, unable to break the spell he was under. She chuckled and spread her thighs, panties barely covering her most intimate places. It had the desired effect, though, because Javi snapped out of whatever hold he was under and finally peeled the black shirt off his body.

And hot damn was he an Adonis. An actual living, breathing Adonis and all hers for tonight. She licked her lips, wanting to lick down his chest to his happy trail to discover the prize that lay beneath.

Javi shucked off his pants while she continued to play with her breasts, moaning. In a matter of seconds, he was on top of her, pinning her down to the bed, with nothing but a thin layer of boxers on. They did little to hide the indent of his cock from her. Her mouth watered, actually watered, for a taste of him.

"Javi..." she whined as he leaned down to kiss her neck, one of the most sensitive parts of her body. She impatiently reached for the waistband of his boxers, tugging them down. But before she pulled down any further and exposed his beautiful cock, Javi caught her hands and pinned them above her head.

She huffed indignantly, which earned her a satisfied chuckle from Javi. "You seem like the impatient type, Lola. Impatient and spoiled. Do you always get what you want, preciosa?"

Her cheeks reddened at the nickname. Her Spanish was minimal, but even she knew that was a term of endearment.

"Not always," she said, but couldn't keep the whine from

her voice. So what if her father spoiled her to compensate for her mother and sister's general shittiness? She liked it and she was not going to apologize for it.

Javi laughed again. "Just most of the time." He said what she didn't. He leaned down so his nose touched hers and when he spoke, his lips brushed hers. "And what is it you want right now?" he whispered.

"You." The word came out breathy and far too quick, but Lola did not want to take it back. She wanted him badly. Wanted to feel nothing but pleasure and his cock pumping deep inside of her until they both reached their peak.

Javi seemed to consider her words and then he nodded, finally releasing her arms. She wasted no time tugging off his boxers and freeing his erection.

"Fuck," she hissed once he was completely exposed to her. "You carry that weapon around with you all day?" She was panting, but she didn't care. She had good dick before, but never the size or girth of Javi's. Would he even fit?

As if reading her thoughts, Javi said, "You'll take it just fine." Clearly, he had more confidence in her abilities than she did, but she was willing to test that theory.

He reached down and ran his thumb along the seam of her panties. Lola ground down on his thumb, desperate for some pressure on her clit. It wasn't enough and she made her dissatisfaction known. Javi took mercy upon her and pulled the lacy number off, discarding it on the floor next to his boxers.

The first swipe of his thumb down her center sent her toes curling. She gripped the bedding, balling it up in her fists to keep from arching too high off the bed.

"So wet for me, preciosa." He purred, one finger diving deep inside her folds. It slipped in without resistance. Another one quickly followed, moving in and out of her at a slow, teasing pace. His thumb continued to circle her clit, bringing her to the edge of orgasm and pulling off before she could take the plummet.

"So damn cruel—" she hissed, just as Javi pinched her bundled nerves again. Her words ended in a loud moan as her legs widened for him.

She thought he would back off again like he did each time she got close, but he didn't. He picked up the pace of his fingers and let his thumb circle her clit until her legs quivered and her back shot off the bed.

Her orgasm came on suddenly, engulfing her body as Javi continued to tease her until she was putty in his arms.

"Your turn," she said and reached her hand down to rub between his legs, stroking his throbbing erection.

Javi grunted and shook his head. "No. I don't want to finish in your hand. I want to be inside of you."

Lola could not argue with that. "Where is your condom?"

Instead of answering, Javi pulled off her, the cold air hitting her exposed body and sending shivers down her back. "On your knees, Lola. Hands on the headboard."

"Yes, sir." Her words were automatic, but she knew Javi liked it because he smirked and slapped her ass when she got up to do as she was told.

"Good girl." She felt Javi move away from the bed and come back a moment later. She heard him rip the foil, tearing the top off to get the condom out. She imagined him rolling the rubber down his thick cock and her body shivered with anticipation.

Javi didn't know this, but she loved being taken from behind. It was both sexy and mysterious. She liked not being able to see because it heightened her sense of touch. Plus she liked how deep men could get from this position.

She felt the first touch of his cock at her entrance, teasing her. She ground against him, her ass pressing back into his hips. "Fuck, Lola, your ass is going to be the death of me," he moaned. Her name sounded so good on his lips. She wanted to hear it again, so she ground back harder.

"Lola." This time her name came with a sting across her left cheek. The mix of pain and pleasure nearly flooded her.

Javi used this opportunity to press into her. Her pussy hugged him tightly. It had been so long since she had gotten any action that did not involve her battery-operated boyfriend. But Javi was so much bigger and deeper and he was only halfway in.

"Fuuuuckkkk," she moaned, her head flopping back to land on his chest. Javi wrapped his arms around her, hands finally going to her breasts, holding them in his very capable hands.

"So tight, Lola. So eager for my cock," he groaned right into her ear. She felt the vibrations of his groan straight down to her core. "Just a little more. You can take it," he said again.

Lola wasn't sure she could, but before she could overthink it, Javi thrusted hard, sending her body pitching forward. She grabbed the headboard harder to keep herself from falling on her face.

Apparently, she could take him all.

She had never been so full before. She did not know where she began and he ended. She also didn't fucking care. Her pussy was stretched, bordering on pain, but she loved every moment of it. To his credit, Javi did not move, knowing she needed a moment—or a century—to adjust to his size.

To distract her, or drive her further into a sexual frenzy, Javi came back to her neck, kissing and biting. He was going to leave his mark on her and she found herself wanting it. A small reminder of what happened tonight, even if that reminder only lasted a few days. Her memory would last a lifetime and she already knew she would not forget sex with him easily.

After a moment, her body grew accustomed to him and she tested out her tolerance by moving her hips. He pulled his cock almost all the way out of her before she pressed her ass back against him. Both of them groaned at the movement. She felt Javi shake and she knew he was doing everything he could to hold himself back.

"Do that again," he commanded.

So she did, but this time faster. She rotated her hips, feeling him hit new spots inside of her, spots she did not know she had.

But then Javi took over and once again, she had no complaints. He moved his hips at a punishing speed, leaving her gasping. She never considered herself loud during sex, but he was bringing out a lot of things she did not know about herself.

"Play with that pretty clit. I want to come with you," he said, taking one of her hands off the bed frame and moving it between her legs. He kept his hold on her wrist, as if afraid she would disobey. Little did he know she was far too gone to even consider being a brat right now.

Her finger went straight to her clit, rubbing small circles in time with his thrusts. She couldn't believe she was going to come again so soon. But the pressure inside of her, the slapping of her ass, and playing with her clit was all too much. "Javi, I'm going to—"

"Me too..." he panted.

She felt the moment he came undone inside of her. His cock pulsed inside of her, his body shuddered, and soon he was moaning her name as he came hard for her. Lola was only seconds behind, her body erupting with white-hot pleasure.

Once again her knees gave out and she barely caught herself as she went down on the bed. Javi snaked one hand around her waist, catching her. "That was—"

"Yeah," she agreed. He didn't need to finish, she knew what he was going to say. Amazing. Earth-shattering. Fucking fantastic.

Javi soon pulled out of her and she whimpered at the absence of him. He got up to dispose of the condom and came back with a bottle of water, which she appreciated.

"Let's rest. For just a moment," she said once she downed the water. She was too tired to wonder if asking him to rest with her was a good idea or not, but frankly, she didn't care. She wanted to be held and aftercare was important.

Javi hesitated for the briefest of moments before joining her back in bed. His warm presence occupied the space next to her and he wrapped his arms around her. She gladly took up the role of little spoon.

"If I'm ever in town again, I'll be more than okay with you rocking my world again," she murmured in her tired state. She didn't hear what Javi said—if he replied at all—because the next minute, she had fallen into a deep, blissed-out sleep.

CHAPTER 4
Javi

Javi hadn't meant to doze off, but when he glanced at his phone tucked away on the nightstand, he noticed it was almost two in the morning. He cursed under his breath when he realized Lola was still wrapped up next to him, completely naked.

Seeing her on full display again made his cock twitch with desire. How could he want someone again after just having her? Lola was curvy. She had a body meant to be worshiped nightly, but he only had a few hours with her. It wasn't long enough to fuck her properly, but it took some of the edge off.

That would have to be enough.

Javi contemplated what he should do. He doubted Lola meant to fall asleep for long and she hadn't invited him to stay the night. He also had to pick Camilia up in the morning to take her to school and this hotel was fifteen minutes shy of an hour away from home. Sleeping over was out of the picture.

What they had just done was meant to be a one-night thing and here he was overthinking it. He needed to get up and leave. Now.

Slowly, so as not to disturb her, Javi untangled himself from the sleeping Lola with all the speed of a sloth. He worried he'd wake her and he didn't want to deal with the awkward goodbyes. Perhaps that made him a coward, but if she woke up, he would want to have her again. He couldn't deal with the rejection of her saying no, or worse yet, her saying yes and him getting another taste of her when he was clearly not ready for a real relationship.

With all the grace of a newborn donkey, he managed to roll out of her bed and onto the floor. He paused, waiting for any signs that he'd woken her, but he only heard the soft snores of a sleeping woman.

Javi pushed himself up, looking around the oversized room to where they'd thrown his clothes. He grabbed his boxers first, finding his jeans next to a vase of flowers and his shirt tossed underneath a leather chair.

He checked to make sure his wallet and keys were still in his pocket before taking one last look at Lola's sleeping form. He understood how creepy he must look staring at a naked sleeping woman, but no one was there to judge him. Lola didn't move much in her sleep and she reminded him of a Latina Snow White. Her full red lips and caramel skin shined in the moonlight. Her black hair was in disarray and her round ass was still tinged red, but that only added to her beauty.

Unable to help himself, Javi approached her once more and leaned down to press the softest of kisses to her forehead. This time Lola stirred, but only to unconsciously grab the covers and pull them over her naked body. She turned away from him, content in her new sleeping position.

"Goodbye, preciosa." He murmured and made his way through her room and down the hallway. Javi left the comforts of their one-night stand and rejoined the real world. Ten minutes and three wrong turns later, Javi was on the road, driving back toward where Camilia waited for him.

CHAPTER 5

Lola

SIX MONTHS LATER

The best scent in the world was old books. Books that had been properly loved with yellowed pages or stains of coffee on the cover. She liked knowing that in her hands she held a piece of history and it always made her wonder who else had touched the book.

Perhaps an elderly man passing the time while his wife knitted. Or a college student who had been told they needed to study the classics in order to graduate with the rest of their class. Perhaps it was a couple in their forties who read together nightly. Sometimes she got lost in all the places books traveled and sat for hours making up scenarios in her mind.

Her love of reading was somewhat of an anomaly. No one in her posh family owned books outside of decorative purposes. The hustle and bustle of work, marketing meetings, business dinners, and charity events stretched their time thin, leaving no room to curl up with a good book.

But Lola had found small moments of peace throughout school, going to the library or reading during lunchtime. It had been her own secret and a time for her to escape to fantasy worlds where dragons existed and Prince Charming was real.

The real world was far less exciting.

"Ma'am?" A gravelly voice startled her out of her memories and caused her to drop the stack of books she held to the ground. They missed her feet by centimeters, sparing her a cracked nail with her open shoes.

A russet-brown face peeked around the bookshelf, large dark brown eyes stared back at her. A feathered brow cocked up, looking between Lola and the burly man standing only a few feet away from her.

"Lo-Lo, you good?" Monique, her best friend since training bras, asked.

"Yeah, yeah, I'm good. Just lost in my thoughts," she assured, knowing Mona—the nickname she bestowed upon her bestie—was quick to jump to her defense. It was a great quality to have in a best friend, but she would rather not displease the contractor she desperately needed in order to get her semi-bad investment off the ground.

"Cool, cool. Sandi and I are going to check out the espresso machine the old lady left behind and see if it works. You need anything?"

"Nope, you and Sandi enjoy," Lola assured and heard a soft meow coming from Sandi. The cat had to be at least ten years old now since Mona was given the calico during her sopho-more year in high school. The damn thing was mean but had formed a special bond with Mona, so now her friend took the old feline everywhere. Sandi only tolerated Lola, which was a lot more than most people.

"Can you repeat what you said? I'm sorry, I didn't catch it the first time." Lola used her best, professional voice—aka her white voice she'd inherited from her father's side. Her Mexican mother had adopted the same voice when speaking to any of her father's influential clients so as not to stand out as the brown girl amongst the sea of Caucasians. Here she was doing the same thing.

She would deal with that identity crisis later. Right now she needed to hear the verdict of the nearly dilapidated bookstore she had purchased.

"Well ma'am, it ain't good." The man said in a southern accent, one she didn't hear much in Berkeley, California. "The foundation ain't all that bad, though you have places of rot and mold. You'll want to fix that before you let any customers inside here. You have an electrical problem, too, stemming from your backroom. It's going to need to be completely reconfigured. Your water is also running brown. That ain't what you want."

Leave it to a man to tell her she didn't want brown water running through her pipes. She knew very little about plumbing, electricity, and foundation integrity, but she knew enough to understand brown water wasn't good.

"Okay," she said slowly, her brain already thinking of solutions. The only problem was that nothing was coming. "So can you fix it?"

"Sure, ma'am. But it'll cost ya. And it'll take time."

"How much time?"

"I don't know. Six to eight."

"Weeks?"

"No, months."

Lola's jaw dropped. She shouldn't be surprised. He wasn't the first contractor to come by and give her a large timeline. The thing was that she didn't have six to eight months to wait around. Each day that passed was more ammunition her mother would use against her to remind Lola how awful this purchase had been. Luciana would then remind her father why she shouldn't have given Lola the money—money that was hers in the first place since the account had been started when she was a baby and given over to her as soon as she turned twenty-one.

"There is no way you can do it any faster?" she asked him, trying to hide the desperation in her voice, but failing miserably.

The man, looking like the country version of Jack Black, frowned, shaking his head. "No ma'am. We have a few jobs that we'd be working alongside yours and this place requires the most of our time. This is our busy season so if you want the job done right, it will take time." He shrugged, clearly never having faced a Mexican mother with a vendetta against him.

So, Lola was back to square one. She refused to let this minor setback cause her to spiral into a full-blown anxiety attack, even if she wanted nothing more than to lie down and have a good cry.

"I can see you need time to think about it," the man said. She wondered how much of a wreck she looked like right now to send a grown man scampering away. "I'll leave you my business card and you can call me back once your mind is made up."

The contractor rummaged through his deep pockets and pulled out a bent business card. She took it from him with a tight smile and led him out. "Thank you for your help," she said as he left, locking the door behind him.

With an audible sigh, Lola leaned against the glass, letting her head hit the hard interior side of the door. Her move back to California and the ancient bookstore was not shaping up like she thought it would.

Lola's obsession with books, history, and learning was the

driving force that had brought her back to California. Florida had been her home for four years, but Berkeley was where she grew up. Her friends and some of the best memories lived here and she made a promise to herself that if the old bookstore on Addison Street ever became available for purchase, she would buy it.

Florida had been a nice break and helped her get over the sudden loss of her relationship with Archie and the expectations her family—namely her mother—had for her. Expectations she knew she would never live up to.

However, her life in Florida quickly became lonely. She hadn't met many people except coworkers. She liked her previous job fine enough, but it wasn't something she wanted to do for the rest of her life. It was something she did because it paid the bills and kept her busy.

Moving back to Berkeley meant she had to tell her parents where she moved and why, and that hadn't been the best conversation. Her father had been confused but supportive while her mother was simply confused.

Owning a bookstore, specifically Phoenix Books, had been a dream of hers since high school when she got her first job as a cashier here. The older woman who ran this store, Mrs. Sanderson, knew of Lola's home life and understood that Lola stood out like a proverbial sore thumb. She had given Lola the job under the guise of extra credit for her school courses and something additional to put on her college applications.

All four years of high school and well into college, Lola had worked at Phoenix Books as one of the only long-term employees. The day Lola quit had been an emotional decision, but keeping up with her course load and working full time had put a strain on her mental health.

Mrs. Sanderson had been understanding and kept her on as

a seasonal employee until Lola moved to Florida for a job in marketing that, admittedly, her father helped her get.

However, two months ago, Mrs. Sanderson reached out unexpectedly and let Lola know she was retiring and closing the store. Lola knew what she had to do. It had taken some convincing to get Mrs. Sanderson to agree to sell, since the store was in rough condition and she had planned to give it over to the city, but in the end, she had talked her way into purchasing Phoenix Books, intending to restore the store to its former glory.

Finding the energy to push herself off her leaning perch, Lola took a quick look around her new store. There was still so much to be done and apparently, it would take even longer than she anticipated, but the inside of the store still held an old charm to it that she wanted to memorialize upon reopening.

Whenever the hell that would be.

"Mona! Please give me some good news!" she groaned, dragging herself away from the front of the store to find Mona behind what was once the register. Mona's back was toward her, but she looked over her shoulder and gave her a thumbs up.

"You, my sweet friend, have a working espresso machine." She smiled triumphantly, holding up a clear plastic cup. Lola had to squint to see the minuscule amount of liquid inside.

"I drank half of it," she said by way of explanation. "The machine did sound like it would take flight, but it made decent espresso. You book people are patient, yeah? So the long-ass time to brew shouldn't be a problem."

"Well, that's something I guess," she grumbled, leaning over the counter. She landed a little too close to Sandi, who promptly swiped at her arm before jumping off the counter. "Your cat is a menace."

"Isn't she though?" Mona cooed and picked up her little devil off the ground, nuzzling the fat cat.

"You realize you have an unhealthy relationship with that cat, right?"

"Only you and my wife seem to think that. I'm thinking you're both just jealous."

Lola scoffed. "Oh yes, Mattea and I are very jealous of your she-demon."

As if understanding Lola's disdain, Sandi hissed at her before wiggling out of Mona's arms and scurrying away, probably to see if she could find any mice in this old building.

"So how'd it go with the contractor? He seem good?" Mona asked, taking a drink of the last bit of her espresso.

"I mean he was fine enough but his timeline is six to eight months. I don't have six to eight months to give," she complained. Her impatience could never allow her to just sit around and wait. She had never been good at being patient.

Mona whistled lowly. "Damn, that's a hot minute. Can we keep looking? I have someone coming into the bakery tomorrow to fix a few broken appliances and an electrical issue I'm having in the bathroom. Want me to scout him out and tell you how he is?"

Lola shrugged. "Sure. At this point, I'll take anything."

"In the meantime, you should really start spreading the word about Phoenix's revival. No use in putting all this money into a place without letting people know. Besides, it'll get your mind off..." Mona paused and looked around the cluttered room. Lola swore she heard a book fall to the ground somewhere. "This mess," she finished.

"And what do you suggest?" She didn't mean to be snippy with her friend, but she was ready to curl up on her cloud-like mattress and binge *Supernatural* until she fell asleep.

Luckily, Mona didn't take offense to her or was simply used to her bullshit that her attitude didn't phase her. "How about you come down to the bakery this weekend? The first weekend of every month, Mattea likes to put on a family day for kids where they make cookies and shit. You could help and read them a story. They would go feral over a good storytime."

Despite her mood, Lola smiled. Children's books had always been her favorite and she enjoyed finding diverse picture books for children who were underrepresented in the media.

"While you're reading, you can make subtle remarks to the parents that you plan on reopening Phoenix. It'll build up some hype." Mona was always the logical one and grounded Lola when her emotions wanted to lead all of her decisions.

"That does sound fun."

"Of course it sounds fun. My wife will make it fun even if it kills us."

"Well we wouldn't want to anger the Mighty Mattea," she deadpanned.

"So, is that a yes, you'll come?" Mona bit her lip, something she always did when she expected the answer to be no.

"Bitch, you know I can't say no to you when you make that face. Plus telling me it's for the children? I'm pretty sure I'd rot in hell if I said no." She laughed, no true malice behind her words.

"That's right, bitch. You'd burn for centuries. Gotta be a good girl and read to them childrens." Mona teased, tossing her empty plastic cup to her. "Now let's get out of here and get some food. I'm starving and ramen is calling my name."

And just like that, her mood increased exponentially at the thought of food.

~

MONA DROPPED her off at her apartment at a quarter past five. The ramen restaurant near Phoenix had been full of college-aged students set up with their laptops on one side and their piping hot bowls on the other. They managed to find a small, cramped booth toward the bathroom, but the table was stationary and gave her little room between the booth seat and the table.

Luckily, the uncomfortable seating arrangement only lasted for about thirty minutes before Mattea called Mona to come help out in the bakery. On her way, she dropped Lola off at the main office in the apartment complex to get her mail. She was expecting a few packages to complete furnishing her new apartment.

Lola had been in her new two-bedroom apartment for a little over a month now. She was adjusting well and often had Mattea and Mona over for dinners and home projects she needed another set of hands and eyes for. They were content as long as she had booze and food, which she always supplied.

As expected, two medium-sized boxes awaited her in the office. She signed for them before walking a few feet over to the mailboxes to gather her neglected mail due to her long hours at the shop. Pulling out a week's worth of forgotten mail was no easy task, especially when the small boxes were filled to the brim. Somehow she managed and made the trek back to her home, only one building over.

When she was searching for an apartment, Lola had called Mona to help her find something big enough so she didn't feel like she lived in a box. Also, she needed somewhere located within the city. She wasn't a country girl and only enjoyed the occasional vacation to less populated areas when she was in need of a break. Otherwise, Lola liked feeling the buzz of crowds and the excitement that inevitably came with city living.

She had sent a few prospects to Mona and Mattea to check out for her, but they had not been thrilled with any of the properties she sent their way. Unknowingly to her, Lola's friends went on a secret mission to find her a place to live and sent her options based on their favorite places. Her current apartment was within walking distance to Phoenix, Mona and Mattea's house, and her friends' bakery. She filled out the application immediately.

Fumbling to get the key into the lock, as well as balancing the mail and packages in one hand, Lola pushed her way into her modern-styled apartment. Pops of pink, yellow, and blue made the living room feel inviting and stylish. She had an eye for colors and bold patterns and never shied away from statement pieces.

Lola dropped the heavy mail and packages onto the bright yellow coffee table after shutting the door with her foot. The mail spilled out over the table, and a navy-blue envelope fell to the floor. She reached for it, but before her hand made contact, she recoiled as if she had been severely burned. The room felt as if it were spinning and she reached back to grip her Tiffany-blue couch, sitting down before she fell on her ass.

She had wondered when she would finally receive it. Her father had been keeping her in the loop about Marisol's upcoming wedding, but she hadn't been quite as prepared as she believed she'd be to get the wedding invitation.

It had been six months since she last saw her family, only keeping in touch with the occasional phone call from her father. Six months since she left their engagement party and hooked up with a stranger. She almost convinced herself that none of it had been real. That her sister hadn't betrayed her in the worst way. Of course, her sister didn't shoulder all the blame. Archie and her mother were just as much to blame for this sinking feeling in the pit of her stomach.

Breathing became a struggle. Her heart raced. Visions of that dinner came rushing back and she didn't know how to turn her mind off. She needed to pick the envelope up off the ground. Did she throw it away and pretend like she never got it? That would create bigger problems with her mother later on, knowing she wouldn't stop calling and guilt-tripping her until she responded. If she responded, then she would have to come to terms with the reality that Marisol was really marrying Archie.

It wasn't as if she loved Archie. She didn't and hadn't for a long time. She recognized that they were two very different people, but there had been a time when she loved him. She had planned a life with the man, only to have the rug pulled out from under her when he said she no longer fit into his life. She had been devastated by losing him, but that pain paled in comparison to the pain of finding out he moved on with her sister.

Marisol had never been a great sister, but Lola would hardly call her a bad one. They did not have the sisterly bond that many of her friends had, and it wasn't for lack of trying. Lola had tried many times growing up to befriend her sister, but the girls were vastly different. It was impossible to find any middle ground when their differences had no commonality.

Despite this, Lola never hated Marisol. She loved her because that was what you were supposed to do: love your siblings because they were family. The fragile relationship and love they may have shared with one another broke the moment she agreed to a romantic partnership with Archie.

She couldn't deal with this alone. She needed to talk this

out, to hear her own thoughts out loud, and for someone else to be a voice of reason. Her family was obviously out of the question, so it only left two people. Lola fished out her phone inside her purse and called.

Not even two rings later, a cheerful female voice picked up. "Hi sweetie. Didn't Mona just drop you off? Are you okay?"

Before Lola could answer, Mona's voice piped up in the background. "Don't tell me your dumb ass locked yourself out of your apartment."

Lola tried to find the words, wanting to joke about how many times Mona had locked herself out of her house or assure Mattea that she was okay. But the only thing that left her mouth was an embarrassingly loud sob.

Crying was a vicious cycle. It hurt to fight back the tears, but crying only pissed her off. Instead of making the tears stop, the anger only made her cry harder. Which wasn't fair because once she started, she found it was hard to stop.

"Oh no, sweetie, no." Mattea's sweet voice came through, along with a few sniffles. Mattea was a sympathy crier and would start crying if someone else was, even if she did not know the reason behind it.

"Let it out, Lo-Lo. Talk to us when you can. Are you safe?" Mona's voice was gentle, though worried.

Lola managed to get out a simple, "Yes," because she was safe, just upset. She had not properly grieved the relationship that ended so abruptly. Even now, the hurt felt like an open wound that hadn't scabbed over yet.

Grief was a weird thing. One moment a person could be totally fine, living their normal life, then the next moment the weight of the world could fall upon their shoulders and nothing was good or right.

After five minutes of embarrassing crying, Lola felt some of her composure come back and she could answer their unasked questions.

"The invitation came." She did not need to say more than that; her friends knew exactly what she meant. She heard Mona swear and Mattea mutter something about "burning his white ass in hell" which caused Lola to smile.

"Throw it away. Don't open it," Mona said.

"I thought about it, but I think that would make things worse. You know my family. They're relentless. I'm not getting out of this shit."

"You also don't have to put yourself in situations where you'll be uncomfortable. They obviously don't give a shit about your feelings, so why care about theirs?"

"Mona!" Mattea gasped and Lola heard a light smack, picturing tiny five-foot Mattea smacking six-foot Mona in the arm.

"Babe, you know it's the truth! Lola's gotta have boundaries."

Lola knew Mona was right. If anyone else in her life treated her like this, she would cut them out so quickly. She knew she deserved better and demanded better, but when it came to her family she always felt and acted differently. It was the one area of her life where she couldn't fix it, no matter what she did. Perhaps it was guilt or the hope that things would be different, no matter how naive that was.

"Have you looked at the invitation yet, sweetie?" Mattea asked, causing Lola to look back at the discarded envelope on the floor. With a reluctant sigh, she plucked it up.

"I'm going to look now." Lola broke the silver seal with her nail, unraveling it until a cream-colored paper fell out. As far as wedding invitations went, this one was simple with silver trimming and a photo of the happy couple locked in an intimate embrace. Lola couldn't deny how beautiful they looked together, but it didn't make the announcement any easier.

"Their wedding is four weeks away," she said softly. "In Colorado." As she said that, two other small pieces of paper fell out of the envelope. One was an RSVP note to mail back. She could not help but notice the plus one on her invitation.

Great.

On top of everything else, she would have to figure out who would be her plus one because there was no way she was going to her ex and sister's wedding alone. The other paper was one announcing she was wanted as a bridesmaid. Leave it to her family to drive the knife deeper into her back.

"There's more. Not only do I need to find a plus one, but I will be a bridesmaid in the wedding."

"Shut the fuck up. Shut all the way up. No you fucking aren't." Mona's disgust, despite everything, made Lola burst out in uncontrollable laughter. She had finally lost it.

"This is perfect. Just fucking perfect." She said after a fit of giggles. "Because why wouldn't my family want to torture me a little bit more? I doubt my sister even knows. This screams my mother. She micromanages everything, apparently even my sister's wedding."

"Well, your mother is a royal bit—"

"Overwhelming," Mattea interrupted before Mona finished her sentence. "All of this is overwhelming and will take some time to process. Do you want Mona and I to come over later and we can binge-watch something on Netflix?"

Lola smiled, her heart swelling at Mattea's words. Her family might be garbage but her chosen family always had her back. "As tempting as that sounds," she started, "I think I just want to head to bed early. I have a full day of errands tomorrow and want to take it easy."

"Okay, sweetie. Mona said we will see you this weekend at the bakery for our Family Fun Day?"

"Of course. I'm thinking of books to bring."

"Good." She heard the smile in Mattea's voice. "We love you and if you end up needing us, don't hesitate to call. We will be there."

She knew they would; she was the luckiest woman in the world to have friends like Mattea and Mona.

They said their goodbyes and Lola hung up the phone. She tossed the wedding invitation under the stack of mail to deal with later. Then she pushed all thoughts of weddings and plus ones out of her mind and enjoyed a relaxing night of watching *Supernatural* and doing face masks.

CHAPTER 6

Javi

For as much time as Javi spent in his old pickup truck, one would think he would be better organized. Yet he couldn't find his unopened box of business cards. He thought he had placed them in his middle compartment, but all he found were two Barbies, three pens, and packets of fruit snacks that had long ago melted in the California heat.

Normally, it wouldn't be a problem if he couldn't find his company's business cards for a multitude of reasons. The most important one being he hated his boss, particularly how he took advantage of the hard-working men on his team. Most of the men, like Javi, had families to support and took whatever job they were offered, afraid that they'd miss their opportunity to put food on the table.

Javi understood that. Understood what it meant to worry week by week, day by day, if he would make enough money to cover his family's expenses. Between food, water, electricity, and his six-year-old daughter, money went quickly. He worked like a dog day in and day out, sacrificing his time with his daughter. His father would say this is the price men paid to provide for the family.

He also wouldn't have cared about the missing business cards because his boss always attempted to overprice the simplest of jobs. Javi never felt right charging two times the price for a simple fix, especially when most of the money went back to lining the pockets of his lazy boss.

However, the missing business cards were not his boss's. They were his. Last week he made the scary, but right, decision to put in his two-week notice and leave his job to work as his own independent contractor. He had built up a rather large and loyal clientele over the years and knew that if he was ever going to make the switch, it would have to be now.

Two seconds after he made this life-altering decision, he called his level-headed sister for advice. She had recently moved back to California from Texas with her husband, Maverick, and provided him with more support than he deserved.

Naturally, Ofelia was on board with his decision—he half expected her to tell him he needed to get his head out of the clouds and keep the job with a steady income. Instead, she insisted he come over so they could design business cards.

His sister was a pro when it came to creating shit like that. Javi had shown up at her house, but that was the extent of his involvement. Ofelia took over, asking him a few basic questions like his email, whether he wanted Javi or Javier, and his work cell phone number, which was his only number.

An hour later, she had not only managed to finish his business cards, but also pay for them to be shipped overnight. He insisted he'll pay her back, but Ofelia would not hear of it and requested he let it go. Begrudgingly, he did.

When they showed up the next day, Javi should have put them straight into the middle compartment of his truck, but instead, he haphazardly tossed them to the back so he could drive his cranky kindergartner off to school in a timely manner.

With a sigh of defeat, he pushed himself out of his car and turned to face his client. She had warm tawny-colored skin, with deep-set dark eyes. Her black coiled hair fanned her face, falling to her shoulders. She had a friendly smile and her bright red, oversized glasses reminded Javi of a schoolteacher.

"I'm sorry. I thought I'd put them in my truck." He mentally kicked himself for being so unprepared after declaring he was going the independent route. He still had a week left, maybe it wasn't too late to beg to keep his job...

The woman waved away his apology. "Don't worry about it. My wife says I would lose my head if it wasn't attached to my body." She laughed good-naturedly and reached into her apron pocket. A moment later she dug out a crumpled sheet of paper and a pink pen. "Can you write down your contact information here? You did amazing inside fixing the water leak and helping design a new cupcake display."

Javi sighed in relief. "Definitely. Thanks for understanding," he said and took the pen and paper, jotting down his information in his best non-chicken-scratch writing. He left two ways to contact him in case one of them was illegible.

"Like I said, it's not a problem. We just need a reliable person to fix shit around the bakery. It's an old building, as you know. I also have a friend who is in need of a contractor. She's trying to open up the old bookstore downtown."

Javi handed her back the paper with his information and raised a brow. "A bookstore? You wouldn't be talking about Phoenix, would you?"

"The very same. Our friend moved back to town and bought it from Mrs. Sanderson. She is hoping to restore it to its former glory but hasn't found a contractor that meets her needs. Love her to death, but she is a hard-ass when it comes to things like that."

Javi wasn't a reader, much to his sister's dismay, but he had been dragged into the old bookstore countless times as a kid. He had hated it at first but eventually found the comic books, which made the visits slightly more enjoyable.

"Oh!" The woman—if his memory served from the job form, her name was Mattea—exclaimed. "She is going to be here this weekend. You could come to the bakery!"

Javi opened his mouth to politely refuse. He had two days off, a rarity for him, and he did not want to spend it doing business. He promised Camilia that he'd spend the weekend with her and he always tried to keep his promises to her. Especially those that involved quality time together.

"That sounds amazing, but I promised I would spend the weekend with my daughter," Javi admitted.

At the mention of his daughter, Mattea lit up. "This weekend we're holding our monthly family day at the bakery. We have cookie decorating and storytime. It's always a hit with little ones. We would love it if you came. Completely free. No pressure on the business side, if you don't want to talk shop while off."

Javi considered her offer. Since his sister moved closer, her mission had been to convert her niece into a bookworm by reading to her, taking her to fun bookstores and storytimes, as well as reading to her each time they were together. It had achieved the desired effect and his Camilia was just as big of a bookworm as her tía.

Add cookies into the mix and he would be crowned superdad. He needed that win. "When does it start?"

The smile on Mattea's face was one of pure genuine joy. "It's Saturday at eleven."

"Count us in."

Mattea clapped, doing a little dance. The woman was pure joy wrapped up in a tiny body. "Wonderful! We are all about getting the community involved. Plus, I love seeing the little ones. I'm trying to subtly hint to my wife that I'm ready for us to start having kids."

He didn't know the woman well, but he could tell she had a big heart and any child would be lucky to have her. "Well, anyway," Mattea said, "thank you again for fixing our bakery issue. I can't wait to meet your little one on Saturday."

"Call me if you find any other problems. I'll see you Saturday." He offered her a wave before getting into his truck. He waited until Mattea went back inside, since it was getting dark, before he took off.

He was off for two days and he planned to make the most of it. He would finally be able to sit and watch his daughter practice cheer, a sport she had been in since she was just out of diapers, and now he could take her to a storytime and cooking decoration activity.

Ten minutes later Javi pulled into his driveway where his father and Ofelia sat outside while Camilia and little Arturo played in the front yard. He attempted to reach for his lunch box, but the zipper wasn't closed properly and his uneaten lunch as well as a white box fell out.

The same white box he had been looking for earlier that held all of his new business cards. Fucking typical.

His body felt tense as newfound stress worked its way through his bones. When he got like this, he knew it meant he was itching for a stress relief. His last relief came in the form of a one-night stand with a gorgeous woman who popped into his head more times than he cared to admit. It hardly seemed proper to seek out another fling when he was clearly not over his last one.

His anger and thoughts of flings lasted a total of twenty seconds though before tiny fists began to pound on the side of his door, accompanied by the sweetest voice he knew. "Papá! You're home."

CHAPTER 7

Javi

Getting three full-sized adults and two kids into his sister's minivan had been no easy task. Arturo decided to have a diaper blowout, making Javi thankful that poopy diapers were something he no longer had to deal with. His father, Ruben, insisted on sitting in the third row of the van, which would have been fine if he didn't move at a snail's pace. He was too proud to admit that he was having a hard time maneuvering his body into the back seat, but Javi knew from experience not to stop him. His father would grow angry and impede progress.

Camilia would only get into the car if she could bring along her doll because she did not want it to be scared alone at the house. By this time, Javi was ready to ram his head through the car's door, but he dug deep within himself to find the last traces of his patience.

By the time everyone was finally in the car, buckled up, and in a sour mood, he was ready to throw in the towel and call it quits. Except that would put a damper on their family day and everyone had been excited when he brought it up. Who knew cookies and a picture book would provide so much joy?

His sister was the last in after putting Arturo back into his car seat with his tablet. "Sorry, sorry! Okay, we are all ready to go," she assured, looking frazzled with her messy bun and rumpled shirt.

Javi bit back the sarcastic retort on the tip of his tongue, knowing that would only serve to cause bickering between the two. He loved his family more than anything, but getting them all out of the house in a timely manner was near impossible. He needed to breathe and trust they would make it through.

Though they were in his sister's van, Javi offered to drive since he knew Maverick, his sister's husband, did most of the driving. Today Mav started spring training for baseball and according to Ofelia, he was adjusting nicely to his new team.

Maverick accepted a job with his San Francisco team nearly a year ago. It had been a huge change for his sister who had lived in Texas for the last five years, but she had been eager to move closer to family. She wanted to raise her children alongside their cousins and be near him and their father when Mav had to travel for baseball.

Javi enjoyed having his sister close again. He hadn't realized how much he missed her until she moved back. It was nice having her close so Camilia would have a woman she loved and confided in if she were ever unable to come to him for some reason or another. Especially during puberty, but luckily they were still pretty far off from that.

Not even five minutes later, Javi heard snoring from the back seat. He snuck a glance in his rearview mirror to see his father in the back, mouth slightly ajar and eyes closed. Arturo was slumped forward in his car seat, tablet nowhere to be found as he too slept. Camilia was the only one awake, looking out the window as they drove.

"Well, next time we need to get them ready for nap time, all we need to do is load them up and drive around the neighborhood." Ofelia laughed, snapping a picture of the sleeping duo in the backseat, no doubt sending the picture to Maverick. "I just hate to wake them up," she said as she put her phone away.

"They are like cats. They sleep all the time." Anytime he walked into the house and Arturo was there with his father, the two were usually curled up on the recliner sleeping. If they weren't sleeping, they were eating something they probably shouldn't be eating. He loved the relationship his father had with his grandchildren. It was special to see him give both Arturo and Camilia his full attention and intently listen to them, even when he had no idea what they were saying. It was a far cry from what he and Ofelia got from him growing up, but he was glad his daughter got this side of his father.

The drive to the bakery only lasted fifteen minutes, but parking would be hell. The bakery was located in the middle of town, one of the busier streets located a few blocks from the university. The only available parking was on the street and so far, he had not come upon a space large enough to fit the van.

After a few times circling the block, a black sedan finally pulled out of a spot and Javi took the opportunity to pull in. The bakery was only a short walk away. He could already smell the delicious sugar wafting from the shop. Camilia apparently could too because she said, "Papá, can I have a cookie?"

"You'll be making your own cookie soon," he answered, which was greeted by a happy cheer.

Getting out of the car did not take as long as getting in, which he was thankful for. His father allowed Javi to help him out without complaint. His sister unbuckled Arturo and placed him down next to Camilia. The two locked hands and Ofelia placed her hand over her heart in awe. "Don't they make you want another one?"

A sad smile touched his lips. There had been a time when Javi wanted more kids, three to be exact, but those dreams died when Estella did. Ofelia clearly noticed his lack of response and shot him an apologetic look. He wanted to tell her he did not need her sympathy; far too many people looked at him with those same sad eyes and it pissed him off.

But his sister meant well. She was in a good place with her husband and their first child. How could she not want more of the ideal family society said they should have. His sister deserved it and he did not resent her happiness, but he sometimes wished things would have ended differently for him.

Not only for him but for Camilia as well. She never knew life with a mother and that, more than anything, pulled at his heartstrings. He wanted to give his baby girl everything, but he would never be able to provide her with the feeling of a mother's love. She deserved that and so much more.

"Papá, let's go!" His daughter's sweet voice made his heart ache.

Despite his changing thoughts, Javi mustered up excitement, which admittedly wasn't that hard when Camilia was a bouncing ball of joy. He reached for her hand and she gladly clasped her tiny hand with his. He wondered how much longer he'd be able to hold his little girl's hand in public.

He really couldn't go down that road of thinking today unless he wanted to bring down the mood of the entire party.

The delicious aroma of sugar and cinnamon greeted them once Javi opened the door for his family. They all trailed in, his father second to last, and Javi took up the caboose. The vibrant pink-and-white styled bakery was packed with so many bodies that made maneuvering from one spot to another an Olympic sport in balancing.

"There's a table over here!" Ofelia called from up front, guiding Arturo and Camilia to the vacant table. Javi took his father's arm out of fear his father would wind up with another family and they'd never see him again. He followed the bob of his sister's messy bun until he made it to the table.

It was a small round table with only three seats, which went to the kids and his father. He did not mind standing and knew his sister wouldn't either, but his father needed the support, or his legs would ache.

"I'm not a child in need of their mother's attention, mijo." His father chastised when Javi insisted he take the seat, but luckily didn't push the matter.

"Javi! You made it!" A feminine voice said from behind them. Javi turned to see Mattea with a giant grin on her face. She carried two plates of plain sugar cookies with icing and sprinkles off to the side. She placed the plates down in front of Arturo and Camilia and pointed to his daughter. "Is this one yours?"

There was no hiding the pride on his face as he nodded. "She is. That's Camilia and my nephew Arturo."

"Well, they are stinking precious. I'm so glad you were able to make it. My wife is somewhere around here and you made it just in time for our story." Mattea's infectious attitude was impossible to ignore and Javi found that he liked the woman. He didn't have many friends, but he could imagine how easy it would be to have Mattea as one.

How the hell did adults even make friends these days? When he was a child, all he had to do was find a particularly nice rock and hand it to the nearest kid and he had a friend for life...or at least for that school year.

A clanging bell sounded, quieting the chatter of the room. Everyone turned to find the origin of the sound and a tall black woman stood atop a chair. He heard Mattea suck in a deep breath and mutter, "She better get her ass down from there. She knows she's uncoordinated." And he wondered if this was her wife, Monique. He had only ever spoken with her over the phone, but all in-person contact had been with Mattea.

"Thank you all for joining us here for cookies and story-time." The woman said loud enough to be heard over the small whines of impatient children and the scooting of chairs. "I'm Monique, co-owner of this bakery. I'm so excited to announce my best friend and the new owner of Phoenix Books—" A few hushed whispers went around the room, wondering when the old bookstore would reopen. He imagined it needed a lot of work before it could open its doors to customers again.

"—Ms. Lola!" Monique finished and a round of applause greeted her last words. She jumped down from the chair to hug the woman who just walked in, carrying a vibrant children's book in her hand.

Javi recognized that deep-golden skin—he'd spent days remembering those curves and the way her ass swayed in the tight pink dress she had worn. He remembered the way she felt around his cock and the way she moaned for him. A warmth shot through his body, reminding him exactly what she did to him.

Standing only feet away, was Lola—the woman he had a one-night stand with six months ago and could not stop thinking about since.

Lola

When Mona first asked her to read a picture book at the bakery's event, Lola envisioned a handful of kids with a few adults on their cellphones. What she walked into was quite the opposite. The bakery wasn't big by any means, but it held about thirty people, according to the plaque on the wall set forth by fire regulations.

Six circular white tables and a long bench seat holding another four tables made up the seating in the bakery. Each table was full of children, ranging from toddler size to around seven or eight. Lola loved kids and hoped she would one day have a family of her own. Just not now. Now, she needed to focus on her dream of reopening the bookstore.

When Mona called her name, Lola took a moment to straighten out her shirt—a pastel pink V-neck with 'Mattea's Bakery' embossed across her left breast. She paired this with dark-wash jeans and open-toed sandals to show off her painted toes.

Mona's arms wrapped tightly around Lola, as if she were greeting her back from a month-long excursion, rather than the two whole minutes they were apart. She loved that about her best friend though, her unbridled passion and need to show her love for others through physical acts. It was something Lola wasn't accustomed to.

Her family rarely showed outward displays of emotions, though her dad was known to give a hug or two on special occasions. Her sister and mother on the other hand? It would be a cold day in hell if they ever showed their affection like a normal family. Touching her might result in gaining extra pounds through magical osmosis and they simply couldn't have that.

"Knock their little socks off, bestie," Mona whispered into her ear. She then left to rejoin Mattea behind the counter, leaving her alone with dozens of eyes glued to her every move.

Lola had never been a shy person, which was probably due to years of standing out. When one went to the most elite of prep schools and everyone looked as if they just walked off the runway while her left thigh was the size of their torso, it gave little room for shyness.

She plastered on a smile from years of experience attending her family functions and doing business dinners for her father and his clients. She had perfected the smile over the years, making sure no cracks peeked out of her armor. Showing signs of weakness was the fastest way for anyone to home in on one's insecurities and pick them apart until they were left bleeding all over the floor. Metaphorically speaking, of course.

Seeing the excited expression on the children's faces made her own smile more genuine. "Hello, friends!" She heard Mona snort behind her because yeah, she might be laying it on a little too thick, but she just couldn't help it. She was surrounded by cuteness overload.

She perched her round ass on the stool provided for her, taking another sweep around the room as she said, "I'm so excited to be reading to you today a book about—" But her words got lost in her throat. Everything seemed to come crashing down around her as her eyes locked on a man she had never expected to see again. A man who had rocked her entire world in one single night. A feat her past boyfriends could not do even after months of dating.

Javi.

Holy fucking shit—Javi is here.

After their time together, she had awoken to find him gone the next day. Sure they were only sharing a single night together and she had not expected him to stay long, but it would have been nice if he had told her goodbye. Instead, she had woken up late the next morning with a delicious ache between her legs and a bed that still smelled like him.

This is not what I need to be thinking about right now!

Her internal freakout almost made her miss the beautiful Latine woman next to Javi. She was curvy, not in the way Lola was curvy, but in a straight-sized curvy kind of way. She was beautiful with long wavy brown hair. The woman was hovering over two children, a boy and a girl. One looked like he may still be in diapers and the other one was old enough to be in school. Kindergarten maybe?

Which begged the question: did she have sex with a married man? And did he lie about it when she asked if he had a partner?

Her cheeks heated, anger coiling low in her belly. There were pieces of shit, and then there were pieces of shit who cheated on their spouses, which made them even lower than the lowest scumbags.

Javi continued to look at her, in much the same way she

was looking at him, like they were Scrooge from *A Christmas Carol* seeing the ghost of Marley for the first time.

A not-so-subtle cough snagged her attention and Lola turned her head to see Mona giving her 'what the fuck' eyes. Apparently, she had been silent for too long and the audience was beginning to wonder if she needed medical help.

She needed help, alright, but there was nothing she could do now but ignore the sinfully hot man staring right at her.

A sinfully hot man with a fucking family! She had to remember that part of it.

Pushing all thoughts of Javi away—far, far away to the deepest crevices of her mind which she wrapped up with extra strength, heavy-duty chains—Lola turned her attention back to the children. They were the reason she was here, after all.

"This is a story about a young boy getting ready for his first dance recital," she said, not missing a beat and picking up where she left off. "He's very nervous about his performance, but his family helps him through those big emotions."

She could use help getting through her own big emotions right now, but she remembered the calming techniques her former therapist taught her when her anger or sadness threatened to overwhelm her. That was easy enough when she focused on the sweet children's book. She changed her voice for each character to give them all different personalities.

As a young child, her abuelita would read her bedtime stories each time she spent the night at her house. It had been one of her fondest memories as a child and the reason she became so invested in reading as an adult. Her abuelita would create silly voices and act out the books she read. Most of them had been in Spanish, and since she never learned Spanish fluently, she didn't ever quite understand what the stories were about. That hardly mattered because she knew how they made her feel. Now that she passed, Lola wanted to continue her abuelita's fun storytimes with others.

When the story came to a close, Lola took in the captive audience as the bakery burst into a friendly round of applause. Before she could appreciate the situation, Mona magically appeared next to her, leading another round of applause. "Wasn't that the *best*?" Her bestie beamed, getting vigorous nods from the crowd. "There'll be plenty more of that once Ms. Lola gets Phoenix Books up and running again. Make sure to check back periodically for updates and follow Phoenix Books on social media!"

Social media? Who the hell had social media? Because she knew her friend was not talking about her. She covertly nudged Mona in the side, trying to look as normal as possible as she whisper-hissed, "There is no social media."

"Looks like your ass is about to make one," her friend retorted, barely moving her lips as she spoke, to keep up the vivid smile. She then gripped Lola's wrist, not in a threatening way, but rather in a gentle squeeze as she continued to speak to the crowds. "Ms. Lola will be here visiting the tables while you create your dancer cookies. My lovely wife will walk you through those steps."

Mattea took her cue and made her way toward their makeshift stage to lead the children and their parents through the cookie activity. Mona took this opportunity to lead Lola away and off to the side. "You were amazing, Lo-Lo. The kids loved you. Did you have fun?"

Despite her rather tumultuous start, Lola did have fun. "It was amazing. They were so invested in the story!"

"Nah, girl. They were invested in how you told the story. You are seriously a natural. Parents are going to flock to Phoenix if you keep up storytime."

Speaking of Phoenix, she narrowed her eyes at her friend. "Yeah, and now I have to make and run a damn social media account, thanks to you."

Mona was not bothered by her annoyance. She waved her off like she did any time she didn't like what she was hearing. "Everyone has social media. Stop being a grandma. I know you be posting some spicy pics up on your 'gram."

"Okay true, but I can't post pics like that for a bookstore!"

"We will figure it out later, Lo-Lo." Once again her hand moved through the air and Lola wanted to snatch it and shake her. But since there were far too many witnesses in the room, she settled for a good ol' fashion pout.

"Girl, don't give me that face. I already have a wife who pouts to get her way; I don't need another."

"That's only because we know how easy you are." Lola giggled.

"Har har." Mona rolled her eyes. "Anyway, I wanted to introduce you to Javier, the contractor guy I was telling you about."

Lola felt her stomach sink...again. This was not happening. Her best friend was not about to walk her over and introduce her to the man she had already slept with. She didn't care how good a handyman he was, there was absolutely no way she would ever consider hiring him. Not because she hooked up with him and he left without saying goodbye—she wasn't mad about that at all. She was pissed at the fact that he was married with kids!

"I don't think right now is a good time. Shouldn't we be helping out with the cookies?"

"Nah, Mattea can run these classes in her sleep. She doesn't need us. And you are the one complaining no contractor can finish on your timeline. So let's see if he can."

"But—"

"No 'buts,' Lo-Lo! I love you very much, but if I have to continue to search for the perfect contractor, I might pass away. We're going."

There was no getting out of her grasp, not when Mona had her mind made up. She could be an adult about this. All she had to do was remain cool and collected, pretend his dick hadn't been a gift to humanity, and she would be alright.

She could so do this.

Mona led her toward Javi's table and Lola swore she was having heart palpitations. Mona tapped Javi on the back of his shoulder to gain his attention. The breath was stolen from her lips when he turned around, his eyes immediately locking on hers. She barely heard Mona say, "Javier? I'm Monique, and I wanted to introduce you to Lola."

She could so *not* do this.

CHAPTER 9

Javi

So much for attempting to avoid her. Javi cursed his horrible luck, even though he wasn't entirely sure why he didn't want to see Lola. It was not as if they left on bad terms. They had an arrangement, fulfilled their agreement, and parted ways on amicable terms.

She had been a ghost living rent-free inside his head for so long though. Never once had he suspected he'd run into her again, but here she was. His dumb-ass self stood there with his mouth slightly parted, looking like the idiot he felt like, and unable to form a coherent sentence.

"Javi." His sister nudged him, brow creased with concern. She gestured to the woman in front of him as if silently saying, *"Speak, pendejo."*

He cleared his throat, buying himself another minute. Was he supposed to pretend like he didn't know her? As if they were strangers and he had never seen her come before? Fuck, those were not the thoughts he needed to have right now. He was a grown-ass adult. He could be civil around a woman even if she had seen him naked before. Easy.

He opened his mouth to speak, but Lola beat him to the punch. "We've met once before." She said, almost begrudgingly. Monique shot her friend a look that clearly said they were going to have words about this later. "I just didn't realize you were talking about him."

It clicked for him then. Why Monique decided to bring Lola over. Mattea had mentioned a friend interested in reopening Phoenix Books during his repair visit. But the odds of that woman being Lola? It seemed so improbable and yet she stood in front of him, looking wildly uncomfortable.

Should it be this awkward? Perhaps Javi was overthinking it all. Apart from the split second of apprehension he spotted on her face when Lola noticed him for the first time, she had shown no other signs of tension, making Javi feel like this was one-sided.

In fact, she seemed pissed that he was here, as he came here today to personally offend her. Even annoyance looked sexy on her, which begged the question, what the fuck was wrong with him? He should not be turned on by her pissy attitude, even if it belonged to a beautiful, curvy woman who he couldn't stop thinking about.

"Well, small world," Monique said after a beat of silence, pulling Javi away from his lewd thoughts. She gestured at Javi, reminding him of a farmer showing off her most prized possession. "So, Javier helped out with a few renovations and fixes the other day. He was able to get them done faster and better than others I have hired."

Pride swelled within him. He knew people enjoyed his work from the continued services they booked and the smiles on their faces when he was done. However, hearing praise for him filled him with the assurance and confidence he needed to know he was making the right decision to leave his job and become his own boss.

Lola seemed intrigued by her friend's words, but almost reluctantly so. Her anger had not faded, he could feel it radiating off her as she scrutinized him from head to toe. "How fast can you finish a job?" she asked.

Javi shrugged. It was a nuanced question because each job was different and required different skills. "Depends on the job. I would have to know what you needed."

"And I suppose you have a waitlist too." She sighed.

That he could answer. Javi shook his head. "I don't. I'm in a transitional period right now. I'm leaving my current job to become an independent contractor. Monique and Mattea are one of my only scheduled clients at the moment."

He hoped more would come his way though. So many people he worked for swore to keep him in mind, but he didn't wait for their calls with bated breath. The industry he was in was saturated and any handyman that could do a quick fix at a decent price, no matter the shitty outcome, usually wormed their way onto projects for unsuspecting clients.

A flash of what Javi could only describe as hope gleamed in her eyes, but when she blinked it was replaced with the emotionless shield she had donned earlier. "I see," she said pointedly. "Unfortunately, I don't think that's going to work for me. I need someone who is both dependable and trustworthy. Sorry to have wasted your time."

Leaving everyone with various levels of shock, Lola turned around, her hair hitting his chest as she walked off toward another table. Monique's head swiveled between Javi and Lola, opening her mouth to say something, but then closing it the next second as if she thought better of it.

Ofelia stared suspiciously at her brother, her hand on her

jutted-out hip. "I don't understand. Did you say something wrong?"

Bless his sister for always having his back and supporting him, but now wasn't the time to get into it. Every instinct in his body told him to go after Lola and demand answers from her. Why was she acting so cold toward him? What did he do to warrant such a response? It couldn't be because he left her six months ago without saying goodbye...could it? They had an agreement and he was following said agreement.

"I'll be right back." Javi said, ignoring the protests from both his sister and Monique. He couldn't hash it out with them right now. He was never one to wait for an answer to show up; he had always been of the mindset that one had to seek answers for themselves. So here he was, seeking the damn answer and hoping it didn't backfire on him.

He found Lola busying herself at a station for extra supplies, trying to tidy up the already impeccable spread. She was actively ignoring him but he didn't understand why she was so angry. He understood that the situation was awkward, but was it that horrible to run into him? Apparently, it was.

"Lola." He spoke her name, and her entire body tensed.

After a few moments, he watched as Lola reluctantly turned around to meet his gaze. Her brows were squeezed tightly together and her lips were pursed together in a tight line. She crossed her arms over her ample chest, pushing together her breasts. Her cleavage was on full display and he did his best to look anywhere but at her chest, no matter how badly the temptation to peek was.

"Lola," he said again, taking her silence as motivation to continue. "I don't know why you're upset with me, but I clearly did something to piss you off. Want to tell me what I did so I can fix it?"

She laughed, her lips forming a cruel smile. "As if you don't know," she spat.

"I really don't," he said through gritted teeth, knowing if he lost his temper it would escalate the situation.

"Right. You are going to stand here and act a fool when your family is five feet away."

"I'm not acting. I legit don't know what you're talking about."

"You're married, Javi!" Her voice was just loud enough that the table nearest to them looked up. The couple gave them reproachful glances before helicoptering over their toddlers again. Lola didn't notice, or didn't care, because she continued on. "And you have two kids. Do they know their dad is a player? Is that what you are teaching your son? I swear men are all the same. All dogs. Only wanting the next shiny thing that walks by. I should cut off your—"

"Lola!" Javi had to raise his voice to be heard over her tangent. She was clearly not happy to be cut off and sent him a reproachful glare. Her anger made sense to him now. It was almost comical that he had not realized how it would have looked like to her from the beginning.

His amused expression only made Lola more fiery with passion. "Oh, don't you look smug now. Just wait until I tell your wife what a bastard you are. She's gorgeous. She'll find better—"

"Lola! Damn girl, I'm not married. She's not my wife." This time Javi was laughing. Not at Lola, but at the situation. He was so used to doing everything with his sister and their kids now, he never stopped and wondered what it looked like to outsiders. Maybe that was why he wasn't getting any dates. Cockblocked by his own sister.

"Ofelia is my sister," he explained, watching Lola's face heat in embarrassment. "The boy is my nephew. The girl is my daughter though, but I swear to you I'm not married and I don't have a girlfriend. I also didn't have those things when we..." He trailed off, trying to find a word for it that was appropriate for their current public setting.

"Fucked," Lola supplied. So much for decency.

"Yeah." He brought his hand to the back of his neck, rubbing out a knot that was forming. "I'm sorry. I didn't realize how it must have looked until you said something."

It wasn't as if he knew Lola was going to be there or had any time to prepare himself for what he was going to do when he saw her, but he hadn't imagined a second meeting with her going like this.

He waited for her to say something, but she chewed on her bottom lip, lost in her own thoughts. He wondered if this was his cue to leave. He took a step back, knowing both Ofelia and Monique were watching the whole exchange. "I should go. It was nice to see you again Lola. I can give Monique some recommendations on contractors for you." Since she most certainly wouldn't be hiring him. That was okay though. She needed to find someone she would be comfortable with.

Javi turned to leave, but he didn't make it two steps before a hand shot out and wrapped its fingers around his wrist, stopping him. He angled his body toward hers, one brow raised in a silent question.

Lola slowly dropped her hand, bringing it back down to her side. "Do you have any availability on Monday?"

Today was Saturday. Even though he wouldn't step back into work until Monday, his day was fairly light and he could squeeze in a visit. "I do in the afternoon."

Lola hesitated and he wondered what was going through her brain right now. He would kill to catch a glimpse of her thoughts. "Then maybe you could stop by Phoenix? Monique was right. I do need someone to help me get it reopened."

"Am I no longer untrustworthy?" he mused, unable to stop himself from teasing her.

Her brown cheeks flushed. "That is...still to be determined, but I don't want to gut you anymore, so I'll take that as a win."

"As will I. Then I'll see you on Monday."

"I'm not saying this is a done deal. I just want to hear your thoughts. I'm also a hard client to please, so don't think this is going to be easy work."

At that, Javi had no doubt. "When it comes to you, Lola, I have a feeling nothing is easy." He winked at her and headed back toward his sister.

Lola

Walking into Phoenix Books should fill her with excitement and a sense of purpose. And it did. Mostly. But these days, it was depressing more often than not, to walk in and find there was still so much to do before her dream bookstore could ever operate. Could she open it now? Yeah, probably. If she wanted to get sued, that is, and she did not particularly want to go through those legal matters at the moment. Or ever.

No, Lola had to wait until the store was renovated and ready to go. Everything had to be perfect, just the way she liked it. She was certain her former therapist would say she was projecting onto this store because she couldn't achieve perfection in her own life and relationships, but she didn't care. Lola had a vision and she wasn't going to let a single damn person stand in her way.

The smell of burnt coffee hit the air and Lola looked down to see the mug she made was full. She doctored the drinks, knowing Mona took her coffee in the same way she did. "Mona, coffee incoming," she said once she was finished.

Her squirrelly friend took the hot mug and began to pace. Mona was never one to stay still, especially when juicy gossip was about to be spilled. To her friend's credit, she had waited two whole days—a record—for Lola to finally be ready to tell her the truth about Javi.

After seeing Javi at the bakery, Mona transformed into a bloodhound, sniffing around for answers. Answers Lola was just not ready to give. She still needed time to process the fact that she embarrassingly accused him of being a cheater in front of a family with toddlers.

Sure, she was quick to jump to conclusions, but she blamed that on her own history of poor choices in men. Specifically, the one about to marry her sister. She was working on herself, but she still had so much trauma to process through.

She did owe Javi an apology though, and that was the first thing she was going to do when he arrived later. Right now, she had a best friend who would soon walk a hole through her floor with her pacing if she didn't open up about Javi.

"So I do know Javi..." she started off, taking a sip of her coffee. It wasn't the best, but it was hot and would soon give her the dose of energy she needed to get through the day.

"Yeah, no shit!" Mona rolled her eyes but was unable to hide her bursting curiosity. "How? And are we going bitch mode on his ass? Do I need to cancel him? Because I will. He's a damn good handyman, so it would suck to lose him, but chicks before dicks, amirite?"

"So you remember how awful my sister's engagement party was, right?"

Mona scrunched up her face in disgust. "Yeah, you mean the engagenent party you didn't know was an engagement party until you arrived?"

"That's the one." She cringed inwardly. It was just

supposed to be a family weekend with a nice dinner. She still couldn't quite believe her sister would betray her in such a big way, but Marisol had never ceased to amaze her. "I forgot to mention when I left the party and went back to my hotel, and I didn't go alone."

Mona's eyes went comically wide. "Shut the fuck up. Seriously, shut the fuck up. You did not just tell me you invited a strange man back to your hotel room knowing damn well how unsafe that is."

"I know, I know! But in my defense, I was sad as hell and wanted to forget. Good dick does that, you know? But I was responsible and took a picture to send to you! I just didn't realize it failed to send. Which is infuriating if you think about it. I paid how much money to stay at that fancy-ass hotel and their Wi-Fi is shitty?" She was getting off topic, but she tended to go off on tangents when she got nervous or excited. Or both.

"Fine, fine. Skipping past the part where you could have gotten murdered, are you telling me that the guy you hooked up with was Javier?"

Mona nodded, walking to the other side of the counter so she could sit precariously on a barstool. Precariously because the moment her ass sat down, it sank lower to the ground. She definitely needed new ones to make them more big girl friendly.

"Girl, you can't just drop a bombshell like that and not give me the details. Was he good? Or was he bad, and that's why you were pissed? I need information!" Mona pouted, discarding her untouched coffee mug on the counter to lean over and prepare for the tea she was about to receive.

A ghost of a smile crossed Lola's face. Leave it to Mona to make anything bigger than what it was. But her moment with Javi had been a monumental experience in more ways than one.

She couldn't shake him over the last six months, and seeing him again this past weekend brought the full force of that night back to center stage. She didn't think her vibrator had seen that much action in weeks.

"No, I wasn't mad because it was bad. I was mad because I thought the woman he was with was his wife. Turns out it was his sister and his nephew. The girl was his daughter though, but he said there was no girlfriend or wife in his life. Ugh, I felt like such a fool! I always jump to the worst-case scenario. Why is my brain like this?" Her dumb, over-anxious brain.

"First off, your brain is not dumb. You've just been in survival mode for so long and your brain is trying to protect you. And secondly, I feel like that was an easy assumption to make. It looked like one big happy family. Technically they were, just in a different way than you thought."

"He probably thinks I'm the stereotypical crazy Latina girl." Which was a stupid stereotype to even have. Expressing any strong emotion as a brown girl automatically made you "crazy." It was harmful and rooted in racism.

"I doubt that. But let's get back to what's important here. How was he in bed?" Mona grinned, moving closer. "If I liked dick, I'm sure I would be all up on that one. But I prefer the pretty kitties, so I'll live vicariously through you."

Lola snorted. She had known Mona all her life and her bestie had never been interested in boys. Ever. It was only ever Mattea.

"That's the worst part. It was amazing." Mona let out an excited little squeal as Lola continued on. "He was so confident and sure of himself. He didn't shy away or make a single comment about my body that wasn't wanted. He fucking worshipped me, and I've tried so hard not to think about how he blew my mind. How did I put up with Archie's five-second-sex bores for so long?

"Seriously. I don't think I've ever had a man make me come like that. I usually have to spend time getting myself off afterward, but nope. This man is magic in bed. Fucking magic." She finished her spiel only to hear another stack of books fall to the ground behind her. She groaned and turned around to see where the noise came from and wondered what broke now that she had to fix.

Lola didn't get to make a full turn when she spotted him, standing only five feet away. He wore dark jeans with a simple white T-shirt that had seen better days. Her stomach dropped as she moved slowly up to the man's face. Javi was here, and he was smirking at her. She swore she heard Mona turn around to laugh into a book behind her.

Fucking hell.

CHAPTER 11
Lola

Now would be the perfect time for the universe to spontaneously combust so Lola would not have to relive this mortifying moment. The damned smirk on Javi's face would be forever etched into her brain. She also wished her best friend wasn't disguising her laughing fit with horrible fake coughs, but this was her life right now and she had to deal with the consequences.

"You're early!" She accused him like a cheater who blamed their infidelity on their spouse arriving home early and foiling their plans. It was the only thing her embarrassed brain thought of.

Javi took his life in his own hands and leaned against the bookshelf. It creaked under his weight but didn't fold like she thought it would. Apparently, even the nosy bookshelves wanted to stay and watch her humiliation.

"I finished a job earlier than expected, so I figured I'd head over here. I'm glad I did."

Ugh, that infuriating, sexy smile was going to be the death

of Lola. Seriously, no one had the right to look that damn good and smug at the same time.

"Have you heard of knocking? Or do you frequently break into people's houses and places of work?" she retorted.

"I knocked. Many times. I figured you didn't hear me. I heard talking so I let myself in. I can wait if you want to finish your conversation though. I think you were at the part where no other man has ever made you com—"

"Oh don't get cocky. You broke my dry spell so I'm just thankful you weren't a dud."

She couldn't believe they only had sex once and he still occupied so many of her thoughts. What spell had this man put her under because she wanted none of it. Unsubscribe her from that brujo fuckery this instant.

"And besides, my last boyfriend wasn't stellar in bed so anyone could have beat him in a competition. Not that this was a competition, but if it was, you would receive a participation trophy."

Stop talking! Stop talking! Why was that such a hard concept for her brain? Instead, it felt the need to word-vomit unnecessary things.

"You aren't helping the situation, Lo-Lo," Mona whispered from behind her, loud enough for Javi to hear. "Perhaps, and I say this with all the love in my heart, shut up?"

Yup, that was what she was going to do. Shut up before she dug herself deeper into a hole. She didn't need Javi to know any more about her pathetic love life and lack of orgasms.

For a second, Javi looked as if he wanted to tease her more, if his cocky smirk was any indication. If he actually apologized for her lack of completion in the bedroom, she would simply roll over and die. It had been a good run, but there was no coming back from a blow like that.

Thankfully, Javi seemed to have noticed her discomfort and instead said, "I'll knock next time."

"Good." That was good. It would have saved her from this embarrassment. "So, we should get started?" she added after, hoping to steer the conversation back to the reason he was here in the first place.

Javi pushed himself off the bookshelf, which gave another groan of protest as he stepped forward, doing his best to tiptoe through the piles of books. That was another thing she needed to get around to doing: taking inventory. Mrs. Sanderson had an archaic way of cataloging books, which consisted of a pen and journal. Lola needed to bring this bookstore into the twenty-first century and put the books onto a database. Those were things she could worry about later.

"Let's start with you taking me through the story and telling me your vision," Javi suggested, stopping in front of her. She had to tilt her head up to get a better look at him. He was so tall. Lola wasn't short. She was 5'8". Having been the tallest girl most of her school life and well into adulthood, she couldn't help but find guys who towered over her attractive. She loved her short kings too, they just didn't typically love plus-size women, in her experience.

"That means walk him around the story, Lo-Lo. Don't stare at him and salivate," Mona unhelpfully supplied from behind her. She made a mental note to kill her later. Or tell on her to Mattea. She was unsure which one would be worse.

Lola—who was most definitely not staring—sidestepped away from Javi. She needed to channel the confident girl she had been when she met him the first time. That girl was still in her somewhere and didn't need alcohol to bring her out. She puffed out her chest some, thinking good posture might help, but in reality it looked like she was presenting her tits to him.

"So I guess we can start here. I want a small coffee area for my patrons. Nothing too fancy, but a quiet place to read and enjoy their drinks," Lola began, showing off the pitiful counter area. It wasn't much to look at now, but in time it would be a cozy oasis for readers.

She then led Javi around. Once she started talking about Phoenix Books, she couldn't stop. She wanted everyone to see the vision she had. She told him how she wanted custom-built bookcases, all complete with LED lights built in to add an extra layer of pizzazz. She did not care how extra it was and that it did not serve any other purpose besides pleasing her; she wanted it.

She also wanted to rip up the floors and put in sturdy wood panels. The current wood flooring was decent, but it was long overdue for a face-lift. Along with updating the various lights around the room. Was a chandelier necessary to have in the center of the store? Absolutely not and that made her want it all the more.

Then there were small electrical and water issues she wanted to make sure they addressed before opening. Lola did not want any surprises happening on reopening day.

By the time she finished showing him around, an hour had passed and her throat was dry from overuse. She desperately wished she didn't forget her bejeweled tumbler on her kitchen table.

Once they arrived back at the makeshift cafe area, Lola finally turned to Javi who had remained silent throughout the journey, only speaking up to ask the occasional question or to clarify her vision.

"So," Lola rocked on her heels, trying to hide her nervousness. She didn't know if she could take more bad news. She didn't mind a long time for construction, she just didn't like the waitlist she was put on or the flat-out refusal because she was too needy. "Do you think you can do it? What would the timeline be?"

Lola all but held her breath, watching Javi's face with the eye of a detective on his final case. She noticed the way he scrunched his lips to the side while he was deep in thought and the way his eyes bounced across the room, taking every one of her demands in.

"Well..." he started and stopped.

That one word alone made Lola's stomach drop. Javi was about to turn her down. She braced herself for the hurt and rejection that would surely follow.

CHAPTER 12

Javi

When Lola spoke about her store, her entire demeanor changed. She exuded confidence and Javi easily sensed the budding small business owner within her. She would be a force to be reckoned with and Javi pitied the bastards who stood in her way.

He didn't speak much during the tour. He was far too enamored with her to do much talking and any questions he had were usually answered with her next sentence. He understood why certain contractors would shy away from taking a job like this. It was time-consuming and relied heavily on attention to small details. There was a fair amount of electrical work to be done too, and finding an electrician with open availability was as easy as finding a unicorn in the wild.

Luckily for Lola, Javi was licensed and had a hardworking group he trusted to call upon when he needed the extra hands. Which he would. He couldn't do the entire makeover by himself. There were many moving pieces involved and Javi wanted to give Lola what she wanted.

Except what she wanted would come at a price. A steep fucking price.

He didn't want to let her down. She was bouncing on the balls of her feet like an excited child about to open their birthday present.

"Well..." he started and that single word wiped the smile off her face. He instantly wanted to take it back, but he didn't want to lie to her either. "This is going to cost you a lot."

The smallest glimmer shimmered in her eyes once again and she perked up at the news. "Okay, cost I can do. That's not a problem."

"It's going to be a lot, Lola."

"And like I said, Javi, that's not going to be a problem."

Damn. What was it like to be so confident in your financial well-being to not even blink when a contractor said a renovation is going to cost you? Good for her for living comfortably, but a small nasty part of him envied her nonchalance.

What did it feel like not having to wonder or stress about paying next month's bills? Or being able to afford new toys for his daughter without having to buy them secondhand? He knew they were lucky to have a sturdy roof over their head and hot meals on the table, but he often wished he could splurge just a little bit.

"I'm more curious about the timeline. How long do I have to wait for you to get started and how long will the reno take? Oh, I should probably also know if you're taking the job." Lola bit her lip, preparing for his answer.

He wanted to suck her lip into his mouth and ease her worry. To pull her into his arms and feel the warmth of her curves against his body. He wanted a lot of things he couldn't —and shouldn't—have.

"A project like this will take me around four to six weeks

with my full team. If you are willing to work with me on unusual hours, I can start as early as next week." Seeing as how this job would be the first he took on independently, he would have to work around his crew's hours until he could figure out the times that worked best for everyone. Yet, he could still start work on getting the ball rolling if she was willing to agree to later times.

Lola's wide eyes and slightly agape mouth made him pause. She stared at him like she was seeing double. He had to look to his sides to make sure he didn't spontaneously grow a third arm. Before he could ask her what was wrong, Lola threw herself at Javi, wrapping her arms around his torso and burying her head into his chest.

He swayed from the sudden impact but soon righted himself. His body acted on instinct as he wrapped his strong arms around her, pulling her flush against his skin. He rested his head atop hers, taking in the sweet floral smell of her shampoo. It fit her.

The way he held on to her, the position of his chin atop her head, and the way that neither of them seemed ready to let go, was far from the professional demeanor he promised to have. But then he heard them talking about their night together and hearing how amazing it was for her, sent pangs of longing through his body. He felt the same way and it was good to know it hadn't been one-sided.

Javi knew he should let go. He had been holding on to her for too long, but it wasn't as if she was in a hurry to pull back either. It was like she needed this hug as much as he did.

A loud cough from someone pretending to clear their throat soon broke the moment between them. Lola snapped away, turning to see Monique smirking at them from the counter. Javi forgot she was there and he couldn't help but wonder what would have happened if she wasn't. How long would they have stayed locked together?

Lola wrapped her arms around herself like she wanted to preserve the warmth shared between them. "Sorry," she murmured and he wanted to tell her to never apologize for hugging him, but she quickly moved on. If she wanted to pretend that she felt nothing when they touched, he'd allow her. For now.

"I'm so excited," she admitted. "I don't care if the hours you need to work are from midnight to 3 a.m., I'll be here. You don't understand how much this means to me. I've been trying for weeks to try and get someone to take on this project, but they kept falling through. Seriously, Javi, I could cry right now."

"But you won't," Monique piped up from the back, moving away from the counter to stand next to her friend. "So what's the next step?"

"I'll need to come back to take measurements and inventory. Then I can give you a better idea of the timeline and pricing. I also need to check with my crew and see what their availability is." Most of his guys he found through working on different projects and often took extra jobs on the side, like him. They were pretty eager to work on new jobs, especially the longer and more profitable ones.

The woman nodded and then Monique said, "Give us one moment." Instead of leaving, they turned around and discussed something in hushed whispers. He stood behind them awkwardly, pretending like he didn't hear them whispering about him. Which was surprisingly easy because he only caught every other word they said.

After a few minutes, both women turned around again to face him. Lola was all smiles and back to bouncing on the balls of her feet, while Monique looked more subdued but equally excited.

"I'm ready to move forward with this. Whatever you need, I'm here for." Lola said, unable to hide her enthusiasm which Javi thought was cute.

"Is there anything else I can help you with? Any questions you have about the process?" Of course, he would go over everything with her tomorrow after he got a better understanding of the layout and his part in this, but he was happy to try and answer anything she might have questions about now.

Lola shook her head no, but Monique spoke up. "Actually, I do," she said. Javi hadn't expected her to speak up and judging by the looks of it, neither did Lola. She raised a perfect brow at her friend which in return was greeted by a wicked grin. "How do you feel about weddings, Javier?"

A look of confusion washed over his face and Javi was rendered speechless. "Come again?"

"Weddings," Monique said like it was the most natural thing to say when talking about renovating a bookstore. Like she hadn't just stunned two people into silence with her wildly off-topic question.

With a roll of her eyes, she said, "Lola needs a date for an upcoming wedding. What do you say?"

What the actual fuck?

Lola

Her brain was still trying to process the fuckery that came out of Mona's mouth. She had not brought up the wedding to her best friend since she got the invitation in the mail a few days ago. The last thing she said about the wedding was she planned on going because not going would be so much worse. She most definitely didn't mention anything about needing a date.

She wanted one, of course, but she didn't *need* one.

"She has a plus one, and knowing her family, everything is paid for. So it would be like a free vacation for you."

"Mona, enough!" Lola couldn't believe her ears. She couldn't look at Javi and see the horrified look she was sure he was wearing. "We need to talk."

"But—"

"Now!" Her words came out forceful and she never spoke to Mona like this. Not once in their twenty-plus years of friendship, but then again her friend had never pushed her this far before.

She didn't wait for Javi or Mona to say anything. She

grabbed her best friend by the wrist and pulled her toward the back of the store, well out of earshot of Javi. Hell, she wouldn't be surprised if he decided to make a run for it while they were preoccupied.

"What the actual fuck, Mona?" Lola hissed once they were alone. She dropped her friend's wrist and settled her hands on her hips, keeping them occupied so they didn't strangle her best friend like she wanted to.

Mona had the audacity to look puzzled. "What? Why are you so angry?"

Why was she so angry? Why *wouldn't* she be so angry right now? "I have every right to be angry with you. What the hell do you think you are doing? What possessed you to think to ask Javi to be my date? In case you forgot, Mona, he is here to remodel my bookstore. That's it."

"Easy. Because Javi is hot and clearly into you, whether you want to see it or not. And I know you, Lo-Lo. I know you don't want to go to your sister's wedding alone. Mattea and I could go, sure, but it's not the same as bringing a date."

"It was one night! He's my contractor, nothing else."

"You obviously have chemistry with him. Who the fuck cares if he is working for you. He can work for you and be your date. Those things aren't mutually exclusive."

Lola had to take a deep breath because she was getting heated. Not just out of anger, but out of embarrassment. How sad was it that she couldn't deal with her own damn love life and find a date to this wedding? She probably looked pathetic and incompetent to Javi, having her best friend ask on her behalf.

She was caught off guard just as much as he was. God, she hoped he didn't think she lured him here just to ask if he would be her date. She didn't need him to think she was loca and for him to stay away from her. She needed him to take this job. Javi was her best bet to open her shop soon.

But maybe if he wanted to also be her date…

No. Nope. She shut down that way of thinking. Why was she even entertaining the idea? It was so unbelievable and unattainable, that she could not afford to put stock into the idea.

"Lo-Lo." Mona's calm voice wrapped around Lola like a soft embrace. She was shaking and hadn't noticed until Mona placed her hands atop Lola's shoulders. It helped center her and from slipping into more gray areas of uncertainty.

"First off, I need you to breathe," she said in a soothing voice. Lola took a deep breath in and slowly exhaled. "Good. Just like that. Now, I need you to look at me when I talk to you. Don't interrupt, just listen. Okay?"

Lola's brown eyes fluttered upward until she was staring into Mona's dark orbs. "Okay," she said softly, afraid of talking too loudly in case Javi was listening.

"I'm sorry I went for it without talking to you first. That was probably not the best way to ask him. But I'm not sorry for playing your wingwoman. This wedding is going to be hard for you and I think you deserve to have some arm candy like Javi. He would be a good buffer between you and your family. I want you to have one person on your side there. I know what a pain your family is and you deserve to have a good time at an otherwise shitty event."

So much anxiety surrounded this wedding. Mona was right. She didn't want to go alone. She didn't even want to go at all, but she wanted to face her mother's wrath even less. Perhaps that made her a coward. The only person she was marginally excited to see was her father. He had always loved her in his own way and his biggest fault was his complacency in their family dynamics. Besides that, he had always been good to her and provided her with money to chase her dreams of opening a bookshop, no questions asked.

A small part of her could picture Javi as her date to the wedding. The way he would look in a tux churned something low in her belly. To be able to spend a week with him all to herself made her squeeze her legs together in temptation. It surprised her how much she wanted that.

Lola let out a half sigh and half groan. "This is a wild idea. He's not going to go with it." If he was even still here. And did she even want to go along with Mona's ridiculous plan? There was no way this could end well.

"It's a tad unusual." Mona shrugged like she was commenting on shorts in the winter rather than a week-long wedding date with a guy she had a one-night stand with. "But I don't think it's such a far-fetched idea. Make it worth his while. Offer him extra money."

"Now you want me to pay for the date? Like an escort service?" Lola asked incredulously.

"Think of it as more of a bonus. Plus, doesn't he have a daughter? I'm sure he could use the extra money as a single dad. Kids are expensive. I've been trying to tell Mattea that forever, but she is insistent on having kids soon."

"Yeah, you'd both make good mamas," Lola said distractedly as she churned the idea around in her head. Of the wedding, not Mona being a mother.

She couldn't believe she was actually considering it. There was no doubt in her mind that she would love to spend more time with Javi in any capacity, but something like this?

But also, what was holding her back? She was a proud, sexy, Mexican American woman who deserved a little fun. Fear had held her back long enough and she was tired of missing opportunities to appease people who didn't give a damn about her in any way that mattered.

"Fuck. I think I'm going to do it," she said at last.

Mona did a weird little excited dance before pulling Lola in for a smothering hug. "Fuck yeah, bitch! Go get him. I'm cheering you on from right here," she said and gave Lola a push forward.

That small push was what she needed to get her feet moving. She needed to do this now while she still had some confidence within her. She prayed to God that Javi hadn't run out, though she wouldn't have blamed him if he did.

When she rounded the corner, escaping the labyrinth of books and scattered pages, Javi was right where they left him with his hands in his pockets. He was pacing quietly and hadn't yet noticed her return.

"Javi?" Her voice sounded small, even to her own ears, but it had the desired effect. Javi stopped his pacing and looked at her. She felt naked under his scrutinizing gaze. The earlier bravado was fading and she didn't want to lose her nerve. "I wanted to talk to you about the wedding—"

"I accept," came his reply before she had the chance to finish. He didn't even know what he was agreeing to and Lola swore she misheard him. But no, he soon repeated what he said, leaving her both stunned and another emotion she couldn't quite place. "I'll be your date, if you'll have me."

CHAPTER 14

Javi

The smell of homemade tortillas permeated the air, which meant breakfast wasn't far off. His mouth salivated at the thought of refried beans and fried papas tossed with scrambled eggs and sausage. Freshly made salsa would already be placed on the table, waiting to greet him as he walked into his sister's kitchen.

Camilia's tiny hand wiggled out of his and she made a break for it. "Tía Ofi!" she screamed, running into his sister's large kitchen. Before Camilia could reach Ofelia, her husband, Maverick, swooped in and picked her up. Camilia giggled, thrashing around to try and escape the man's grasp as he peppered her little cheeks with teasing kisses and tickled her sides.

"Good morning, my loves!" Ofelia dusted the flour from the tortillas off on her apron that once belonged to their mother. She moved to hug Javi and he—not for the first time—thought about how much he loved having his sister close by. Camilia was a great tía to his daughter and Maverick was proving to be a great tío and father. He was happy for the little family they created and even happier he could experience parenthood with his sister.

"Thank you again for watching, Camilia. I owe you." He said once he released his sister from the hug. He looked down at his dark clothing to find some of the flour from Ofelia lingering on his clothes and absentmindedly wiped it off.

"Nonsense. I want all the time with my sweet Camilia. She's growing too fast, you know."

Oh, how he knew it. Just last week he was wrestling with a rambunctious toddler and now all of a sudden he had a kindergartner? He desperately wanted time to stand still, but he also loved watching his princesa grow up and look more like her mother every day. It was a beautiful reminder that Estella was still partly with him.

"How's papá?" Ofelia turned her back to him, grabbing a plate from the cupboard to dish up breakfast for him before he left. No use in telling his sister he was going to a coffee shop and would undoubtedly eat something there, but according to Ofelia, a pastry was not a suitable breakfast item. He was inclined to agree with her.

"He's fine. I thought I would give him a bit of a break this morning." His father was good to watch Camilia in a pinch, but he was getting older and he wanted to respect his father's time. Ofelia loved having his daughter over, so leaving her with his sister was never an issue. He figured she was making up for lost time.

Ofelia handed him a bowl and shooed him over to the table where Arturo sat in his highchair, eggs and ketchup all over his face. He had bits of tortilla stuck in his hair as well. "Mijo, so messy." Javi laughed and ruffled his hair.

"He gets that from me." Maverick beamed, placing a squirming Camilia down in the available seat next to her primo. Fatherhood looked good on Maverick. He picked up his son and whisked him away, probably to clean him up.

Soon another plate of food was placed down in front of Camilia and Ofelia sat down in the empty spot next to her. "So, what are you up to this morning?"

Right. So he had not exactly told his sister why he needed her to watch Camilia this morning because he was still trying to make sense of it all. He didn't know if he was foolish or just plain dumb. Who in their right mind would agree to a whole wedding and be the date of a woman he barely knew and only slept with once?

Lola had requested they meet today to go over the finer details of their agreement. He suspected she meant their wedding date agreement, though he supposed it could also mean her bookstore renovation. Speaking of which, it was unclear if he was still hired on as her lead contractor. He needed to make sure of that.

Ofelia continued to stare at him expectantly, waiting for his answer. He didn't make it a habit to withhold information from her, but he figured it wouldn't hurt in this situation. Soon he would tell Ofelia everything, but he needed to figure out what he agreed to first. No use in getting her worked up for no reason.

"I'm meeting with a client about a remodel. This would be my first big renovation outside my current employer, so I want to make sure it all goes well," he lied easily enough.

The warm smile Ofelia sent him sent pangs of guilt through his body. He needed to remind himself he wasn't lying to her...he just wasn't ready to give her the full truth yet. "Oh, Javi, that's wonderful. You have to tell me how it goes," she said in between bites of her breakfast.

He most certainly would tell her how it went and come

clean about everything, in time. He wanted today to provide clarity to something he agreed to without any hesitation. The idea of a sad Lola alone at a wedding was enough to drive him into a fit of rage. She didn't deserve such torture.

Scarfing down his sister's breakfast—which was much better than his father could ever make, but Javi would be damned if he ever told his old man that—he cleared his plate and placed it in the sink, running water in it. "I'll text you when I'm on my way."

"Mav wanted to take Arturo down to the field today so he can see where Daddy works, so we might be there depending on when you're done. If we are, I'll drop her off at your house once we're done."

"We get to see tío's baseball field?" Camilia's head snapped up, bits of egg hanging off her lower lip.

Ofelia chuckled and took a napkin to clean her face. "We do. And I heard the mascot will even be there." Her words were met with more cheers. She would have way more fun with her tía and tío than she would hanging out in the house with her abuelo.

"Thank you again, Ofi." Javi came over to kiss his sister's temple and then gave Camilia a giant hug. She squirmed in his arms but hugged him back. He hoped she would never be too big to hug her daddy. "Be good, princesa. Papá will take you for ice cream later." Ice cream always made him the coolest dad and he will rue the day the simple gesture no longer works its magic.

"Good luck. Happy for you, li'l brother," Ofelia called out to him. He needed all the luck he could get.

～

THE COFFEE SHOP was surprisingly empty for a weekend morning. Typically, the line was out the door and every table and available service was occupied by a college student or a professional-looking person conducting work from their personal laptop.

Today only a few of the tables were occupied, mostly by friend groups catching up. The line only extended out to two people and for once Javi heard the soft jazz instrumental music playing. Off to the corner, sitting by herself with a journal, two large mugs, and several pens laid out in front of her, was Lola.

She hadn't noticed him yet, which allowed him time to stare without repercussions. Today she wore her curly hair in a half-up, half-down style with little strands framing her face. She wore a pair of blue jeans that looked as if they were painted on her body, hugging her thick thighs and soft belly perfectly. She wore a white button blouse that tied in the front, right under her breasts, exposing the black bodysuit underneath. She was effortlessly beautiful and Javi wanted to take in every inch of her.

He couldn't deny that Lola's physical appearance was the first thing that attracted him to her, but he was starting to learn more about this outspoken businesswoman and her passions. Each facet of her personality she revealed to him left Javi yearning for more.

Lola must have felt him staring, because she soon raised her head from looking down at her journal and spotted Javi. She offered him a tight smile and gestured to the chair in front of her.

"I wasn't sure what you liked, so I ordered you coffee," she said in a way of greeting once he took the seat in front of her. Javi wasn't much of a coffee drinker, but he also didn't mind the taste.

"Thank you."

"Yeah, not a problem," she said before they lapsed into an awkward silence. He knew she was thinking the same thing he was and they would have to address the wedding date sooner or later.

When he left the bookstore the other day after agreeing to her crazy plan, they shared no more words about the matter and she promised she would call him to set up the details soon. He still couldn't believe he agreed to be her date. What possessed him to willingly put himself in a situation that could compromise their working relationship? He couldn't deny the allure of a week with Lola.

After a few days went by and he had yet to hear from her about the wedding or bookstore renovation, Javi began to worry that he fucked up. Until she called yesterday out of the blue and asked to meet him at the coffee shop.

"We should—"

"I want—"

They both spoke at once, laughing nervously, but it eased some of the tension away. "So, I guess I'll start," Lola said, placing both hands atop her journal. He couldn't see much underneath her arms, but he caught a few words and her feminine handwriting.

"I wanted to give you an out before we take this thing any further. I realize how inappropriate the situation was and understand if you are uncomfortable moving forward." Lola looked up at him through heavy lashes. He saw how stressed she was over this whole conversation and he wanted to alleviate that.

"I don't want an out. I stand by what I said. If you'll have me, I'd love to be your date to this wedding." He had no idea whose wedding this was or where it would be held, but he figured those details would be coming soon.

"Well, in that case." Lola grabbed a sparkly pink pen with a fuzzy pom at the top of it and turned to a blank page in her journal. "We need to discuss ground rules."

CHAPTER 15

Lola

A well-planned checklist was Lola's idea of a good time. To-do lists, grocery lists, book lists...there were endless possibilities and it kept her tasks manageable and organized. With so much of her life in the hands of others and her unable to hold the reins, Lola desperately wanted some semblance of power back.

Hence, the checklist.

"So I think we should start with compensation," she said, ignoring Javi's cute, confused face. His brow furrowed and he scrunched up his nose as if deep in thought. She had not been prepared to see him looking all sexy in his denim jeans and long-sleeved white shirt. He made it hard to concentrate while the fabric pulled taut over the muscles he hid underneath.

She had practiced what she was going to say with Mona last night, probably a million times before her friend threatened to call the cops on her for torture.

"I would like to hire you as both my contractor and my date for my sister's wedding," she started, giving Javi a tiny insight into the wedding. She wasn't ready to give him all the details yet, though they would come in due time. "I would like to offer you two hundred thousand dollars. One hundred thousand to one hundred and twenty thousand going into my shop and labor for your workers, and the rest to you for all the trouble I'm causing you. I'll pay you half now and the rest after the wedding."

Javi completely short-circuited. Was he breathing? He had to be breathing. His eyes were the size of saucers, staring unblinkingly at her. His mouth opened and closed but no words came out, none that were coherent anyway. Not even his chest rose and fell with his breathing. Had she successfully broken the man?

"Javi? You good?" She thought about poking him to make sure he was still with her, but felt like that might send him overboard, so she kept her fingers to herself.

"Lola. I—you can't—you—I..." he babbled, his brain going faster than his mouth. She had expected some pushback because it was a lot of damn money. Enough to change a person's financial situation for a while.

"I can, actually," she said as he continued to sputter. "My father gave me access to a good sum of money to invest in my new business. It is more money than I will ever need and I can only use it for work-related purposes. Granted, my father probably didn't think about having my contractor escort me to my sister's wedding as work-related expenses, but here we are. The money is yours, and I'm prepared to give you half now to start on the renovations, and the other half at the end of our deal. Before you say no or try a bullshit attempt at telling me how I should spend my money, you should know that once my mind is made up, I rarely ever change it."

Mona told her she needed to be firm. There was no place for a wishy-washy attitude when it came to this amount of money. It was also important that both parties knew where they stood.

"Please say something. I need to know I'm not wasting either of our time. If you don't want to go through with the date, I understand and still want to offer you the renovation job." Lola's leg began to shake, a nervous habit she picked up in childhood that always made her mother smack her leg to keep from bouncing.

Javi miraculously learned to speak again and put her out of her misery. "That's a lot of fucking money, preciosa. I should turn it down because I'm getting the far better deal. You don't get much out of this."

Lola snorted, trying not to conjure up memories of the last time he called her preciosa. The way it lit a fire deep inside her, made her wish she could hear him whisper it in her ear.

She quickly shooed those thoughts away. "Don't I, though? I get my dream bookstore and I don't have to lift a finger. I also get saved from endless discussions with my family about how if I only ate more salads and less burgers and exercised every once in a while, I would have a man. The crazy thing is, I don't even like burgers and I do yoga every day!"

Javi rolled his sleeves up, exposing more of his toned arms. His body stiffened and his arms flexed. When she met his gaze again, his lips were pressed together in a thin line, eyes narrowed. "They comment on your weight?"

"I mean, yeah. Mostly my mom. My sister will give back-handed compliments, but my mother instigates it." She shrugged like it was no big deal since she had been living like this her entire life. It was just one of her mother's many quirks.

"And you're fine with excusing her behavior?"

The question was so unexpected and frankly uncalled for that it stunned her, taking her longer to compose her thoughts. "Well of course I'm not okay with it. It's not like I ask my mom to comment on my weight. I'm tired of fighting back. After you've lived with it your entire life, you become desensitized."

There was no mistaking her anger, and Javi had the decency to look thoroughly reprimanded. "Right. Sorry. I just don't like that someone makes you feel inferior about one of the most beautiful parts of you."

Fucking swoon.

What person didn't like being told they were beautiful every now and again? To feel desired and cherished. It wasn't a bad thing to want someone to lust for her body and she wouldn't feel ashamed in thinking so.

"You're forgiven, but now you know just a fraction of what I'm up against. Your presence is going to be a big help. Honestly, when you meet my family, you'll feel cheated out of more money. I assure you."

Javi still didn't look comfortable and she wished she could read his thoughts. She wanted to know what was going through his mind and try to help ease his worry. She would never ask him, but she didn't know how much he made and with a daughter, she imagined the bills added up. Being a single dad was a full-time job, and an expensive one, so if this could help him, she wanted to make it happen.

Lola didn't pressure him. She let him stew in his own thoughts as she marked compensation off her checklist. The next thing she wanted to talk about was the wedding dates. She guessed Javi would have to make arrangements for his daughter and she wondered if that was going to be a problem. A small part of her also felt guilty for stealing time away from the girl when his time seemed limited as it was.

"The wedding is three weeks away," she said, looking up at him to gauge his reaction. If he was surprised by the sudden date, Javi didn't show it. "It's being held in Colorado, but airfare, hotel rooms, and most meals will be provided. I booked us separate rooms for obvious reasons. We are going to be there for a week, is that going to be a problem for you with your daughter?"

Javi shook his head once. "No. Camilia will be in school most of the time and between my sister and father, she will be in good hands."

She placed another check in the box and looked at her last topic of discussion. "As far as renovation goes, we can start on your schedule. Mona is going to be helping out a lot so either one of us will be in the shop with you to answer questions or to address whatever you need from us. I'm not good with last-minute plans, but I know there are tons of them in construction, so I'll try to remain as level-headed as possible. This is my apology in advance if I get snippy. It's not you."

There was nothing left for her to say. She had gone over the most important parts of her plan and later—if he agreed—they would have to make a list of things that were appropriate to do as a fake dating couple and things they weren't comfortable with. She didn't have a lot on the not-comfortable list for them, but she suspected sex should be off the table for obvious reasons.

"So, what do you say? Do you agree to this crazy plan or would you rather not associate with my family drama? Totally understandable if you want no part in it. This is so out of pocket. It's not like—"

"Lola, I'm going to need you to calm down and take a

breath for me. Can you do that?" Javi grinned, reaching out a hand to place over hers.

She listened, taking in a deep breath and thankful that he had the decency to cut her off before she could babble on more.

"I already agreed to this and I'm not backing out of it. But...I do have one stipulation." That caught her attention and she raised a brow, gesturing for him to go on. "I want to take you out on a date first."

The laugh that left her lips was involuntary and way too high-pitched. "You don't have to do that."

"No, I don't have to. I want to. Think of it as a trial run before the big day. Don't you think we should get to know one another before we pretend we are madly in love in front of your parents?"

"Well, no one said anything about being madly in love." She blushed, but he had a point. They needed to know the basics about one another so they didn't come across as complete frauds. She should at least know his favorite color before presenting him in front of her parents. "Fine, I agree to a date. When and where."

The smirk that crossed his face was nothing short of amused. "You and me, preciosa. I'm taking you to bingo."

"What the fuck. Are we ninety years old? How about you pick me up from my retirement home and maybe I can charm the nurse into sneaking you back into my room I share with Agnes? The three of us can knit and talk about the good old days before the war."

"You have jokes." Javi took her teasing in stride. "But you are missing out and I would hate for you to have never experienced the adrenaline rush of your first bingo. Do we have a deal?"

This man was odd and damn her if she didn't find that extremely attractive. "We have a deal." She held out her hand to shake, but Javi took it and pulled her hand to his lips, giving it a gentle kiss. This man was going to be the death of her and their deal had barely begun.

CHAPTER 16

Javi

Two hundred thousand dollars was a lot of fucking money. He had the inkling suspicion that Lola was comfortable financially, but he had *no* idea just how comfortable she was. He not only had more than an ample budget for her renovation, but enough money to catch up on bills, pay Camilia's cheerleading fees in advance, and get his baby girl new clothes and toys.

Yet he still could not help but feel guilty each time he thought about taking the money. Before he left the coffee shop that day, Lola had handed him a crisp check for the amount of one hundred thousand dollars to get started on the bookstore. It still lay atop his nightstand, tucked under the lamp as he grappled with his conscience.

A few days after their coffee shop meeting, Javi had visited Phoenix Books to take measurements and start prepping for renovation. That meant packing up the books and leftover furniture to clear out a workable place for him and his team. There was only one problem: he didn't have a sitter for Camilia. His sister left to accompany Maverick to one of his games and his father was visiting with old friends in town for the day.

He hoped it didn't seem unprofessional showing up to Phoenix with his daughter at his side, equipped with a bag of activities. Today was a teacher planning day, meaning no school for kids. That left Javi with no other option but to bring Camilia along. Lola had noticed Camilia immediately because how could she not? Javi felt his body heat with embarrassment. "Sorry. I didn't have any childcare."

But Lola waved off his excuse and at first, he thought she would tell him to leave, but then she moved and crouched down in front of Camilia with a friendly smile. "Want to help me sort books? I may or may not have candy. We can also read some of them if you like."

Camilia's eyes grew wide at the mention of candy and followed Lola toward the back of the store, disregarding Javi altogether. He didn't know if he should be insulted or impressed that Lola jumped into watching his daughter while he worked and how easily Camilia left him. He went with the latter.

After several hours of clutter removal, Javi finished for the day. He followed the two voices he heard from the back and found his daughter and Lola neck-deep in books. Her hair was tied back in a messy bun with strands hanging out in all directions. The look of sheer concentration on Lola's face—eyes squinted, nose scrunched, and lips pursed—was enough to give Javi pause. He didn't know how he was going to survive the renovation and wedding with her looking good enough to eat, but he would find a way.

Somehow.

"I'm sorry to interrupt, but I'm all done for today," he had called into her office, both girls jumped at his silent entrance.

Camilia made a sound of protest. "But papá, we were just getting to the good part!"

Before he could answer, Lola held out the book to her. "Here. I have another copy and maybe your papá can read this to you tonight."

"Really?" The excitement in his daughter's expression warmed his heart.

"Really. I have an extra copy and I think this one needs to go home with you."

"Thank you, Ms. Lola!" Camilia jumped up and gave Lola a hug. She seemed surprised by this, but Javi watched as she relaxed her body and hugged back. "I'll go put it in my backpack right now!" She giggled and rushed out of the room.

Once alone, Javi took a step closer to lean against the doorframe. "Thank you for entertaining her. I hope she wasn't too much trouble."

"Not at all. Actually, she helped me sort all the children's books, so she was a great help. She earned her prize."

They fell into a natural silence, Javi in awe of how comfortable his daughter was around Lola. From the looks of it, Lola had seemed to enjoy their time together too.

Finally noticing him staring, Lola cleared her throat. "So, I'll see you next week then?"

"No," he said, causing her to frown. "You'll see me Saturday when I take you out on our date."

"Are you seriously going to take me to bingo?"

People slept on bingo and she would understand that soon. He winked. "Seriously." And left without another word. He took Camilia's hand and loaded her into his truck.

He spent the next two days with Camilia, taking her to a park and ice cream after. The distraction helped keep his mind occupied and eased the dad guilt of leaving her for a few hours tonight as he took Lola out on a date that wasn't really a date. Granted, she would be asleep and not even realize he was gone, but still. Being her only living parent, Javi took her safety and happiness into consideration at all times.

Thankfully his papá agreed to babysit and not even an hour ago the two of them waddled with blanket capes around their shoulders to Camilia's room to watch *Beauty and the Beast* for the millionth time. Both of them would be asleep before the credits rolled, snoring peacefully.

Javi needed to get his ass ready and stop thinking about all this damn guilt he was carrying around like a hard hat. His only concern should be what the best shirt was to wear on his non-date date.

Javi thought back to his sister's first date with Maverick. She had called him on the phone and he had to sit for hours, alongside her best friend Willow, to decide on the outfit Ofelia would wear. He would like to think he wasn't that obsessive over his choices, but after the third shirt he discarded with the others, he was starting to worry.

After a solid five minutes of staring into his unorganized closet in hopes that something would jump out at him, Javi settled on a maroon crew neck and his only pair of non-work jeans. After another ten minutes in the bathroom, he was ready to go.

It felt weird not picking Lola up, but she requested they drive separately. She said she liked having her own vehicle in case of emergencies, which he understood so he made sure to give her the address. Thinking of Lola waiting for him at an unfamiliar place made him leave the house twenty minutes earlier than he anticipated, but he'd be damned if she showed up alone.

The bingo parlor was downtown, a few blocks away from

Phoenix. Finding it wouldn't be a problem, but rather like anything downtown, parking was a complete nightmare. Luckily there was a garage right across the street to accommodate the various entertainment buildings downtown. Javi parked his truck on the second floor, noting the various open spots for Lola. Then made his way across the street and waited just outside the parlor.

He had been skeptical about it at first until one of his work buddies dragged him here a few years ago. There was a large bar that served beers, cocktails, and wine, as well as a rather impressive menu of street tacos. He remembered dragging Ofelia here a few times after to get her to experience bingo like it should be played. Admittedly, he knew bingo was an odd choice unless you were a ninety-nine-year-old grandpa.

Inside would feel like a small fiesta predominantly full of locals from various Latine cultures. Cumbia music played softly in the background and Javi felt at peace here. Like he belonged. The last thing he wanted to do was walk into a white-dominated bar and get looks because he didn't fit into their perfect little mold.

He hoped Lola felt comfortable too and that he didn't make a mistake bringing her here.

Not even five minutes later, she arrived. Lola was in a black dress and red heels, her hips swayed with each step she took closer to him. Her sweet red lips turned into a shy smile when she saw him. "I think I'm a little overdressed."

Her black dress—he was starting to think black was her favorite color to wear—was skintight, accentuating her curves. She wore her hair down in loose curls. She was beauty incarnate, and Javi felt like a dog, salivating after a particularly juicy steak. He didn't feel worthy enough to be in her presence, but he was damn glad he was.

"No, you look perfect." The words fell from his lips like freely given secrets. The deepening red tint to her cheeks made him obnoxiously happy to know he had made her smile like that. Not another man. *Him.*

"So, bingo. Care to explain why? I don't think I've ever played bingo as an adult," she said, looking up at the building with the flashing neon lights. The parlor itself wasn't much to look at, but the ambiance and food more than made up for it.

"It's easier to show you." Javi offered his arm to her. Lola did not even hesitate as she looped her arm through his.

He opened the door and walked them to the counter where he purchased their bingo cards and markers. The man told them the next round of games would happen in thirty minutes, giving them enough time to get their food and drink.

The bingo man gestured for them to walk inside where a lively crowd had formed. The cumbia music from outside had grown louder, reverberating through his body. Inside felt like a little slice of Mexico, with papel picado decorating the ceiling and terecitas scattered throughout the tables in little clear vases.

"Oh, wow." Lola's voice barely carried over the music, but he could still hear the awe in it. It was how he felt when he stepped foot in here for the first time. Seeing one's culture represented and celebrated in a positive light always left him breathless. He remembered why he loved coming here and made a mental reminder to start coming more frequently.

"Are you hungry?" Javi asked, leading her further inside.

Lola still looked like a kid in a candy store, taking in all the delectable sights and sounds. She nodded at him, though he suspected she was only half listening. "Let's—" she started, but then her eyes went wide and her body tensed.

Javi's own body was on instant alert as he swept his gaze around the room, wondering what made her react like that. He didn't have to wonder long because she said, "Is that...that one baseball player? Maverick Wilson?"

Of course his date would be a sports fan and he not know.

Javi's stomach dropped as he turned in the direction she was pointing out. He sent a silent prayer to God that Lola was mistaken and that his brother-in-law was not here on bingo night. But the moment he looked, there was no denying the familiar face of him and the woman sitting next to him.

"And—holy shit! Is that your sister?" Lola gasped. He remembered she had seen Ofelia once at the bakery.

Both Maverick and Ofelia turned toward him at the same time. His brother-in-law immediately noticed the woman next to him and smirked, but Ofelia's eyes widened in shock. "Javi?"

He was truly and utterly fucked, not yet willing to answer the barrage of questions his sister would undoubtedly ask him about Lola. He wanted to turn around and take Lola to one of those fancy bars he was complaining about. Ofelia must have seen the startled look in her brother's eyes because she moved from her perch at the table and hurried over to him, pulling him into a bear hug.

From over his sister's head, he tried to convey how sorry he was to Lola and how he hadn't planned this at all. But Lola was holding back her own laughs and shrugged as if to say, *"Well, what are ya going to do?"* He supposed this would be their first test in whether they could convince family members they were dating. Javi just wished it didn't have to be right now.

CHAPTER 17

Lola

It wasn't every day you got to go on a fake date and meet a sexy as hell baseball player. She only knew Maverick played baseball because her father was a big sports fan and whenever they were together, he always had a game on or gushed about his favorite players.

Javi had been mortified that his sister and her husband happened to be at the same place, but Lola didn't mind. It actually eased some of her anxiety. She didn't feel like she had to be "on" the whole night and find ways to carry the conversation. Lola thrived in larger crowds because there were always enough people to take the attention off her.

Javi begrudgingly led them over to his sister's table and she reassured him for the umpteenth time that she wasn't upset. Unlike some of her other dates who attempted to hide her or pretend she did not exist. Javi didn't do that. He let her keep hold of his arm as he introduced her to his sister, Ofelia, and her baseball player husband, Maverick.

"Why didn't you tell me you were going out tonight?" Ofelia said the moment they sat down. The table had long bench seats and as soon as Lola sat down, Javi squeezed in next to her. Two large half-drunken beers and untouched carnitas tacos sat in front of her, permeating the air with an oniony aroma.

"Or tell me you had a date with the woman who could hardly stand you at the bakery?" Ofelia continued, whispering the last part. Lola heard it as clearly as if she were sitting right next to her and felt her cheeks redden in embarrassment. She might not have made the best first impression.

"I told you I was going out." Javi shrugged, opening his phone to scan the QR code crudely taped to the table. It brought up a full drink and food menu. He passed his phone over to her with a smile. "Order whatever you like."

"So chivalrous," Lola teased, scrolling the extensive list of alcohol.

"You told me you were going out, but not on a date!" Ofelia chastised like only older sisters could do. At least that was what she thought anyway. She didn't really have a bond with her sister, but she imagined this is what a healthy sibling relationship looked like.

"Baby girl, leave him alone. I'm sure he didn't expect us to interrupt his date," came Maverick's deep tenor. How did Ofelia listen to that voice every day and not want to jump him? Not that Lola did, of course. She was more than happy to be fake dating Javi who made her heart skip a beat with a simple touch.

Ofelia grimaced. "Shit. We're crashing your date. Do you want us to find a new table?"

Javi said, "Yes" just as Lola said, "No." They stared at each other and shared a smirk before Lola continued, "No, please. Honestly, it's fine. It's refreshing to see siblings get along so well."

"Are you not close with your own siblings?" Ofelia asked, cocking her head to the side as if not able to compute that type of relationship.

Lola smiled to ease the knot in her throat. "We've never seen eye to eye." Lola settled on, not wanting to burden these strangers with her family woes. She felt Javi's eyes on her, but she was too much of a coward to meet his gaze. He didn't need to know how bad things were yet. In time he would be able to experience the drama of her family firsthand.

Maverick leaned close to his wife, placing his hand atop hers and giving it a gentle squeeze. "Don't grill the poor woman. We are trying to have fun tonight."

Ofelia's eyes widened. "Right. I'm so sorry. Sometimes I'm so nosey. I haven't had many days away from our son in a long time. Mav's mom is in town and offered to babysit so we jumped at the chance to get out of the house together. I need to remember how to socialize."

"Socialize less, loca, and let us find something to eat," Javi teased his sister with ease and then flashed his smile Lola's way. Her stomach did a weird flip that wasn't entirely unpleasant. One second she thought she was over his charm and the next she was putty in his hands. He was going to give her whiplash.

"Have you decided on what you want?" Javi asked. In truth, she hadn't paid much attention to the menu. The sights, aromas, and chatting had distracted her, but her stomach growled reminding her how hungry she was.

"What do you suggest?" Despite Lola's mixed heritage, her mother went to great lengths to whitewash her and Marisol. White was privileged and Luciana clung to that ideal like a too small dress. The white privilege never quite fit because their skin was a few shades too dark and their hair was too unruly to ever fit the mold, but that didn't keep Luciana from trying.

Lola often suspected that was the reason her mother was drawn to her father.

"You can't go wrong with anything, but my favorite is the birria tacos. Super juicy, a little messy, but so damn good."

Lola didn't know what birria was but a quick Google search told her the tacos were typically made from goat meat or beef and she liked both of those things, so that seemed like an obvious winner. She placed the order on the app, as well as a white peach margarita, and handed Javi back his phone so he could place his own order.

Ofelia and Maverick set up their bingo cards. They both had three each and spread it out among their side to get a good look. Ofelia popped off the lid of one of the markers and placed a neon pink dot on all the free spaces.

Of course she understood bingo but she had never played like this before and was intimidated by the three cards she would have to monitor. At least she had a pretty pink dotting marker to draw with if things went horribly south.

"So, I know about Camilia, but are there any other family members I should know about?" she questioned, raising her brow. Maverick and Ofelia were consumed with each other and not paying them any mind, so she felt now was the proper time to ask Javi about his family. As his fake date, she needed to know these things.

"Just my papá. We don't have any immediate family close by and Camilia's maternal grandparents live in Puebla so they don't see her much." There was a story there, one that Lola was not yet privy to. She wanted to know and wondered how much Javi would tell her, but she didn't feel like this was the place to bring it up.

She moved their discussion into what she hoped was more neutral territory. "Have you always wanted to be a father?"

His features softened, eyes crinkling in the corner. There was a soft peacefulness in his expression and not for the first time Lola wished she could catch a glimpse inside his mind. "I knew I wanted to be a papá, but Camilia was an unexpected blessing. My fiancée at the time, Estella, and I had just fallen in love and were starting our lives together when we found out she was pregnant.

"When Camilia was born, I knew that this is what God, or fate, or whatever you believe in, had in store for me. I was chosen to be her papá and I take my job very seriously. She's been my greatest gift and it's so fun to watch her grow into her big personality."

The love behind each of his words when he spoke of his daughter, tugged on her heartstrings. Every child deserved a father like Javi. "She is a special little girl. I hope she comes around to the bookstore more," she said and was surprised to find that she meant it.

A man with a greasy off-white apron soon approached their table, cutting off any reply Javi might have said. He said something in Spanish that Lola didn't understand, but it made Javi laugh. He then placed down the tastiest-looking tacos in front of her, with a side of broth for dipping. Like a dog, she salivated, nearly panting from the meaty aroma.

Maverick reached across the table and placed a large pile of napkins down in front of her. "You're going to need these." And he was right. The first bite she took after dipping the tacos into the broth, sent juices straight down her arms, all the way to her elbows.

Before she could grab the napkin to clean herself up, Javi beat her to it. He trailed the napkin down her forearm, making sure to soak up every last drop. Heat blossomed on her skin where he touched. There was no hiding the physical reaction her body had for him.

"Careful, preciosa, wouldn't want you to ruin that beautiful dress." Javi's voice sounded right in her ear and butterflies erupted within her belly. Her cheeks reddened and if Javi noticed, he didn't comment—thankfully. She took another bite, more carefully this time, and kept the mess at a minimum.

The music soon died down as a female voice came over the speaker. "Señoras y señores, welcome to another night of bingo!" Loud cheering answered the woman's voice and Lola found herself cheering alongside them. "We will be getting started in just a few minutes. Make sure your cards are out in front of you and your markers are working. Any problems and one of our employees will come to help you. Just raise your hand."

The music turned on after that and begrudgingly, Lola pushed her food to the side to spread out her cards. She must have looked nervous because Javi placed a hand on her thigh and Lola had to squeeze her legs together. "Don't worry. I'll help you. It can be a lot to look over at once."

"Just don't try to cheat me out of my prize."

The man's cocky smile made her forget his sister and her husband were sitting right in front of them. "Oh, I would never."

Her cheeks ached from all the damn smiling she was doing around him. No man had the right to be this smooth. Neither one of them addressed the hand on her leg and she wasn't in a rush to move him away. He brought her comfort and she wasn't one to turn that down.

After a few minutes and once the employees of the parlor made sure everyone had the necessary tools, the woman came back on stage, dressed in a metallic silver dress that reminded

Lola of a disco ball. She once again wondered what she had gotten herself into, but since everyone else seemed to be chill with the talking disco ball lady, so was she.

Disco Lady didn't hold back. As soon as she started calling numbers, it was a mad dash to mark them off, and multiple times Javi had to take over one of her cards to make sure that all the numbers were scratched off. She had gotten so close to bingo multiple times and groaned when someone called out a bingo while she was one or two spots away.

The only time Lola had to eat and enjoy her margarita was between passing out cards, and even then it was only a minuscule amount of time. They didn't fuck around with their games here.

The next round of bingo started off slow. None of her three cards had much of anything and she muttered a curse under her breath. She didn't know where this newfound competitiveness was coming from, but apparently, bingo brought out the need to dominate her opponents.

After a few more calls, Lola looked down to realize she was only one away on all three of her cards. Her excitement took over and she accidentally elbowed Javi in the ribs. She ignored his grunt of pain and grabbed his arm, the nervous-excited energy getting to her. Her body buzzed as Disco Lady called out another number. "B-19!"

Lola scoured her three cards and found the number on one of them. She blinked once, then twice, because... "You won!" Javi beamed, causing both Ofelia and Maverick to look over at her cards.

Ofelia gasped the moment she saw the bingo. "You won!" she repeated what her brother said. "You have to say bingo, Lola. Get your prize!"

If she hadn't just been guzzling the largest margarita

known to man between games, she probably wouldn't have been comfortable raising her hand and screaming, "Bingo!" at the top of her lungs. But the alcohol coursing through her veins brought out her extrovert side and she didn't mind all the eyes on her, even some of the pissed ones because she called out bingo before they did.

"We have ourselves a bingo! Let's go check." Disco Lady said, sauntering off the stage and walking over to Lola's table. She shimmied her way between Javi and her, leaning down to check out her cards. Less than a minute passed before Disco Lady grinned and straightened her posture. "A winner!" she announced and the crowd erupted into cheers, Javi and Maverick whistling as if she had just performed an amazing stunt, while Ofelia whooped.

Digging into her chest, Disco Lady produced a gift card. "Here you go, muñeca." She winked, handing over the card that was once nestled between her boobs. Lola tried not to think about that and dampen the moment.

"Congratulations, preciosa!" Javi smiled and then as if acting on instinct, leaned in to place a soft kiss on her cheek. It happened so fast that neither could react. She felt the moment Javi realized what he did because he tensed, slowly pulling back. "Uh, sorry. I wasn't thinking—"

Before he could pull further away and finish his sentence, her own instincts kicked in and she grabbed his wrist, pulling him back and placing a soft kiss on his lips. Just like that. She didn't even second-guess herself. At least not much because it felt right.

"Here, I want you to have this." She handed him the gift card. His smile instantly vanished and it took her a moment to realize how that might have looked. She didn't want him thinking she thought he needed the money more than she did.

"For Camilia," she clarified, "let her buy a toy or two. That's a far better use of the money than what I could use it for."

Hearing his daughter's name made him relax. "That is very sweet of you. Thank you. She is going to love it." He tucked the gift card away in his jacket pocket, securing it with his zipper.

"This calls for a celebration. Next round of drinks on me. Lola, another margarita?" Maverick asked, standing up and stretching his tall body.

"Yeah, but maybe something a tad smaller? I still have to drive home." She laughed.

"You got it." He leaned down to press a kiss against Ofelia's mouth before heading to the bar.

Perhaps it was the adrenaline from winning or the margarita from earlier, but Lola laid her head down against Javi's shoulder. "Thank you for bringing me here. This has been so much fun."

"Good. I like it when you smile," he said, giving her thigh another gentle squeeze.

At first, she had been skeptical of the date, but she had never expected to have such a good time, even running into his sister. The rest of the night produced no more bingo winners, but that hardly mattered. She ate far too much and didn't regret it, got to lean against Javi, and laughed until her face hurt. It was one of the best nights she had in a long time.

CHAPTER 18

Javi

I t had been three days and Javi still felt the press of Lola's lips against his. It wasn't a particularly fantastic, mind-blowing kiss. It was chaste and hurried, and yet he couldn't stop thinking about it.

It ran through his head the entire drive to the parent line for morning drop-off. He had a rare morning off and was able to take Camilia to school. She was normally a bus rider, but Javi loved the early moments before school when he could spend some extra time with her.

He helped her get ready for her school day and drove through to get donuts for breakfast, something he didn't do often because Camilia and sugar were a dangerous combination. He felt bad for her teacher, but the smile his daughter gave him was worth it.

"I'll pick you up after school. Papá has to talk to you about some things." The "some things" being him leaving for a week and having to break the news to her.

"Am I in trouble?" she asked, pink icing from the donut covering her mouth.

"No, mija. Nothing like that. I can't stay mad at you."

She gave him a toothy grin. "I know." She had him wrapped around her little finger and they both knew it.

Javi pulled up in the line and an older black woman opened the door. He thought he recognized her as the principal, but he wasn't sure. "Well hello, Miss Mendez. No bus today, I see." Her cheery voice rang throughout his truck, reminding Javi that educators did not get paid enough. Who in their right mind could be that cheery at seven in the morning while greeting children?

"No, papá took me to get donuts!" she exclaimed while her principal helped unbuckle her.

He turned his body, catching Camilia before she sprung out of the car. "I'll see you after school. Love you, princess. Be good." He kissed her temple seconds before she swung her backpack around, nearly decapitating him in her efforts to get out of the car.

"Goodbye, Mr. Mendez. We'll make sure she doesn't take the bus." With that, the principal shut the door and Javi was prompted to drive forward. He stayed to make sure Camilia got into the building safely before driving out of the school parking lot, hanging a left at the stop sign.

Although he was off from his normal job, he still had a bookstore he had to renovate. He'd also be lying if the thought of seeing Lola didn't awaken a primal part of him. He wondered what she'd be wearing today. If she had decided to leave the house with makeup or sport her messy bun and puffy eyes. Both were incredibly sexy to him.

He pulled up to the bookstore ten minutes later, miraculously finding parking right outside. He grabbed his clipboard and a few tools he would need to start working on the cafe area. He had a crew coming in tomorrow to get started on the custom built-ins, since those were going to be the heart of the store.

The chime above the door—recently installed—alerted anyone who may be inside to his arrival. He only had to walk a few steps to see that the woman lounging in an old leather chair was not Lola. Disappointment settled over him like the cobwebs hanging from the corners of the shop. He tried to hide his reaction though when Monique looked up from her book and nodded at him.

"What's good, Javi? Lola won't be here today—she's dealing with a dress issue for the wedding. Her family's fucked, let me tell you." She rolled her eyes, letting him know just what she thought about the situation. Curiosity seared through him, as questions burned on the tip of his tongue. It wasn't his place to ask and he doubted Monique would provide much insight anyway.

"Anyway, she left you this," Monique added, reaching for papers on the table and handing them over. Javi looked them over, discovering a plane ticket as well as a note from Lola that read:

Javi,

I'm going to be busy with dress shopping and last-minute wedding preparations over the next few days, so I don't think I'll have a chance to give this to you in person. Here is your plane ticket for Saturday. Please be at the airport early and I'll meet you at our gate. Feel free to text me anytime.

Lola

Holding the plane ticket made their situation a reality. As much fun as they had together the other night, and as much as his body yearned for her, this was a job. She hired him to renovate her bookstore and be her date to a wedding she couldn't face alone. Lola hadn't told him the reason for that yet, but he planned to ask her about it as soon as they were on the plane. It was perhaps a dick move since she literally had nowhere else to go and couldn't excuse herself from answering, but he needed answers.

"Thank you. If you see her, will you tell her I sent over a schedule for the shop for the next few weeks? Someone's going to have to be here while we are at the wedding to answer any questions my guys might have."

"It'll be me or Mattea. I'll have her forward that email to me. Imma head to the back, if you wanna get to work. Just let me know when you're done." Monique grabbed her book with a half-naked woman on the front and a stained mug filled with coffee and headed to the back.

As much as he wanted to see Lola, this at least provided him an opportunity to be productive. He began the tedious, yet stress-relieving task of removing parts of the cafe area to make way for new furniture and counter area. He lost himself in his work, thinking about Lola's vision for the shop and feeling the strain of his muscles with each movement.

School ended promptly at 2:45 p.m., but apparently parents started lining up so much earlier. Except Javi didn't realize this, so by the time he finished up with his work and let Monique know he was leaving, it was already 2:30 and the line was wrapped around the school.

One would have thought the president was in town, but no, the mile-long line was full of impatient parents waiting for their children. Though, if there was one thing the school knew how to do, it was getting the kids out of the building in a safe, but fast manner.

It took about twenty minutes before he was pulling up to the same lady from earlier. Camilia stood next to her, Elsa backpack draped over one shoulder as she ate the grapes he packed for a snack. Her entire round face lit up the moment she saw his car.

"Hi papá!" She greeted him as soon as the door was opened for her. "We got to touch frogs in school today! They were slimy and a little smelly." She then went on to list all the facts she learned about frogs today, while her principal finished getting her in the car, waving a hasty goodbye, and closing the door.

"Can we get a pet frog?" she asked as he drove off. It was her thing to ask about any new animals she learned about and Javi was not about to try and keep up with a frog. He could only imagine where it would end up.

"Let's keep frogs at school."

A dramatic sigh from the back answered him, and he couldn't help but laugh. He only hoped his next words got him a different reaction. "Are you hungry? Why don't we go out to eat?"

Camilia's hazel eyes grew wide, her long eyelashes fluttering. Going out to eat was a novelty that they rarely did, unless it was Maverick and Ofelia taking them. Then they would pay the bill after some protests from Javi, even knowing damn well he didn't have spare money lying around to pay for the fancy-ass places they liked.

Lola had given him financial security and although it felt

weird to use the money on such trivial things, Camilia enjoyed going out to restaurants. He didn't want to deny her because he was uncomfortable spending money.

The excited hollering coming from the back seat was all the indication he needed to know she liked his idea. The Italian restaurant down the road from their house was one of her favorites and a large greasy pizza sounded like exactly what the two of them needed.

Not even fifteen minutes later, they arrived at the restaurant and Javi requested a booth by the window so Camilia could look out and people watch. Water for him and juice for her were brought to the table and Javi waited until they ordered their half cheese, half sausage with onions pizza before he continued on with their conversation from the morning.

He hadn't yet told her about leaving for a week. Partially because he wanted to make sure it was still happening and partially because he was afraid of her reaction. After telling his sister, only a day after their accidental double date, he was grilled with dozens of questions, each of which he had to answer to avoid suspicion.

Ofelia was smart; his sister knew how to read him better than anyone else, and although she seemed skeptical about the situation, she agreed because she loved spending time with his daughter. Especially now that she had a son she could play with. How a two-year-old and six-year-old played together, he didn't know, but they always had a good time.

"Mija, you remember what I said this morning about having to talk?" Camilia looked up from the Barbie she snuck into her backpack this morning and nodded. "Well, papá has a friend who needs my help. She—"

"What's her name?" Camilia interrupted. "You have

friends that are girls?" His six-year-old looked flabbergasted and it made him laugh. She was a perceptive little girl.

"Her name is Lola. Remember her from the bookstore?"

Camilia scrunched up her nose, deep in thought. "Yes, but why does she need your help?"

"Well..." He trailed off, thinking of the best way to tell his kindergartner this, but also not wanting to lie. "She really needs a friend and I'm available. But it does mean I'll be gone for a week." He hadn't ever been away from her for more than a day, so he was anxious about how this would turn out. He trusted no one like he trusted his sister, but Camilia was his daughter and he couldn't stop the guilt bubbling within his chest.

"How many days is a week?"

"Seven."

"Oh." Camilia's forlorn gaze amplified the guilt. She picked at her Barbie's messy hair before her face brightened suddenly. "Wait, does that mean I'll stay with tía Ofi and tío Mavy?"

The tension eased, but only partly as he nodded. "And Arturo. Abuelo will be around too if you need him. You are going to have a lot of fun and I promise to call you every night, mija. But if you don't want papá to go, just say the word."

He waited on bated breath. He didn't believe in making all the decisions simply because he was an adult and excluding his daughter's opinion. She got a say in what happened to her too and if she wasn't comfortable, he wanted that to be known. Of course, that would mean losing out on one hundred thousand dollars and potentially any relationship he might have with Lola, but...

"That's okay. I'll have fun. You'll bring me back a surprise?" Relief washed over him like a tidal wave. Knowing Camilia was comfortable with his trip eased a tightness within him he didn't know he was holding on to.

"Of course, anything you want," he said, which launched her into an explanation of a new racetrack she just had to have for her Barbies and described it in great detail before making Javi pull out his phone and look up the exact racetrack she needed so he could commit it to memory.

Thankfully their pizza soon came out, sparing him another lecture on which racetrack was the best, for the time being. He chose the cheesiest-looking piece and placed it on the plate in front of her, while he grabbed two slices for himself. He couldn't remember the last time it was just the two of them out to eat, but he needed to cherish these moments. They went by too quickly.

Enjoying their night out together was much easier now that he got the secret off his chest and they began to brainstorm everything she needed to pack for a week-long trip to her tía's house. What clothes, toys, and bathroom products she needed.

They ended their dinner with a slice of chocolate cake and once they were done, Javi carried her and the leftovers to the car. They hadn't even pulled out of the restaurant when he heard soft snoring from behind him.

CHAPTER 19

Lola

One would have thought there was a death in the family with how distraught and erratic her mother and sister were being. No one had died, apart from many of her brain cells and her patience, but dealing with the stress of a funeral would be preferred over dealing with the unnecessary chaos of finding the perfect bridesmaid dress.

More than once, Lola had burst into angry tears after a grueling phone call with her mother and her sister's hysterical voice in the background. "Tell her she needs to find a dress that will fit her before she gets here! I need to see pictures!" It was the same lines from her sister each phone call since her mother had informed Marisol that Lola would be a bridesmaid.

Her mother and sister had no idea how Lola was going to dress her size eighteen body. They insisted she needed someone to make her a dress because *"no boutiques would carry her size."* And therein lay the problem. They only ever stepped foot into high-end boutiques or designer clothing stores, knowing damn well they never carried anything for larger bodies.

So Lola had to have the same damn conversation she had

countless times before. Yes she would be able to find a dress, but no she couldn't shop in the same boutiques as them. If her mother didn't want all this added "stress" Lola was supposedly giving her, she shouldn't have made her a bridesmaid.

Lola didn't even bother to mention how hypocritical her family's statement was, considering nobody but her father gave a damn about her unless their image was called into question. She also didn't remind her that Marisol was marrying her ex because it was not a fight she wanted to have.

Finding a dress wouldn't have been so hard if she didn't have a looming cloud over her, ready to rain down and dampen any potential dress she picked. Lola had lived in a curvier body most of her life; she knew which places carried her size and where to find the cutest clothes for her body type.

She started off at multiple bridal stores that carried plus-sizes and tried on an armful of dresses. She video called her mom because her sister was far too bogged down with important wedding matters to pay her any mind. The reactions were much the same, all far too critical and finding something minor wrong with the dress.

The dress hugged her tummy too tightly. This dress was too short. That dress's neckline was too low and her boobs were going to pop out. The list went on and on.

It was on day three when Lola lost her composure with her mother, scaring the poor fitting room attendant in the process. "I have tried on every goddamn navy-colored dress in a thirty-mile radius from my house and not one of them is good enough for you. You get this dress or you don't get anything. Make your choice, right now, because I'm so tired of hearing you belittle me and my body."

As soon as the words left her mouth, she wanted to take them back and apologize. She didn't speak to her mother like this—ever. It didn't matter how snide her mother's comments were, she held the aggression deep inside herself, letting it fester until, apparently, this moment. The screen was a big reason for her newfound courage, but she still found herself clamping her mouth shut with invisible nails to keep herself from taking it all back.

Her mother's stunned expression stilled on the screen with her brows raised high to her hairline and lips pressed in a tight line. Lola thought she was frozen and went to tap the screen as if that would somehow make her mother move.

"The dress is fine," her mother's demure voice said after a moment, shocking the hell out of her. "Get the white heels you showed me earlier. I'll see you at the hotel in a few days." After a curt goodbye, her mother hung up the phone.

Not an hour later, Lola was back at her house, packing two suitcases for her weeklong Colorado trip. Her mother would have thrown a fit if she saw the folded bridesmaid dress at the bottom of the suitcase, so she made a mental note to take it out as soon as she got to the hotel.

The contents of her closet were strewn across her bedroom floor and her bathroom was in complete disarray as she began to pack toiletries and makeup. Sometime throughout the night, she managed to send Javi a text asking if he received the plane ticket she printed out for him.

He replied almost instantly with a thumbs-up emoji.

Make sure to be at the airport two hours before takeoff. You never know what the crowds will be like.

See you then, preciosa.

Preciosa. Every time he called her that, her heart did a

somersault and she thought back to their first night together and the way he dominated her in bed. No man should have this much power over her and yet, if he asked her to slide into his bed naked, she wouldn't fucking hesitate.

And that was just sad.

Not for the first or second time since Javi unexpectedly came back into her life did she have to remind herself that everything between them was just an illusion and despite the fact that it felt so right, it had an expiration date. Did that mean she couldn't enjoy him while they were together?

Yes. That was exactly what that meant—she needed to push all horny thoughts away and finish packing. She mentally packaged up all thoughts of Javi and filed them away in her mind so she could go back to getting her things into suitcases.

It was nearly midnight by the time she finally crawled into her unmade bed and fell fast asleep. What felt like only seconds later her four a.m. alarm roared to life, bringing her out of the midst of REM sleep.

Her clothes were already laid out from the night before and she mentally thanked her last-night self for the preparation. Lola rolled out of bed, hair wild and matted to her head and last night's leftover eyeliner smeared across her eyes. She relieved herself before washing her face and brushing her teeth. She placed those items into her toiletry bag and gently tossed them into her suitcase.

Lola discarded her clothes into the hamper and put on cheeky panties and a white lace bra that made her boobs look great. The gray sweatpants she chose for comfort and slipped them up her legs and over her ass. The white crop top she made from a vintage band shirt she found at the thrift shop. She completed the look with a black tracksuit jacket in case it got cold on the plane.

Although she was no stranger to flying and airports, she still felt a tremendous amount of anxiety. Flying made no sense to her. How did a giant ass metal bird remain in the sky when all she could picture is plummeting to her death at the slightest bit of turbulence?

The alarm on her phone beeped again, letting her know she needed to get her ass in her car. Mona had offered to drive her but she was barely functional in the mornings, so Lola opted just to leave her car at the airport. Now that she was thinking about it, she probably should have offered to pick Javi up, but she trusted he would meet her there.

Loading up her big suitcase and carry-on, Lola checked once more to make sure she had her phone, chargers, and AirPods. She did. Which wasn't surprising because she checked ten times and each time they were at the bottom of her purse and didn't magically jump out like her brain kept telling her they did.

Her brain was extra nervous today because in a matter of hours, she would be face-to-face with her family. Once again she would have to see Marisol with Archie looking perfect and beautiful together. Marisol was the type of woman who would make any rich entrepreneur happy. Looking back now, she would never have fit into Archie's lifestyle, but she would have tried until it consumed her and spat her back out.

All of her feelings for Archie had faded long ago, so seeing him would no longer feel like a knife wound to the heart; however, being around her family while they flocked around Marisol and silently compared the sisters was enough to bring on the panic attack bubbling near the surface.

She had to remember that she wasn't going to face them alone. Javi would be there and despite the fact that she was paying him to be at her side, Javi liked her. He calmed her in ways she had never experienced before and Lola was hoping that would continue during their week together.

Lola pulled up to the parking area she prepaid for, scanning her barcode before the barrier went up to let her in. The parking area was only half full, so she took that as a good sign and hoped that Javi wouldn't have any trouble finding a spot.

Getting her stuff from her car, onto the shuttle, and through baggage drop-off took twenty minutes, but she had not seen or heard from Javi yet. She sent him a quick text letting him know she was there as she waited in the TSA line. Her nerves skyrocketed when the sleep-deprived TSA agent barked orders at everyone to take off their shoes and remove all large electronic items from their bags. Not really knowing what counted as a large electronic, Lola dumped the contents of her purse out and tossed her carry-on onto the conveyor belt, and hoped for the best. Five minutes later she was through.

Their flight would take off from Gate 20 and judging from the numbers hanging on the walls, she wasn't too far. A small crowd had already begun to grow, all seated with their headphones on and their noses in their phones. Not one of them was Javi.

Dread began to bubble in her belly as she pulled out her phone to check the time. There was still an hour and a half before takeoff and she had to remind herself that not everyone was crazy like her and arrived well before their flight. Javi would be here. He wasn't the type of guy to just leave her hanging.

At least, she didn't *think* he was...

No, not him. She hadn't known him for long, but from their work interactions and their date, she knew Javi wouldn't just leave her stranded. To put her nerves at ease, she sent him another quick text to let him know she was waiting by their gate. He had not replied to her first text, so she wasn't holding out much hope he'd replied to this one.

Thirty minutes went by and the crowd around the gate began to grow. She expected a full flight and knew it would be a mad dash to the boarding lines, even though they all had assigned seats. It was always that moment when they started calling boarding numbers that her anxiety began to spike and stayed high until they landed safely at their destination.

Lola's knee began to bounce, trying to dispel the pent-up energy inside of her. Another look at her phone told her that Javi still had not responded. If she were being stood up, this was literally the most crappiest scenario.

"Fuck this." She murmured under her breath and picked up her phone to call him. It started to ring immediately. And ring. And ring. And—

"Lola."

Lola jumped in her chair, nearly chucking her phone at the poor elderly woman next to her. She scrambled to catch her phone and bring it up to her ear. "Javi? Javi, you there?"

A low chuckle came from behind her and a moment later the seat next to her was filled. The familiar scent of citrus and clove filled the air. He wore something similar to her, dark gray sweats that made her eyes wander down to the impressive bulge between his legs. Her body flushed as she averted her gaze up to his long-sleeved black shirt and up to Javi's smug face. Clearly, he saw her checking him out, but she didn't shy away from his gaze.

"Sorry I'm late. I had to drop Camilia off at my sister's and I stopped and picked us up some breakfast. Did you eat?" He reached into the small duffle bag on his lap, pulling out a greasy white bag. How he got that through security, she wouldn't know. Her stomach growled at the sight and she shook her head. "Good. I like feeding you."

Javi unwrapped her breakfast taco and when he asked if she liked salsa and Lola nodded her head, he opened up the tortilla and poured salsa on her taco. All she could do was watch as his man prepared her food. It was a simple gesture, but he still went out of his way to do it for her.

The taco was delicious and she avoided any spills on her shirt. The moment they finished their breakfast, Javi took the trash and tossed it away for them. When he came back, he placed his calloused hand on her shaking leg. "Are you okay? You seem...tense."

"I hate flying. It stresses me out," Lola admitted in a soft voice. She hated that she never knew if the seats would accommodate her, but she felt too embarrassed to say that, even to Javi.

"Ah," Javi nodded his head like he understood. "Well, I've never flown before, but if you need a hand to squeeze, I have two ready."

An involuntary smile spread across her lips. It surprised her that Javi had never been on an airplane before, but she was inexplicably excited his first time was with her. Maybe if she focused on his excitement for flying for the first time, some of her fears would slowly dissipate.

That theory was debunked the moment a woman's voice came over the speaker and announced they would start boarding first class. Lola sucked in a breath and reached for Javi's hand on instinct. He squeezed back gently, getting up and pulling her to her feet. "You ready, preciosa? I'll be right next to you."

His calming voice gave her the strength to move to the line and scan their boarding passes. Javi took the lead once inside the walkway, but he never once dropped her hand. That small gesture made her feel something she had not felt in a long time. Something she was not ready to identify quite yet. Instead, she pushed those new feelings aside and let Javi put their carry-ons away as she took the window seat.

CHAPTER 20

Javi

Leaving Camilia had been harder than he expected. His little girl didn't cry when he dropped her off, but she did pout and hug him extra hard right before he left. Ofelia assured him that she would be fine, and Javi had no reason not to believe her, but it didn't lessen the hurt at all. He promised to call Camilia tonight once they landed and were settled in their hotel rooms.

When he arrived at the airport—arguably too close to boarding time—the first thing he spotted at Gate 20 was a stressed-out Lola. She jumped when he came up behind her and he hoped the breakfast he brought would ease her nerves. It did for a while, until boarding.

Now Lola sat tucked against the window, hands in her lap, bouncing her leg up and down. He was beginning to realize that was her go-to when she was anxious or worried. She shut herself down, keeping the fears within and he refused to have her suffer alone.

When the plane began its takeoff, he reached for her, tugging her hand to pull her body his way. Her eyes squeezed shut and her breathing became slightly erratic. He didn't speak; he continued to hold her hand, rubbing soothing gestures with his thumb.

It wasn't until they were far enough above the clouds that she finally opened her eyes. He wasn't going to invalidate her feelings by saying takeoff wasn't so bad, so instead, he said, "Thanks for holding my hand. It made takeoff easier."

The surprised smile gracing her face would forever be etched into his brain. He wanted to always be the one to elicit smiles like that. To make her feel safe when they were thousands of feet above the ground. Perhaps this was the machismo in him, but he didn't care. Not when Lola was looking at him like that.

"I'm sorry I'm so nervous. I swear I'm not normally like this," Lola said, embarrassment coloring her features.

It bothered him that she thought she needed to apologize for her very normal human feelings. "It's okay to be nervous, Lola. I want to get your mind off it. How about we quiz each other? We were supposed to do that on our bingo date to get to know one another before the wedding, but then my sister prevented that."

"She did, but I still enjoyed our time together. Hmm, let's see," Lola said, biting her bottom lip while she attempted to think of a question. Javi tried not to notice, but failed spectacularly and had to covertly readjust himself in his seat. All because she bit her damn lip. "Ah, I have a question. Have you always wanted to work in construction?"

"I've always been good with my hands and I enjoy building things. I don't know if I've always wanted to do construction, but I grew up around it. My father worked for various construction companies and would tell me about the projects he worked on. I thought it was so cool. Once I got into the job force, I still felt that way, but I didn't like my management. It's taken me a while, but now I'm in a place to go independent." And now a lot of that had to do with Lola and the amount of money she was paying him for his first big job.

Part of him still felt bad for accepting the outrageous amount of money, even as he finally took it to the bank to cash last week. But another part reminded him how he was caught up with bills for the first time in a long time. He put most of the money in savings to pay for expenses and labor, still unsure if he was willing to accept the entire generous amount.

"Well you're good at what you do, and I'm excited to see what you do with my bookstore." Lola's words filled him with an insurmountable amount of pride. His chest puffed out like a damn peacock, ready to strut his feathers in front of the ladies.

"Speaking of the bookstore, you are going to be amazed at the changes already. The guys are taking care of it while I'm away." He smiled. Lola had been busy for the past few days and Javi had accomplished a lot, like completely stripping the interior until hardly anything from the original store remained. "Also, I noticed the plan you left out on the counter. The one for a large kids area. Will it be for more storytimes?"

"You noticed that, huh?" Lola's eyes twinkled with amusement. "I didn't realize how much fun reading to kids was until I did it at the bakery. I think I'm obsessed now. My grandma would read to me as a kid, and I want kids in the community to be able to experience that as well."

"What was your favorite book as a kid?"

"Oh, that's a hard one. We read so many, but I think my favorite was a book called *The Tortilla Quilt*. My grandma read it to me all the time. It was about a little girl and her friend learning how to quilt from her grandma. It reminded me so much of the relationship I had with my abuelita that I made her read it to me constantly." Lola laughed, a far-off look in her eyes as if she were transported back to a little girl with her grandma. "What about you?"

Javi didn't read much. He wasn't like his sister who could devour an entire series in a week, but he had enjoyed the bedtime stories his mother read to him as a child. "I think mine is *The Giving Tree*."

It was as if he said he kicked puppies on the weekends for fun by the reproachful look Lola glared in his direction. "Absolutely not. Your favorite book cannot be *The Giving Tree*."

"And why is that? I didn't realize this choice was so controversial." It was one of the only ones he remembered his mother reading to him because he liked how soothing her voice was when she read it.

"Well it is!" Lola all but shrieked. "It's a horrible story for kids. Promoting the idea that it is okay to give everything you have and expect nothing in return. Which, sure, a nice topic in theory, but the tree literally gave the little boy everything until she died. Where is the justice in that?"

"Well, damn, I wasn't thinking like that as a kid. I just liked the way my mamá read it to me before bed. It was like our little moment together," he explained. "She died a few years ago, so I try to hang on to her memory in different ways, you know?"

Lola grimaced and sank into her chair. She shocked the hell out of him by leaning her head against his shoulder. The touch shouldn't have felt as intimate as it did. "Well, now I feel like a dick. The book is so terrible, but your mother sounds like she was a wonderful woman. I'm glad you were able to have that time with her."

Javi thought back to the moments he had with his mother. She shaped his entire childhood and although they didn't have much extra money, Javi never felt like they suffered or missed out. His parents had made sure they were well taken care of and loved. He hoped Camilia felt that way, too.

"My mom was a great woman. She loved picture books too. She didn't read much unless it was to us, but I remember her taking us to the library, and Ofelia and I would spend hours with her looking at the books and reading them. Of course, my go-to was *The Giving Tree* before I knew how controversial it was." He laughed, tilting his head to better see Lola.

She didn't respond. Javi waited and watched the slow rise and fall of her chest, accompanied by soft snores. She had fallen asleep. Considering how high-strung she had been, Javi wasn't surprised or insulted.

A smile spread across his lips as he angled his body, moving his arm around her so she could nestle into the crook of his neck. Lola did just that, not waking up as she made herself comfortable against his body.

Javi leaned down and pressed a featherlight kiss to the top of her head. She smelled of lavender, reminding him of his abuela's house during spring.

The woman in his arms was beautiful. He didn't know what awaited them in Colorado, but whatever it was, he had a strong suspicion her fear wasn't entirely about flying. Perhaps it was what awaited them once they landed. He vowed right there and then to be her rock, no matter what was presented to them. She deserved the best and if her family couldn't see that, Javi would make sure he showed them.

Lola

Lola hadn't realized she had fallen asleep until Javi's gentle voice and soft caresses woke her up. She noticed a small spot of wetness on his shirt and was immediately mortified that she'd drooled on him. Thankfully he made no comment as she pushed herself off him and attempted to tame her hair.

Lola reached in her pocket for her phone and to check the time. She quickly turned off airplane mode and her phone buzzed. The screen lit up in her hand as missed calls and texts began to pour in. Most of them were from her mother and sister, but a few were from her father asking if she was able to board the plane okay and if he needed to send a car to pick them up. She smiled at his thoughtfulness and sent him a quick reply that she would arrange for an Uber. A few moments later her father responded with a heart emoji.

When the plane door opened, Javi stood up and stepped aside to allow Lola to get off. She didn't argue with him when he took her carry-on because her mind was clouded with thoughts of her upcoming meeting with her family.

Up until this point she had done a good job at blocking all thoughts of seeing her family, but now that they were only minutes from seeing each other, she no longer had the security of miles between them. How was she going to act when she came face-to-face with Archie? Had she steeled herself enough to face her mother's scrutiny? What jabs would her sister throw at her for stealing the man she thought she would marry?

Her body moved on its own accord to baggage claim. She sensed Javi next to her and felt his gaze bore into the side of her head. She could feel the unasked questions lingering close to the surface and she feared if she made eye contact with him, her resolve would crumble. Like a coward, she pulled out her phone and busied herself with ordering them a pickup to the hotel.

"I'll grab our bags." Javi said after another beat of silence passed between them. He walked ahead of her, and she knew he was giving her space to breathe. She appreciated that he didn't demand answers from her or pry. She couldn't put what she was feeling into words and didn't want to try to untangle the web of emotions dampening her mood. It would require too much backstory and though Javi deserved to know it, she wasn't quite ready to tell him.

She didn't want him to see her for how pathetic she was.

By the time Javi returned with her bright pink suitcase and his sensible brown one, their car was waiting outside. She led him out and slipped into the back while Javi and the driver took care of the bags. A few minutes later, both got in and they were on their way to the hotel.

She hadn't even realized she had been bouncing her leg until she felt a hand on her thigh. She recoiled and Javi pulled back, but not before she missed the hurt expression on his face.

Regret and shame washed over her like a tidal wave and she instantly reached for his hand to pull it back to her.

"I'm sorry. My family always makes me jumpy. It's not you." Above anything, she needed him to know that her tumultuous feelings had nothing to do with the man sitting next to her and everything to do with the people awaiting their arrival.

His face was set into a hard expression, brow furrowed, and jaw tense. "What are you not telling me, Lola?"

And wasn't that the million-dollar question? She wanted to open her mouth and blurt out why she was acting like a skittish cat around water, but if she did that, the tears would start coming and she didn't want to face her family with red-rimmed eyes. They didn't need any more ammo against her.

She should tell him. She wanted to tell him, but her lips weren't forming the words. She fought the tears that stung her eyes, avoiding his piercing gaze. "I can't..."

She didn't finish that thought because the car came to an abrupt halt, nearly throwing her against the seat in front of her. "Here," the man said from the front, looking at her through the rearview mirror.

She hadn't paid any mind to where they were and it surprised her how quickly they got to the hotel. It was a typical luxury place her parents would stay at with a slew of valet drivers waiting to park cars that cost more than their houses. It was at least fifteen stories tall and if she had to guess, she would presume their hotel had a spa area and several dining locations. One she was certain her parents bought out for her sister's rehearsal dinner.

Lola was prepared to ignore Javi's question and had her hand on the handle when he reached out and placed his hand on the door to keep her from leaving. The heat of his body radiated off him and couldn't keep herself from looking in his direction.

He was angry, but her gut feeling told her he wasn't angry with her. "Lola," he started again, "are you going to be okay going inside?"

She would have to be, wouldn't she? Lola dug deep within herself and pulled out what she hoped would be a convincing smile. "I'll be okay. Let's get through the initial meeting and I can fill you in a little more when we are in our hotel room."

Javi didn't seem happy, but he released his hold on the door and let her out. She took her opportunity to escape, hearing Javi move behind her. The door to the truck had been propped open and she started getting their things out. Or at least she tried to until Javi shooed her away and got them out himself.

"I can take my own suitcases, it's really not a problem," Lola tried to argue, but Javi shut her up with a searing look that sent her squirming under his gaze and squeezing her thighs together. She stopped arguing after that.

Steeling herself for what was coming, Lola took a deep breath and led Javi into the lobby of their hotel. A giant rock waterfall cascaded down the first floor into a small koi pond. Off to the right was a bar with a seating area, leading out to a courtyard.

Sitting at a circular table in the middle of the bar were four people she recognized. Only her father noticed her at first. Travis Roberts stood up, shaking the table in his excitement. Lola found herself smiling back at her father, a little of the earlier tension easing...that is until her mother, Luciana, and sister, Marisol, turned around.

Sitting next to Marisol was a tall, white man with dirty-brown hair. She had believed seeing him wouldn't affect her because she held no love for Archie, yet her stomach churned, threatening to discard her breakfast from earlier.

Lola could picture his hooked nose and thin lips. The way his eyes reminded her of a murky swamp. Her body froze as Archie slowly turned around. When he saw her, he scowled, before quickly changing his features into a toothy smile he used a lot with clients.

"Dolores, so glad you could make it," his voice—had it always been that smarmy?—greeted her from across the room.

Before she had the chance to address him, her father engulfed her in a hug. She smelled the cigar smoke on him and it reminded her of summer nights at their childhood home in Florida when she would cuddle next to her father under the stars. "Princess, it's been too long." Her father pretended to scold her, but the gleam in his eyes gave him away. "You are such a sight for sore eyes."

"I didn't realize you were bringing anyone." Her mother's voice invaded her senses, coming up beside her father.

Luciana and Travis could not have been more at odds with each other—appearances-wise. Her mother was of Mexican descent. Thick black hair that had been straightened almost every day of Lola's life. She remembered seeing her mother's naturally wavy hair once and how much her mother complained about it. Her mother was slender with soft curves. She had large brown eyes and lashes that nearly touched her eyebrows.

Her father was a white man whose family immigrated from England in the nineteenth century, opening up their own business that specialized in wine production. Her father inherited the company as his birthright and it would now be passed down to Marisol and Archie. Which was fine with Lola, she told her father as much when he tried to make the sisters partners in the business. Lola vehemently refused, knowing there was no universe she could work well with her sister, especially now that she would be marrying Archie.

"Dolores, did you mention bringing a plus one on the invitation? We are only allowed a certain number of people into the venue and—"

"Mother, I made sure to add a plus one." Lola kept her voice level as if the roles were reversed and she was the mother to a petulant toddler. "I sent it back and let Marisol know. I also mentioned it on our phone calls during dress shopping."

Her mother looked affronted as she turned her attention to her oldest daughter. "You didn't tell me this." It was her go-to response each time she wanted to deflect accountability.

"I'm sure I did, but you know I have so much going on." Marisol was the only person who could roll her eyes at their mother and get away with it.

"Ladies, ladies. Enough of the bickering. Our family is together. This is cause for celebration." Her father tried to ease the tension by encouraging them to sit down and enjoy a round of drinks, but Lola could tell her mother wasn't over the fact that she brought a date. The way she looked at Javi made her skin crawl, as if Javi wasn't good enough to be the dirt under her Chanel high heels. Her sister insisted they needed to check on the flowers since they hadn't gotten an update from the store in over twenty-four hours.

Archie, for once, left his nose out of the family discussion and nursed the alcohol in front of him. Lola wanted to dump the contents over his head, but she did her best to restrain herself, even though her sanity was hanging on by a thread.

"Maybe tomorrow, Dad. It's already been a long day and I just want to check into our room and rest."

Her father's face fell, but only for a fraction of a second. "Of course, Lola. Tomorrow we will catch up and I would like to know more about this boyfriend of yours, yeah?" Unlike her mother, his interest seemed genuine and not condescending.

"Right, of course," she murmured and gave him a quick hug. For appearance's sake, she gave her mother and sister an awkward hug and nodded vaguely in Archie's general direction before taking Javi's hand and leading him toward check-in.

"Lola—"

"Not now, Javi. Please." She didn't mean to snap at him, which she had been doing a lot since leaving the plane. She heard his intake of breath, but Javi didn't try to say anything. She didn't know if him talking or not talking was worse.

She let those thoughts leave her mind as she checked into the room. The chipper young woman hummed as she input her information into the computer. "Okay, Ms. Roberts. Your poolside king bedroom is ready for you. You'll be on the sixth—"

"King bed? There are two of them, right?" Lola interrupted her spiel.

The woman shook her head after glancing down at the computer. "No ma'am. Just one bed."

"I booked two queens, though. Could you see if you have anything else available?"

"I'm sorry ma'am but we are booked for multiple weddings this weekend. This is the only room we have available right now." She didn't actually sound sorry, more like she hoped that Lola wouldn't press her about it anymore.

The dam holding her tears back was going to break any

second. She needed to be far away from this lobby when it did. "That's fine." Her voice sounded hoarse and far too small.

"Great. Once again, I'm so sorry about that. You will be on the sixth floor on the left. Please call down if you need anything and thank you for choosing us for your Colorado stay."

Lola turned her back on the woman before she finished, making her way to the elevator. She pressed the up button and immediately expected the elevator to open for her. When it didn't, she pressed it again and again and again…

"Preciosa." Javi's large hand covered hers, pulling her back to his chest. She didn't fight him, she just let it happen. Not a moment later the elevator door slid open and Javi walked them both inside. It was a bit awkward to walk pressed up against his chest, but she no longer trusted her own legs to lead her.

He pressed the button for the sixth floor and let the elevators close. Neither of them spoke after that. She listened to the steady beat of his heart and counted backward from thirty to keep her composure for a little bit longer.

The elevator dinged, signaling they had made it to their floor. This time she pulled away from him so Javi could lead them to their room. She trailed behind him as if each step cost her dearly. She watched in silence as Javi opened up their door, propping it open to allow her in.

The room was beautiful, as she knew it would be, and very spacious. The small hallway held a bathroom off to the right and at the end opened up into a sitting room with a couch and two chairs with a coffee table. A coffee bar sat on the opposite side of the wall. Past the sitting area was the bedroom with one large king-sized bed overlooking the balcony.

And that's when Lola lost it. The stress of the day, preparing to see her family and her ex, and finally the stupid mess up of rooms pushed her over the edge. She couldn't stop the panic attack if she wanted to. Anxiety was stupid and nonsensical. Each hole in her perfectly curated dam had weakened her resolve. Now it was destroyed and she unleashed the bubbling sobs in her throat.

Javi

From the time they boarded the plane until the moment they made it to the hotel, Javi had felt the tension rolling off Lola in waves. Each time he attempted to provide comfort, with the exception of the plane ride, she flinched at his touch or snapped at him. He didn't take it personally though because his girl was so deep into her own head that she was barely registering reality.

It just didn't make sense why she was icing him out and that bothered him. Lola had given him very little to go off and though weddings and families could be a stressful thing, the degree to which Lola felt anxious wasn't normal. So what was he missing?

He hadn't expected a welcoming committee upon his arrival, but at the very least he expected more than the reproachful looks he got from her mother and sister. The three women all held a striking resemblance to one another. All had a thick head of midnight-black hair, but Lola was the only one who wore it in its natural curly state. They had the same plump lips and hazel eyes. The other two women lacked the curves Lola had, curves Javi found extremely alluring.

Her father was the only one who seemed interested in meeting him. The only other person Javi couldn't quite get a read on was the other man sitting with the family. He assumed he was the groom-to-be, but Javi noticed the way Lola's body stiffened when she acknowledged him. Javi made up his mind right then that he didn't care for the man.

He didn't get the chance to talk to her between her checking them in, assaulting the elevator button, and entering their room with only one bed. Admittedly he didn't mind only having one bed, but since she seemed uncomfortable with it, he was going to offer to take the pullout couch.

At least he was until he turned around to see full-body sobs wracking through Lola's body. It happened so fast it nearly gave him whiplash. One moment she was quiet, lost in her own thoughts, and the next her cries rang out around the room, nearly bringing him to his knees.

"Preciosa." The nickname tasted vile on his tongue. He didn't deserve to call her that, not when she was crying and shuddering so violently he thought she'd come crashing to the ground.

Not even a second after his thought, Lola's legs gave out and she crashed onto the couch next to her. Her sobs only grew louder, her body shaking as if caught in the cold. Javi crossed the room in two long strides and sank down on the spot next to her. "Lola." Her name sounded like a plea on his lips. A plea for something he couldn't quite put into words.

But now was not the time for talking. No words could form through that avalanche of emotions. He did the only thing he knew how to do, the only thing that didn't need words. She didn't fight him when Javi opened his arms and pulled her to his chest.

There were times when Camilia got so worked up that she couldn't form any words and reasoning with her proved impossible. Javi struggled for a long time because he had always been one who needed to talk things through, but Ofelia helped him realize sometimes emotions were too big, too vast, that no words could break through those barriers.

Nonverbal communication was better at that.

The sobs rolled through her body into his. Lola gripped the front of his shirt, bunching it tightly in her fists. He rubbed her back, hoping the single action conveyed everything he was feeling and couldn't say. The anger for her family. The frustration with himself for not being able to do more. The curiosity to learn what made her feel so overwhelmed.

For twenty minutes they stayed like this, him just holding her until her sobs turned into soft hiccups. She was far from better, but it was a start. One he could work with if nothing else triggered her.

"When Camilia has had a bad day, the only thing that makes her feel better is a long soak in the tub with her tablet. My mom used to do that for me and Ofelia after we cried on her shoulder. I don't know what it is about baths, but it always did the trick. She would also read us *The Giving Tree*, but I know you have a personal vendetta against it, so can I prepare you a bath?" He looked down, meeting her red-rimmed eyes. She didn't speak, but she also didn't ignore him. A single curt nod was her reply and that was enough for him.

Untangling himself from her, Javi got up and headed to the bathroom. He hadn't gotten a good look at it when they walked in, but now he was able to take it in. The room was two times his bathroom back home, accompanied by a large walk-in shower with a waterfall shower head. The tub was detached and could easily fit a whole family. He sat at the edge of the large tub and turned on the warm water, putting the stopper in at the bottom.

While he allowed the water to fill, he searched the small cabinets and drawers in the bathroom. These fancy hotels always had free shit laying around. Besides the sinfully fluffy white towels, he also found a robe he hoped would work for Lola. It was made from the same materials as the towels, so it would envelop her like a warm hug.

After laying out her towel and robe and turning off the water, Javi stuck his head out to make sure she was still okay. Lola had a vacant look in her eyes, staring ahead at nothing while tears streaked down her cheeks. "Bath's ready." His soft tone still managed to startle her, and Lola flinched. As if in a trance, she got up and walked past him. He stepped aside to give her privacy and as soon as the doorway was clear, she shut the door with a resounding thud.

There was nothing more to say. At least not right now and he knew better than to pry. If she wanted to tell him, which he hoped she did, it would have to be on her own time. She had reached her limit with other people's expectations and he refused to be another stressor in the equation.

To keep his mind off the woman in the bathroom, he took a seat on the bed, letting his back rest against the headboard, legs outstretched. There were a few texts from Ofelia, wondering if he made it alright.

He replied back to let her know he was at the hotel and to let Camilia know he loved her. That resulted in a thirty-minute phone call where she spoke animatedly about the pizzas she got to cook alongside her tío and how he burned his pizza, but hers came out perfectly.

Forty-five minutes later he was off the phone, but Lola hadn't come out yet. He was half tempted to check on her, but then he heard water swishing and someone moving around in the bathroom. He waited and his patience paid off. Lola opened the door, stepping out with her robe on and her hair cascading down around her shoulders.

The tightness of her face from earlier had eased, leaving her more relaxed and although not completely at ease, better than when they started. Her eyes were no longer red rimmed, just puffy from crying. When their eyes locked, her chin dipped down and she grimaced.

"I owe you an apology."

He couldn't have been more shocked if she turned around and showed him she sprouted a tail in the bathtub. An apology? For what? She did nothing wrong and it bothered him that Lola would feel the need to apologize for having feelings. "You don't owe me shit, especially not an apology. I'm worried about you, Lola, not angry."

She seemed to consider his words before nodding. "Still, I doubt you were prepared for me to snot all over your shirt and break down without any warning." She crossed the room to stand in front of him. She hesitated for only a fraction of a second before taking a seat next to him. Her white robe rode up dangerously high on her thighs and Javi couldn't pretend not to notice, not with her smooth brown skin on display for him.

"My eyes are up here, Javier." He heard the smirk in her voice, before he saw her expression. Her lips were upturned, holding back a laugh.

"Dolores, I'm a gentleman. I would never do something as heinous as look at your deliciously exposed thigh. What kind of man do you think I am?"

"Oh, I have a pretty good idea about the type of man you are."

Seeing her smile made him want to capture this moment and lock it away. She deserved to laugh and smile and having that taken from her made Javi see red. He couldn't explain this new streak of violence when it came to Lola, but it made him more curious about what he was obviously missing.

"Listen, you don't have to tell me anything. Nothing at all. But if you want to talk about what happened earlier, I'm here to listen."

The soft hum of the AC was the only sound in the room. Lola rubbed her hands up and down her thighs, seemingly contemplating what information she wanted to share.

"I didn't tell you the real reason I didn't want to go to this damn wedding alone. I had ample opportunity, but I couldn't bring myself to admit it to you. I guess I didn't want you to see me differently. Which is stupid, I know, but my anxiety around this whole ordeal is fucking astronomical.

"So you met my family downstairs. They aren't the most welcoming of people unless your pockets are lined thicker than Oprah's." Javi snorted. He had the inkling that her parents surrounded themselves with people who used twenty-dollar bills to wipe their asses. And Lola had grown up in that environment. He couldn't begin to imagine what that was like.

"I don't talk about it often because everyone kinda rolls their eyes at the rich girl's problems," Lola continued, "and I get it. I was extremely privileged growing up and I never lacked for anything...well material needs anyway. My emotional needs were hardly ever met and I've been in therapy for it for years.

"Anyway, that's not what triggered the panic attack from earlier. It was seeing Archie."

"Archie?" The name didn't ring a bell to him.

"He was the man seated at the table next to my sister. He's the one she's marrying and..." Her voice caught and a tear rolled down her cheek. A self-deprecating laugh left her lips. "Fuck, I'm not even sad over him! My emotions are just all over the place right now."

He reached over to the tissues on the bedside table, offering it to her. She quietly thanked him and used a tissue to dab at her eyes. "What I'm trying to say is I used to date Archie— don't look at me like that, I was young and stupid. We dated for a few years and I swore he was the one...until he broke up with me and almost immediately started to date my sister. I guess she fit his image better."

It was as if a volcano erupted inside of him, scorching every surface of his body. He had known anger before, most notably after the death of Estella, but that felt different than this. He wanted to wring Archie's neck. Not fit his image? As if the goddess in front of him needed to fit any damn image but her own. A man like Archie couldn't possibly love a woman like Lola properly. He knew men like Archie. Ones who wanted a pretty little wife by their side to advance their own career. Lola deserved better.

"Javi, say something. It looks like you want to break a lamp." Oh, he definitely wanted to break something, but not a lamp. Simultaneously, he wanted to thank Archie for being a pendejo for letting Lola slip through his grip. She fell into Javi's arms. It didn't matter that he only had this week with her and their relationship was fake; this week was very much real and he would see to it that she was treated as she deserved.

"If you want me to punch him in the veneers, I will." That got a bark of laughter out of her and a smack to his arm.

"Hasn't anyone ever told you that violence isn't the answer?"

"Actually no, someone told me that violence is sometimes the answer." Another smack, this time to his chest. "Ah, preciosa, you don't live by your own teachings."

"Hey, I'm only good at giving other people perspective. My life is a shit show." She shrugged. "But now you know why I have been on edge all day and had a panic attack. Thank you for everything. I've never had a panic attack in front of anyone but my therapist before. You handled it well."

"Camilia sometimes has moments like that. We call it her big feelings. I think she got it from her mother. Estella had bad anxiety, so I tried to learn ways to make it easier for her."

"You don't talk about her. Estella," Lola said softly and Javi's body stiffened. It wasn't as if he didn't talk about Estella. No one ever brought her up and asked about her. He didn't have many friends to confide in and he didn't like the way people looked at him with pity in their eyes. Like he was the one who died and not her.

A soft hand wrapped around his own and he realized he had been silent for a beat too long. "You don't have to speak about her. I just thought since you saw me ugly cry, I could return the favor." Her smile was delicate, but she didn't push. She didn't need to. Javi found himself wanting to talk about her.

"Estella was my high school sweetheart. We met in middle school and hit it off. By ninth grade we were inseparable. When we graduated high school, she went to school for nursing and I started in construction alongside my dad. I wanted to help her pay off her loans and we wanted to start a family eventually."

He remembered the exact day Estella had gotten into nursing school. He had come home from a late-night shift and found Estella curled up on the couch crying over her laptop. Javi's mind immediately went to someone dying and ran to her, pulling her into his arms. But she pushed him away and showed him the acceptance letter she received. They were both crying after that.

"A year later she got really sick, so I took her to the doctor. Turns out we weren't as safe as what we thought we were and she was pregnant."

"Who picked Camilia's name? It's beautiful." Lola smiled, squeezing his hand.

"Thank you, and Estella did. It was her grandmother's name. Estella spent nearly a year with our little girl before she was taken from us."

Lola's eyes filled with unshed tears. Her heart was just so damn big and he loved that about her. He just didn't want her crying for him. "If you don't mind me asking, what happened?"

It was a question he had to answer and hear hundreds of times, but it never got easier. He could recite her death in his sleep for how many times he played it back in his head. "Estella had just dropped Camilia off at my dad's house. He agreed to watch Camilia while I worked and Estella went to school for nursing. She only had a semester left.

"It was a rainy day, bad conditions on the road. From what I'm told, she had stopped at a stoplight and the light turned green. She went to go, but a semi-truck off to her left had lost control of his vehicle or something was wrong with his brakes. I'm not sure which. Whatever it was, he sped right through the light and straight into Estella's car. The first responders said she died instantly, so at least she didn't suffer. The worst part was she wasn't even supposed to be on that road. I should have taken Camilia to my parents that morning, but she let me sleep in. If only..."

"Oh Javi." Tears rolled down Lola's eyes. He was surprised

to find his own cheeks wet. Lola moved so she was in his lap, arms around his neck. "You can't blame yourself. It wasn't your fault. You had no way of knowing this would happen. Please don't beat yourself up over this."

He had heard that numerous times from his family. He didn't think the pain or the guilt would ever go away, which is why he worked extra hard to make sure Camilia was well looked after and loved. It was hard not to feel like he took her mother away.

"Javi, look at me." Lola cupped his face and forced him to turn in her direction. Their faces were inches apart. He could lean down and brush his lips against hers, but he held firm. "You are a good man and a great father. Camilia is so lucky to have you. What happened to Estella was a horrible accident. It never should have happened and I'm so sorry it did, but you can't blame yourself. You can't live with that guilt."

Healing was a weird process. It wasn't linear and sometimes it didn't make any sense. One second you were fine and the next you were crying in the arms of a beautiful woman. And he fucking hated crying. It wasn't so much due to toxic masculinity but more because it always made his eyes itchy and his nose run.

"I'll make you a deal," he said, wiping his eyes with the back of his hands. "I'll work on forgiving myself if you work on not letting their opinions dictate your feelings about yourself."

"Well fuck, Javi. That's asking for a hell of a lot." But even as she said it, she held out her pinky to his. "Pinky promise?"

Javi wrapped his pinky around hers. "Pinky promise," he repeated, leaning forward to press a soft kiss to her hand. She smiled at his touch, letting her fingers linger against his before she slowly pulled away.

"Now that's enough soul-searching for one day. How

about we take advantage of my father's credit card and order a shit ton of snacks and rent a few movies?" She grinned and reached for the hotel's phone.

"Now you're speaking my language. Let's get our own party started." And that was exactly what they did. Lola ordered far too much food and they watched the first two movies in the *Lord of the Rings* series after Javi found out she had never seen them before. By the third movie, Lola had fallen asleep on the bed and Javi covered her up. He went around to turn off the lights and television before making himself a nice bed on the couch. Not five minutes later he was asleep with thoughts of a certain big-hearted woman on his mind.

Lola

Lola awoke the following morning to the sound of soft snores and an empty bed. She was still in the robe from yesterday and must have fallen asleep during one of the *Lord of the Rings* movies, though she couldn't remember which. They all blurred together after a while.

Although the bed was huge, she only occupied a small portion of it, not once moving throughout the night. The bed would have been more than accommodating for the both of them, but she had fallen asleep before they discussed it. Javi, always the gentleman, took the couch and she doubted it was as comfortable as the feather mattress she was atop of.

A soft buzzing sound grabbed her attention. Her phone lay on the bedside table, but it was not plugged in. She hadn't had the chance to get her charger out last night and she was sure it was almost dead. Reaching for it, Lola brought the buzzing phone to her ear and saw that it was her mother calling. She groaned, nearly letting it go to voicemail, but thought better of it last minute and answered.

"Mother, hi," she greeted her as formally as if the Queen of England had called her.

There was a pause on the other end and then the sound of shuffling papers. Knowing her mother, she was still neck-deep in wedding planning, even days before the actual event. "Good heavens, I hope I didn't wake you. It's nearly noon."

One quick glance at her watch told her that yes, she had slept until noon. What the actual fuck? She hadn't slept that late since she was a teenager. Flying and breaking down in the middle of her hotel room really took it out of her. "Oh, I was just lounging," she lied, "did you need something?"

"Yes, I wanted to call and remind you that dinner tonight will be at the second-floor restaurant. Do you need me to send someone to retrieve you when it's time? I know how forgetful you can be when it comes to things like this."

If it were possible for eyes to roll all the way to the back of her head, this would have been the moment. She had been late once to one of the functions her mother had put on, simply because she was out doing errands for *her*. She had yet to live it down and now her mom always asked if she needed to send someone to escort her like a babysitter.

"I think between me and Javi, we'll manage to make it to dinner."

"Oh, yes, the young man you brought with you. He'll be joining us?"

"Yes, Mother." If there was a reward for forced patience, Lola would win in every category. "He's my date, of course he's going to be part of the wedding activities."

"It's interesting we have never heard of him, that's all. No need to get so pressed. Anyway, I actually called you for a different reason. Your sister and I are going out to look for shoes. Can you believe that she hasn't found her wedding shoes yet? You would think everyone is getting married and buying up all the semi-decent shoes in town. But that means I won't be able to retrieve her earrings arriving today. The front desk graciously agreed to keep them safe. Would you be a dear and check periodically throughout the day? You can bring them to dinner. Are you sure you don't need me to send for you when it's dinner time?"

"I'm certain. And yes, I'll get the earrings. Anything else?"

"No, nothing I can think of. Make sure you and your... erm, boyfriend are dressed appropriately."

"Perhaps you want to come in and dress us yourself." Lola tried to hide the bitterness in her tone, but failed.

"Dolores Cecilia Roberts," her mom reprimanded, throwing out all three names like confetti. Except there was nothing celebratory in her tone.

"Kidding. Yes, I promise my *boyfriend* and I won't embarrass you. I'll see you tonight and don't ask me again if I need someone to remind me about dinner. I'm not going to forget. Bye, Mother." She cut the line before Luciana could ask her to do anything else.

"Boyfriend has a good ring to it, don't you think?"

Her soul jumped all the way out of her body, ascending far into the heavens. She could hear her spiritual self now, telling the golden angel that she died of fright. "How long have you been awake!?" She shrieked and pulled the covers tighter around her as if they could protect her from a smirking Javi.

"Long enough for your mother to call me your boyfriend. Though she didn't sound fond of me." Despite having slept on the couch, he looked fully rested and not disheveled like Lola was certain she looked. Her hair alone would take time to tame the bird's nest it probably was.

"Well you are technically my boyfriend this week, so her assumption is correct."

"Does being your boyfriend this week earn me a good morning kiss?"

Despite herself, she smiled at his lame attempt at flirting. "Honey, you do not want to kiss my morning breath mouth."

"Oh, I don't know about that. Just a taste, preciosa. I'll be a happy man." How this man could make her stomach flutter upon waking up, she would never know. She was certain there was a permanent flush to her cheeks now, thanks to Javi.

She flipped over the blankets, freeing her tangled legs and got up to walk toward him. She stopped right in front of the couch and leaned down, placing a swift kiss to his forehead. "That's all you get. Now, if you would kindly stop flirting with me so I can get dressed, that would be amazing. Don't think about checking out my ass when I turn around."

"Never would dream of it. What type of man do you take me for?"

"Hopefully a decent one. Feel free to get ready here. I'm going to be hogging the bathroom for a bit. We're on earring duty, by the way." She turned her back to him and felt his searing gaze on her ass as she walked away. That might have made her swing her hips a bit more dramatically than normal.

MUCH TO HER mother's dismay, Lola had kept her word and made it to dinner alongside Javi and the damned earrings with five minutes to spare, successfully preventing Luciana's beloved lectures. Her father and mother lingered outside the hostess stand, waiting to be sat. Marisol and Archie were nowhere to be found, so her mother pegged the wrong sister as tardy.

"My girl," her father said, wrapping his bulky arms around her. He was the only one in the family that could wrap around her torso and it made her feel safe within his arms. When he pulled away, he shook Javi's hand with a vigorous handshake. "And Javier, isn't it?"

"Yes sir. Javier Mendez. Nice to meet you again."

The conversation lolled soon after that with still no sign of her sister. Lola wasn't surprised by this though. Marisol had always been notoriously late. It was like time held no meaning for her and when she showed up, that was simply the time she was meant to be there. Oh, how Lola wished she could operate like that, but anxiety made her arrive at everything at least five minutes early.

Their stunted conversation came to an abrupt end when the red-haired waiter came by wearing a smile the size of Texas. Working with a population of people who made money in their sleep, Lola too would smile like that in hopes of a good tip.

"Welcome and thank you for dining with us tonight. If you'll follow me, I'll lead you to your booth," he said in an English accent. Lola's stomach churned at the word booth, but she tried not to think too much about it.

Their waiter led them through the expensively decorated restaurant with a stocked bar off toward the right. In the center was a large crystal fire pit with a burning blue fire that added to the ambiance. They were led to a row of booths and she held back a groan.

Her mother's petite frame scooted in first, followed by her father. Her father had a rounded belly that she always loved. The table pressed up against his stomach and he laughed, patting his belly. "Gotta lay off the Oreos," he joked. If Lola made that joke, her mother would have died on the spot, but since it came from her husband, Luciana was all smiles and tickled with laughter.

Lola had said it once and she would continue to say it. Booths at fancy-ass restaurants—or most restaurants for that matter—were not built with plus-size people in mind. They were often placed too close to the table in order to fill more of the space with booths and customers.

Javi slid into the booth first and she sent out a silent prayer as he did. Javi was straight sized, but he was tall with big arms, so scooting down the leather seat had not been an easy feat. Lola felt her mother's judgmental eyes as she slowly lowered herself down to the bench. It was humiliating having her mother watch her as she struggled to wiggle into the tight space. She accidentally hit the table with her elbow, nearly knocking down a wine glass.

Javi snatched his hand out with all the reflexes of Spider-Man and caught it before it crashed to the ground and broke into a million different pieces on the floor, saving her from the judging stares of the other patrons.

When she squeezed in enough, Javi offered her a smile and placed his hand on her thigh reassuringly. Her mother still wore the look of thinly veiled disgust and took this opportunity to not-so-subtly bring up the gym membership she researched the moment Lola told her she was moving. "Have you checked out the gym I sent you, dear? The one with the classes and personal trainers."

Next to her, she felt Javi stiffen, but she clamped her hand around his to ease his temper. "I told you, Mother, I'm loving the yoga studio I go to and have no desire to go work out with a bunch of sweaty strangers. Especially there."

"Oh, but Dolores, it would be so good for you. Don't you want to be healthy?"

It always came back to health. When a fat person existed in a place for straight-sized people, everyone was a doctor. Thin didn't equal healthy and she wished her mother understood that. She knew for a fact that she was in better shape than Mona and Mattea, even if they were both smaller than her. Yet, her mom would only see their size and think they were the epitome of health.

"I'm quite fine the way I am. But if my body insults you, maybe you should work on fixing your own biases when it comes to plus-sized individuals." Outwardly she hoped she projected strength and badassery because inwardly she was freaking out that she even humored her mother in the conversation.

"Now ladies, enough fighting. Let's discuss what we want as an appetizer. Personally, I don't think we can go wrong with a charcuterie board," her father, ever the optimist, said. Lola loved him, she did, but he could be so dense at times. He never saw how her mother treated her and thought to himself that it was wrong. He tried to be a buffer, but she doubted he knew the root of the problem.

"I'm just saying it is something you should consider." Her mother always had to have the last word. Before Lola could respond, Luciana's face lit up and that only meant one thing. Dread nearly immobilized her body, but she forced herself to move.

She turned in time to see Marisol and Archie head their way. Marisol was in a knee-length red dress that hugged her body perfectly, no roll in sight. Archie wore his standard dark business casual, like he was prepared to go to an interview at any time. Even she had to admit they looked pretty together.

Marisol took one look at her sister, giving her a simple nod before heading over to their parent's side of the table. The booth seat should have only been big enough for three people to fit comfortably across, but both Marisol and Archie slid in.

"What are we drinking?" Archie laughed good-naturedly. He was met by a chorus of chuckles as his father went into a deep analysis of every wine on the menu.

"Did you pick up my earrings, Dolores?" No hi, no how are you, just straight to the point. It was her sister to a T.

Lola searched through her silver clutch and pulled out the black velvet box and handed it over. Her sister inspected it, opened it up, and gasped. "Oh these are perfect! Archie, don't you think these are perfect?"

Judging by his disinterested look and quick glance at the box, Lola didn't think Archie gave a flying fuck. "Yes, very nice. What are they for?"

"The wedding, Archie. The whole reason we are here." Marisol frowned.

"Right. Well, I'm sure they will compliment your dress." He offered her a dazzling smile that might work for his clients, but not a fiancée. Lola felt the anger roll off her sister and, despite their personal problems, wanted to stand up for Marisol. Until Marisol took her ire out on her, the black sheep of the family.

"Dolores, you never showed me your jewelry for your dress. You know I hate those big hoops you wear. Please tell me you got something more sensible."

The night had barely started and already Lola was tired. Between her mother's hurtful jabs at her weight and Marisol's misplaced anger, Lola knew she was in for a verbal beatdown. She just wished Javi wouldn't have to witness these horrendous attacks.

CHAPTER 24

Javi

From the way he gripped the table, Javi was surprised that the edge hadn't snapped off in his hand. The only thing keeping him grounded was Lola's hand atop his as he listened to her family demeaning her with every other sentence. How she simply sat there and took their jabs with as much grace and poise as she did, he would never know. Because all he saw and felt was red rage.

"So, Javi. What do you do for a living, son?" Travis's gaze looked him over, sizing him up. Out of all the Robertses, he was so far the most tolerable. At least he seemed to love his daughter, though he was ignorant when it came to how his wife and other daughter treated her.

He had also been the only one to take an interest in Javi. Luciana stared in disapproval, as if she could smell the poverty on him. Not that he was at the poverty level, but compared to these people he might as well be. Marisol only glanced his way a few times but was otherwise occupied by Archie and her phone, which seemed to be an extension of her body.

"I work as an independent contractor," he said, getting a nod of approval from Travis and a furrowed brow from Luciana.

"Ah, good work, indeed. Always a good sign when a man is good with his hands. Never a bad thing to put some grease on ya," Travis tutted. It was clear the man had a very old-fashioned way of thinking, but it served in Javi's favor this time. Not that he needed his approval or anything since he wasn't technically dating his daughter, but it would make their time together more pleasant if Travis didn't want to run him off.

"He's the one I hired to help me renovate the bookstore, Daddy, remember?" Lola chimed in and he tried to ignore the lurch of his dick when Lola said the word "daddy." Now was not the time to be sporting a major hard-on. "He has a few guys working now and when we get back my bookcases should be nearly finished. Isn't that right, Javi?"

"If everything goes according to plan." He made a mental note to check on his crew later. Just because he wasn't working, didn't mean the guys he hired to take charge of the built-ins weren't.

"The bookstore? What is this about a bookstore?" Marisol's voice couldn't sound more condescending if she tried. Her well-manicured fingers stopped flying across her phone long enough to catch the tail end of their conversations.

With more patience than her sister deserved, Lola explained the renovations taking place back home. He liked the way she spoke about his work, with admiration and happiness. His heart swelled in response, knowing she trusted him this much with her dream store.

"So you opened a bookstore, huh?" was Marisol's only response. Her tone bordered on amusement and astonishment, sounding as if she didn't see the value in what Lola was doing nor understand the concept of a passion project.

Because that was what the bookstore was to Lola. It was a way to turn something she loved into a full-time career. A place where she could spend her days lost in books and the customers. Where she could read to children and find the perfect book for anyone who walked through her door.

"You must send us some progress pictures. I would love to show some of my golf buddies the work you are doing. They were impressed to hear you starting on your own little entrepreneurial path," Travis said, eyes glinting with pride. Marisol narrowed her eyes. Obviously, she had not been expecting that response from her father.

"Yes, you really must show us some progress photos. Such an interesting thing, a bookstore," came a new voice. Everyone's heads swiveled toward Archie. Javi felt Lola tense next to him and he felt his own body move closer to her, as if trying to shield her from the smug smile on Archie's face.

Javi didn't consider himself a violent person, but something about Archie made the hairs on the back of his neck rise. He wanted nothing more than to put the man in his place, but he knew that would embarrass Lola and possibly get him kicked out of the wedding. He wasn't willing to risk that.

"It's admirable. We all have to start somewhere. It is hard to start new businesses these days; most end up failing. But I'm sure that won't be the case with yours," Archie said the last part as if it were an afterthought. Javi hadn't realized he was clenching his hands into fists until he felt Lola's hand covering them.

She was trying to comfort him when it should have been the other way around.

The rest of the table quieted until Travis and Archie

launched into work talk about the upcoming grape season. None of it piqued his interest so Javi let his mind wander to Camilia and how much fun she was probably having with Ofelia. To the men back in California working under the watchful eye of Mona or Mattea. And finally to Lola, how she appeared so calm and collected, but how her family had caused an abundance of anxiety.

Their dinner saved him from reliving anymore from yesterday. He hadn't remembered what he ordered until a large lamb chop was placed in front of him, with a veggie combo and a baked potato. His mouth salivated. Lola was given the same except instead of the baked potato, white rice was placed in a single mound on the plate.

Travis and Archie both received similar meat platters while Marisol and Luciana ordered a large salad with what looked to be apricots and almonds, along with a reddish vinaigrette. It didn't appeal to Javi, but Luciana stared pointedly at Lola's plate.

"Sweetheart, are you certain you ordered that?" she pried, even though they had all listened to Lola's order.

"Oh, no. Did I make a mistake?" their waiter asked.

Lola's cheeks tinged red, signaling her mortification from her mother putting her on the spot once again. "No, no mistake. I ordered this."

"Are you sure? I don't mind getting the correct order," the man assured, not realizing he was making the situation worse.

"Looks right to me. Lola was always an...adventurous eater when we were together." Archie commented and it took everything in Javi not to jump across the table and plant his fist between his eyes. His anger only flared when Luciana laughed, seeming to find his words charming rather than hurtful.

Javi saw the panic set in, the way all eyes were on her and

how Lola slowly retreated back into her shell. He wouldn't stand for it. "This is exactly what she ordered. Thank you." His voice held a certain dismissal that could not be ignored.

The waiter seemed taken aback by his abrupt answer, but composed himself swiftly. "Of course. Enjoy your meal. Please let me know if you need anything," he said and quickly made his way to a different table.

"Thank you." Her voice came out low, barely above a whisper, but he caught the relief in her features. He, however, was far from relieved. Javi's body tensed up even more than it had been only moments ago. He felt like a too tightly wound rubber band that was about to snap at any moment.

How the fuck could she be so goddamn calm during all of this? How the hell did she grow up in a household that made belittling comments her entire childhood? If Javi had been subjected to that, he doubted he would be half as bubbly as Lola. Not when he carried so much hurt and trauma with him from the very people who should have loved him unconditionally.

His words should have been the end of it, but Luciana Roberts couldn't read the fucking room and had to make one more comment, not knowing that Javi was seconds away from bursting. "Just remember you have a dress to fit into for your sister's wedding. There wouldn't be enough time to properly alter it now."

Javi had enough and threw his hands down on the table. The glasses and silverware shook and everyone jumped to attention, staring at him with wide eyes and open mouths. "I have only met you guys twice and in that time you have done nothing but make offhanded comments about Lola."

He knew he should stop. Knew that this wasn't his place, but the lava within him had bubbled over and he couldn't stop the flow now. "What gives you the right to police and comment on her body? Because frankly, Lola is the most beautiful woman I have ever laid eyes on. That's the least impressive thing about her though, because she also has a huge heart and anyone would be lucky enough to call her a friend. Which, you would know if you both stopped trying to tear her down for two goddamn seconds and got to know her.

"And you—" his eyes darkened, narrowing to slits, as he turned to Archie "—keep your unsolicited comments and dick-head behavior to yourself. You have no goddamn right to speak to or belittle my girl. Hell, you aren't even worthy enough to be in the same room as her. I highly suggest you keep your mouth shut when she's around."

His passionate proclamation and threat were met with stunned silence. Everyone's faces had different degrees of aston-ishment, but then the spell broke and Luciana and Marisol began to sputter their retorts back at the same time.

"I never—"

"How dare—"

But Javi didn't give a shit what they had to say. He turned to Lola, barely registering her expression, saying, "I need a moment."

Wordlessly, Lola scooted out of the booth and Javi followed her. "I'm sorry," he managed to say in passing, listening to the chaos he left in his wake. Perhaps he should turn around and apologize for his behavior. Maybe he made it worse for Lola, but going back now wouldn't repair anything. He would only make it worse. Better to beg for forgiveness later when his head was clear.

Javi stormed out, passing disgruntled patrons attempting to locate their seats. He thought he heard someone calling his name, but he didn't dare look back. He didn't stop until he was out of the restaurant and back at the elevators. He found a hallway that only led to bathrooms and hooked a right, using the space to pace back and forth, allowing his anger to dissipate.

Fuck, he blew it. He had always been a hothead when it came to people he cared deeply for and he tended to act first without thinking. If he was a better man, he would walk right back in and apologize and offer to give back the money. The money he needed, but didn't deserve because he wasn't upholding his end of the bargain.

"Javi!"

He didn't know how long he had been pacing when he heard his name. He stopped abruptly and turned toward the voice. Lola stood there panting, eyes blown wide with an emotion he couldn't quite place yet.

The apology fell from his lips immediately, his anger turning into embarrassment. "I'm sorry, Lola. Fuck, did I make it worse? I just couldn't sit there and let them talk to you like that a second longer. I swear—"

"Javi."

He was rambling and he knew it. Lola marched right up to him again after calling his name for the second time. He didn't know if this was the part where she kicked him out. He would go, and although he was embarrassed with how he handled the situation, he didn't regret his words. They deserved to be called out on their toxic behavior.

"If you want me to go, I will."

"I want you to shut up." Her words were a command. One moment she was standing right in front of him and the next she was in his arms, kissing him and stealing the breath from his lungs.

He didn't respond at first, far too shocked to make any sudden movements. But then his brain kicked in and instinct took over. A low growl left the back of his throat and he kissed her back, moving her against the wall. A low moan left her lips as her body curved to his.

This wasn't the reaction he was expecting, but it was far better than he deserved.

CHAPTER 25

Lola

Because frankly, Lola is the most beautiful woman I have ever laid eyes on. That's the least impressive thing about her though, because she also has a huge heart and anyone would be lucky enough to call her a friend.

Those words rang through her ears, sending shivers down her entire body. With a few sentences, he had managed to render her senseless, moving only so he could escape the travesty that was her family. Four sets of eyes stared back at her in astonishment, though Archie looked more amused than anything, hiding his smile behind his glass of wine. If only he knew how badly Javi wanted to hurt him. She could feel it in the way his body tensed when he all but threatened him.

As soon as Javi was out of distance, her mother and sister started in on her. "How dare you bring someone so rude and inappropriate to your sister's wedding week. Do you think of anyone but yourself? And for him to insult Archie? Unacceptable." Her mother's scorn cut deep, but she had spent most of her life hardening herself when it came to her. Yet, this time her mother's anger wasn't at her...well, not entirely. When Javi was involved, she found herself steeled against her ire.

To her complete amazement, before she had the opportunity to talk back to Mom and inevitably make the situation worse, her father beat her to it. "Enough, Luciana. You are always too hard on Lola. Both you and Marisol"—he shot her sister a disappointed expression—"have grilled Dolores since she arrived. Her young man has had enough. Frankly, I have too."

She couldn't have been more stunned if her father had announced he was running away to join the circus. His features relaxed when he turned back toward Lola. "Go check if Javi is alright, princess. And please give him my deepest apologies. This is not how our family normally behaves." Well, she wasn't going to burst his bubble and let him know this was exactly how their family behaved, but she appreciated the sentiment regardless.

"Thank you, Daddy." Lola was tempted to kiss her father, but she would have to lean over Archie and Marisol to do that and she didn't want to be anywhere near them. The only person she wanted to be with now was Javi. If she knew him like she thought she did, he was off blaming himself for his mishap and probably thought she was pissed.

She wasn't upset though, not in the least. What she wanted was him, but getting through the labyrinth of the restaurant had been no easy feat. She maneuvered herself through waiters and waitresses and squeezed her ass through too tight tables and chairs nearly on top of one another. At one point she was certain she hit a glass and knocked it over, but she didn't look back to confirm.

When she finally made it out and didn't see Javi, she got worried. What if he went home? He wouldn't leave her without saying goodbye. Hell, she hoped he wouldn't leave at all. Without him, the rest of the trip would be unbearable. And if she was being honest with herself, she had liked having him by her side for reasons unrelated to her family. She liked the way he made her feel and the safety he offered. She also liked how he looked at her when he thought no one was watching.

Maybe there was something there between them that needed to be explored. She just didn't know how to take that plunge or if she was ready to admit her feelings. It was still too soon; her feelings were too strong and all over the place.

Once she reached the elevators, she found Javi pacing back and forth. He had not noticed her yet, lost in his thoughts. Once again she was struck with a sense of wonder. Standing so close amplified her feelings for him tenfold, passion like she had only felt once before sprang to the surface and she clenched her hands into fists.

Then he noticed her and all the unsaid words he couldn't share came tumbling from his mouth. Her suspicions had been correct and he thought she was mad at him. The whispered way his name left her lips did nothing to stop the onslaught of his tirade.

"Javi." Lola tried his name again only to get the same outcome. He wasn't seeing her. If he was, there would be no question about what she wanted from him. There was only one way to get to him. One way that was a surefire way to get his attention.

Her feet acted of their own volition. Like a hungry viper, she stalked her prey until she was right up on him. One look into his dark eyes and she attacked. Her lips were on his before he could finish his sentence, tasting the dinner he barely touched. Her tongue eagerly parted his lips, exploring the taste of him.

Javi's body went rigid against hers and not in a sexy way. Had she done something wrong? If she read the signals wrong and was accosting this man, she would never forgive herself. Lola went to pull back, but it was as if a light switched on inside of Javi.

His hard body pressed her back until she hit the wall behind her with enough force that it sent tendrils of pleasure and pain through her. His hands went to her hips, squeezing. They were a mess of tongue, teeth, and saliva. There wasn't anything light or sweet about this kiss. It was dominating and rough. Everything she needed.

She felt wanton next to him and when he moved closer, pressing his leg between her thighs. Her pussy fluttered for him. Wetness dampened her panties at the friction his knee made.

"Preciosa." Javi sucked her bottom lip between his, tugging on it. She let out a strangled moan. Any moment anyone could walk by them and see the way Javi had her pinned against the wall and her legs straddling his thigh. They were fully clothed but exposed in so many different ways.

Despite knowing—or maybe even due to knowing— someone could walk by them at any time, it did not stop the proverbial fire that had been lit underneath them. She grabbed his neck to pull him back down to her, kissing him deeply. A long stroke of his tongue met hers and his hands dipped lower to cup her ass.

It was still not enough; it would never be enough. She began to rub herself against his leg, hoping to apply some friction to her needy clit. "Fuck," Javi growled and that's when she felt his hard cock press into her leg. "Look at what you do to me, Lola."

She wanted to show him what he did to her and that

started with them getting the hell out of the public hallway. His thigh would not keep her satisfied for long, no, she wanted his head buried between her legs.

"Lola, we should stop." The words did not register at first. Stopping seemed like the opposite of a good idea. They had the chance to chase their pleasure so why wouldn't they?

"I don't want to stop." She couldn't keep out the wine in her voice. It didn't matter that it made her sound pathetic, she was horny and in need of release.

"Trust me, preciosa, I don't want to stop either. But I don't think I would be doing my job if I didn't remind you of our business arrangement. I don't want you to do anything you aren't comfortable doing."

Business arrangement.

Those words hit her hard. It hardly seemed fair that she was this close to release, only for her own words to come back and haunt her now. But she hadn't taken the time to consider how this might feel for him. She gasped in horror and shook her head. "Oh fuck, I swear I'm not paying you for sex. Holy shit."

A gruff chuckle met her mild freakout. "No, I know. Believe me, I want to. But when I get you back into bed, I want it to be because you want me and not because I stood up for you in front of your family and you feel like you owe me."

She didn't feel that way...did she? Fuck, her head was all fuzzy with big emotions and horniness. Damn, this man and his chivalrous nature. "I hate you a little bit," she muttered.

"Trust me, I hate myself too."

"Then I guess we should go back to our room."

"Yeah, it does seem like we should."

"Our room with only one bed."

"Just the one."

"That couch couldn't have been comfortable."

"It wasn't," he agreed with a small smile tugging at his lips.

"Then maybe," she bit her lips, squirming under his gaze. She had just been rubbing herself against him and now suddenly she was shy? Make it make sense. "Maybe you should take the bed."

"And kick you out? Nah, I wouldn't dream of that."

"I said nothing about being kicked out. I said you should take the bed. With me. It's a big bed."

The man was full-on smirking now, his lips plump and still shiny from their kisses. "You want me to sleep with you?"

"Just sleep. As you said earlier. We shouldn't jump into anything right now, but I think we are both mature enough to share a bed and both be on our best behavior."

"I'm nothing if not a gentleman," Javi said and Lola had to keep herself from rolling her eyes. What they had been doing seconds ago was the furthest thing from gentlemanly she could think of.

"Then it's settled. You'll sleep with me and tomorrow I will deal with my family."

Javi's cocky smile dropped. "Yeah, about that. Again I'm sorry—"

Lola stopped him with a smack to the chest. "No, do not apologize for standing up for me after they showed you their true colors. No one has ever done that for me before and I will not let you *"sorry"* yourself out of this."

"Well, when you put it like that, I guess you're right."

"I'm always right. It would do you well to remember that." She winked and slowly—and very reluctantly—began to untangle herself from Javi. Once she put a bit of distance between them and straightened out her clothes, as well as pretending as if she didn't see Javi's erection through his pants, she spoke again. "Now, let's head back to the room and order a pizza since we didn't finish dinner. We can continue watching your silly movie from last night.

"Silly? That's *Lord of the Rings* you're talking about. Show some respect." He winked at her. Lola laughed and turned on her heels, heading straight toward the elevator. She didn't look back, but she heard Javi's footfalls as he followed behind, just like he promised.

CHAPTER 26

Lola

Javi was a cuddler and that made her inexplicably happy. After the terrible dinner incident that resulted in being pinned up against the wall and kissed until their lips were swollen, Lola led them back to their room. Javi immediately went to the bathroom and stayed in there for a questionable amount of time doing God knows what. Her mind conjured up images of Javi braced over the bathroom sink, cock in hand as he pleasured himself to thoughts of her.

A girl could dream.

When he finally came out, dressed in black sweats that hung low on his hips and a gray T-shirt, the explosion of passion from earlier had simmered down to only a mild annoyance. Thoughts of the damn business agreement provided enough of a cockblock for now, but she didn't know how much longer either of them could ignore these feelings.

While Javi got into bed, Lola slipped away into the bathroom. She took off her makeup, making sure to scrub her face clean. Sleeping with makeup on was a big no-no for her because it caused irritation to her skin. She then changed out of the stuffy dress she only wore around family and into her pink, silk, matching pajama set.

When she returned to the room, she felt Javi's heated glare on her body, taking in every inch of exposed skin. She made no comment as she made a show of putting away her phone and getting comfortable in bed, all the while feeling his eyes on her.

Lola squirmed under his scrutiny, attempting to hide the blush creeping along her cheeks. "So, we should order that pizza now," she said and dialed room service. Not an hour later, the two of them were in bed, eating a deliciously greasy pizza, and watching a movie.

About halfway through, Lola grew tired but tried to keep her eyes open and attentive. Apparently she was failing because Javi gathered the pizza box and paper plates and got up to toss them away. "We should sleep," he said, his voice gruff but she wasn't sure if that was from being tired or something else entirely.

"Goodnight, Javi," she said right before she reached to turn off the light, leaving them in complete darkness. He didn't respond to her, not at first. For ten minutes they lay in silence, only the sounds of their breathing comforting one another. Lola was certain he had fallen asleep and moved to make herself more comfortable, when two strong arms wrapped around her, pulling her to a hard chest.

She had never been held like this before, where the other person didn't expect anything in return. Hot breath hit the back of her neck and Javi's chest rose and fell in a slow rhythm. His grip around her tightened, not painfully, and not enough to keep her from moving away if she was uncomfortable. The small gesture made her feel important and safe.

She had no problem falling asleep that night.

In the morning, the sun crept through their curtains,

cascading rays of light onto her face. The sun brought with it a new day and a new day meant she would have to face her family. If it were up to her, Lola would spend the entirety of their free day together in bed. But she knew from experience that letting unneeded tension fester between herself and her mom and sister would only result in a bigger scandal.

As if sensing her alertness and wandering thoughts, Javi's arms tightened around her and pulled her flush against his chest. Every part of him was awake and ready to greet her and she couldn't stop the slight wiggle she did to tease him. That earned her a groan and lips against her neck. "Don't go."

Soft lips explored her neck and she was inclined to just go with it. Lola let her head fall to the side, exposing more skin to him which he greedily took. "Stay," he said again, his lips brushing against her ear.

How easy it would be to stay here and pretend things like her family or their business arrangement didn't exist. How desperately she wanted to feel instead of thinking about the complicated set of emotions swirling through her brain and heart regarding him.

"I have to go check on my family." The flimsy excuse sounded bad, even to her ears. But she did need to put out fires so the rest of the trip wasn't harder than it had to be.

"Or...you can stay here and we can do more of absolutely nothing." He bucked his hips against her backside and she had to hold back a moan. Wasn't this the same man who told her they needed to cool it yesterday before things got hot and heavy? And now he was instigating something and her body so desperately wanted to give in.

Maybe just a little taste...

"No," she had not realized she said it out loud until Javi's lips and body stopped moving against her. Heat rushed to her cheeks and she quickly clarified. "I need to check in today. I don't like conflict and I know they can be miserable people, but they are still my family. I want to make sure they don't dislike me any more than normal and then I'll be back. We don't have anything planned for today, so we can spend the day doing whatever the hell we want," she assured, hoping that would please him.

His arms dropped from around her and he rolled to his back. The absence of his body was immediately felt and she nearly took back her words. "You're right. If you need to check on your mom and sister, I'm not going to stop you. Do you want me to go with you?" He didn't seem excited about the idea, but it was sweet of him to offer.

"No, you stay here and get some more rest. I don't think it will take too long." She planned to find them, apologize for how things ended yesterday, and make sure they didn't need anything from her. She didn't think having Javi there would help and she couldn't blame him for being wary around them.

"I'll shower when you leave. Then I'll be ready to go when we decide on our plans."

"Perfect." She reached to squeeze his hand before getting up. Last night she had set out simple jeans and a faded black crop top with a pocket on the breast. She escaped to the bathroom to relieve herself and get dressed. Her curls were curling today and there was no taming them. She wore her hair down proudly, thickness and all.

Sending a quick text to her dad, she found out her mother was in Marisol's room making last-minute calls to guests and making sure the rest of her bridesmaids would be landing tomorrow.

"I'm leaving! I won't be too long," she called as soon as she opened the door.

"If you need backup, call me," he said, sitting up in bed now. He caught what she had on and smiled approvingly. "Seriously? There is no reason you should look that damn good at all times."

She hadn't known she needed that boost of confidence and appreciated his words. "Enjoy your shower." She winked at him and left, closing the door without waiting for his reply.

MARISOL's front room was in complete disarray, at odds with the other rooms of her flashy penthouse suite that screamed of Daddy and fiancé's money. She had thought her and Javi's room was lavish, but it paled in comparison to the apartment-like accommodations her sister had. On her way in, she spotted two untouched rooms. Who needed two extra bedrooms? Clearly her sister.

Marisol and their mother were seated at a round glass table, the hotel phone and Marisol's purple laptop between them. They ended a call with an uncle she believed to live in Tijuana, but she could be confusing him with one of the many other cousins her mother had. She was a bit surprised her mother considered inviting the extended family since they didn't fit in with her new, flashy lifestyle.

"Good morning." Lola's voice startled both women, her mother's dramatic shriek and hand to her chest as if she just had a heart attack never failed to make Lola cringe. Her mother was extra in the worst ways possible.

"Who let you in?" Her sister's accusatory voice could have been aimed at a poorly trained assassin who announced he came to kill them instead of her baby sister who wanted to make sure they had recovered from yesterday.

"Daddy met me downstairs and handed me a key." She showed the plastic key, holding it up in front of her like a shield that would protect her from her sister's wrath. Marisol continued to look annoyed, but no more than normal.

That had to be a good sign.

"Are you alone?" her mother asked, peering around Lola, no doubt searching for Javi to round the corner at any minute.

"Yeah, Javi's back in the room. I wanted to come down and apologize for how things were left last night. It wasn't my intention to cause a scene at your dinner, Marisol." Did she feel like she did anything wrong? Not particularly. But this was her sister's engagement week and despite everything, she didn't want to taint these memories for her. Emotions ran high last night, but she hoped it wouldn't happen again.

Marisol offered her a smile. Not one that met her eyes, she doubted her sister was capable of a full range of emotions, but a smile nonetheless. "Yes, all is forgiven. Daddy wasn't happy about the incident."

No, she suspected he wouldn't be, though she didn't think his anger extended to her and Javi.

"I still don't understand why you allowed that man to speak to us like that. If you had a problem with our words, you should have come to us. You know we love you and only want what's best for you," her mother cut in.

The thing was, she truly did believe her sister and mother loved her. Or perhaps that was the hopes of a naive girl talking who desperately wanted a loving mother and sister. Their love came with conditions and Lola often found herself coming up short of their expectations for her. She stopped trying to please them long ago, but she would be lying if the thought of giving in to their demands didn't cross her mind every once in a while.

"Javi felt like you were attacking me—"

"Attacking?" Her mother gasped, shaking her head like that was the most outlandish idea to have ever crossed her mind. "Oh, dear, you know that isn't it at all. He needs to better understand our family before he puts his nose into places it doesn't belong. I would hate for that to end badly for him."

"Jesus, Mother. Must you always be so dramatic?" Marisol muttered under her breath, displaying a rare case of sibling support.

Of course, her mother was never one to reflect on her behavior. "That man ruined your entire dinner. I don't think I'm being dramatic when I say Lola needs to pick better men."

A very unladylike snort left her lips. She couldn't escape the irony, could she? "Are you kidding me?" She scoffed, her face grew hot with pent-up anger. "Need I remind you that my last boyfriend is about to marry my sister? So he was only a bad pick for me, but not Marisol?"

"Lola, please. Let's not do this now. This week is not about you, and it's unfair to your sister to bring it up. I thought we were all over it?"

"How can we be over something we never discussed?" Her voice rose with each word. "But it's not even about that. It's about how you two constantly treat me. I'm sick of it and I've been living with it my whole life. Javi was only at dinner for less than an hour before the way you treated me pissed him off. He cares for me, Mother. Openly. Something you could stand to learn from him."

This wasn't why she came into this room, though she knew seeing them would bring along the possibility of another argument. She was sick of being in survival mode all the time. Sick of caring and not being able to let go, even now she had the strong urge to push everything under the rug and survive until the end of the week.

"I said what I needed to and I don't want to discuss this anymore. If you need me, you know where to find me. I'm going back to the kindhearted man who appreciates me and doesn't point out all of my flaws." With that, she spun on her heels and left the room. No one tried to run after her, not that she thought they would. Her goal had been to mend the tear in the relationship, but she only made it worse.

No, not her. *Them.* They made it worse.

How hard was it to be a decent fucking human? Her mom would piss and moan about her attitude and make some offhand comments, then they would go about the same cycle they always fell into. It was toxic, but it was comfortable. All that either one of them knew.

Just once she wished her sister would stand up for her, more than expressing annoyance in their mother. She couldn't quite blame Marisol. Her sister was just trying to survive too.

Lola stormed back to their floor, slamming her key against the reader until the green light shined. When she pushed the door open, she heard water coming from the shower, but that didn't stop her from calling out, "Javi!"

She was on edge and needed to come back down. Needed to experience something other than this negativity coursing through her veins and there was only one man who could help her. A special man she was beyond tired of denying and one who made her feel things she was sick of shying away from.

The water suddenly cut off and she heard him scramble inside the bathroom until the door slid open, exposing a very wet and half-naked Javi, a tiny towel the only thing covering his lower half. His eyes were blown wide with concern as he looked around the room, stopping once he reached her. "What is it? What happened?"

Seeing him, his chest rising and falling rapidly because he

rushed to check on her, was the last bit of evidence she needed to know that this man would do anything for her. It was a scary, but exhilarating thought.

"Fuck the business deal."

"What?" Naturally, he was confused by her choice of words, and probably worried. After all, she just stormed into the room and demanded his attention.

"I said fuck this business deal. I don't want to think. I don't want to be around people who can't accept all of me because I'm too much. I fucking want you. This has nothing to do with you being my fake date. I want *you*, Javi. I want you to help me forget. Just like you did six months ago."

Silence met her plea. Heat rushed to her cheeks as she wondered if she had just overstepped. They had been good yesterday, so maybe Javi didn't actually want to be with her. Maybe she had completely read the room wrong and she was making a fool of herself.

But a few seconds later, a low, seductive laugh left Javi's mouth. She watched as his eyes took her in, every inch of her body. She felt herself grow hot from his gaze alone.

Just when she thought the tension was going to be the death of her, Javi stepped closer. "You want to forget, preciosa? I can manage that." In the next instant, he was on her.

CHAPTER 27

When Javi heard Lola yelling his name, he didn't even hesitate as he sprung into action. He swore if he ran out and she was on the verge of another panic attack, he'd book them the first flight home. None of this was worth her mental health, no matter how much she wanted to try and reason with her mother. Frankly, Luciana didn't deserve shit from Lola.

Javi barely got the water turned off before he was out the door, grabbing a towel that he tied haphazardly around his hips. One strong gust of wind would send it to the ground, but in that minute nothing mattered but getting to Lola.

He flung open the door, taking in the scene. Lola's cheeks were red and her eyes were glazed over, staring at him with the utmost concentration. Water dripped onto the floor around him, creating little puddles that he would need to clean up later.

"What is it? What happened?" His voice was gruff as he assessed the room for a threat. As if her mother and sister would round the corner and start swinging at him.

But that wasn't what happened and when she spoke, his mind was slow to process what she was saying. *"Fuck the business deal"* repeated in his head over and over like a broken record. A horrible part of him, one that he would never admit to out loud, reverberated through the back of his mind. *What about the money?* And fuck if he didn't want to punch himself right in the face for thinking such vile thoughts when Lola was offering herself up to him.

She wanted him and it had nothing to do with their little deal. She wanted to forget and Javi wanted to indulge her. "You want to forget, preciosa? I can manage that." The words left his lips before he could think them over. There were reasons they shouldn't do this. It would muddy their relationship and leave them with more questions than answers. They had yet to talk about these real feelings they both felt. Were they ready to ignore all the red flags and jump into bed together?

Yes. The answer was yes.

In two long strides, he bridged the space between them, pressing her back against the wall, recalling last night. Only this time they weren't in public and he wasn't going to put a stop to it.

His lips crashed against hers. There was nothing sweet in the way he kissed her. He kissed her to claim her, to feel her heartbeat through her lips. The soft moans he elicited from her went straight to his cock which was hardening against her.

"Javi." She was breathy and panting. It was sweet, tortuous music to his ears. "Please," she begged him as his hands roamed her body.

"Please, what?" Perhaps he was being cruel, but he wanted her to say exactly what she wanted. There could be no mistaking because once they went down this road, there was no turning back.

Lola rolled her lip between her teeth, gaze sinking to the floor. Oh hell no, he was not having any of that. Placing his finger under her chin, he forced her attention back onto him. She was a big girl and could look into his eyes when she asked him for pleasure. Lola stiffened under him but didn't try to move out of his grasp.

"I want..." She trailed off, losing some of her bravado. She wouldn't feel so self-conscious if she only understood what she did to him. Javi rolled his hips against her, his erection digging into her belly. The towel miraculously staying on as he ground into her.

"You want what, Lola?"

"You. I want you to fuck me."

And there it was. The last of his resolve began to crumble and the dam holding back his feelings broke. He was done denying himself and apparently, she wanted him just as much. Javi was prepared to give her what she wanted—but only on his terms.

In one fell swoop, he picked Lola up and threw her over his shoulders. Lola shrieked and pounded his back playfully. It shouldn't have been as arousing as it was, but his cock ached for her. He wanted to be buried deep inside her pretty pussy until she came around him.

"Javi! What the fuck?! Put me down; I'm too heavy."

That statement earned her a swift smack to her ass and once he reached the bed, Javi did put her down. Not because she asked, but because he needed to see her beautiful face when he scolded her. He leaned forward, his arms caging her in on either side, causing her to lean back to get a good look at his face. "I don't know what *boys* you've been fucking around with, but there is nothing too heavy about you, Lola. If I want to throw you over my shoulder and carry you to bed, then that's what I'm going to fucking do. Understand?"

"Fuck, that was so hot."

"Do you understand, Lola?"

"Yes."

He leaned in and kissed her gently. "Good girl." Then he pushed himself up, standing in front of her. His hands went to the towel, but his gaze never left hers as he pulled at the end of the towel and let it fall around him. Lola sucked in a deep breath as she took in his hard cock. All for her. Only for her.

"Do you want something in your mouth, preciosa?" he asked, moving to wrap his hand around his shaft, giving his cock two long strokes. It felt good, but not nearly as good as what her velvety lips would feel like around him.

"Yes."

"Get on your knees." It had been a long time since he got to command anyone in the bedroom and he realized how much he fucking missed it. Lola didn't need to be told twice; she scooted off the bed, sinking to the floor and chased his hands away from his cock. He gave up his stroking as her hand took over.

"Fuck." His groan came from deep in his throat. His muscles flexed and he kept himself from grabbing the back of her head and pushing her down until he was deep down her throat.

As if knowing what he was thinking and wanting to tease him, his girl wore a cute little smirk and brought his tip to her mouth. She flicked her tongue out, spreading the bead of precum around his head. It felt so good, too damn good, and then his brain short-circuited as she took him inside her mouth.

Javi felt like a damn teenager, ready to explode at the first contact with a woman's mouth. Lola's cheeks hollowed out as she bobbed her head to take down almost every inch of him. With her free hand, she reached up to cup his heavy balls and he roared with pleasure. "Fucking hell, Lola, you're going to be the death of me."

She hummed in response, alternating between taking him down her throat to only teasing his tip. Both felt equally good and if she kept this up, he would come in no time.

But he was not ready to come yet. Not until she got what she deserved. His pleasure could wait until he got a taste of her.

Without warning, Javi pulled out of her mouth. Precum and spit rolled down Lola's shocked face. "Was I not doing it well?" The embarrassment was evident in her tone and he quickly shook his head.

"You were doing too good, but when you are with me, you get to come first." Her shocked face told her that she hadn't been accustomed to treatment like this before. It made a primal part of his brain inexplicably happy that he could be part of one of her firsts. "Clothes off, beautiful. Let me see that body you are trying to hide from me."

"I'm not hiding anything from you," she shot back, rolling her eyes but stood up up to do as she was told. He watched as the crop top came off, showing off her lacy red bra. He had never been attracted to a color before, but red looked fucking sexy on her soft brown skin.

Lola then undid her jeans, kicking them off with ease. "Matching set?" he mused, seeing the red thong she sported.

"I like feeling sexy underneath my clothing." She shrugged, undoing the bra and letting her large tits spring free. The last to go was her panties and soon she stood in front of her in all of her glory.

Lola wasn't petite. She had a round belly with the slightest hints of stretch marks. Her thighs were thick, and he wanted to bury himself between them. Everything about her demanded his attention and worship. He couldn't help but notice how she didn't shy away from his gaze but instead allowed him to drink her in.

"You are the most beautiful fucking person I have ever seen." She deserved to be treated like a queen every day and know her worth. Not what her mother and sister tried and failed to drill into her head, but her actual worth. How her body was perfect, a temple to be worshiped by anyone she deemed worthy. He thanked God she chose him.

"And what do you want to do to the most beautiful person you've ever seen?" Her voice was like honey, caressing his senses. He wanted to do a lot with her and didn't know where to start. They had all day, but that didn't seem like enough time to give her all she deserved. Still, he knew where he would start.

Easing her back down on the bed, Javi spread her legs, exposing her sweet pussy to him. It glistened with her arousal and he leaned forward and smelled her sweetness. "So wet for me," he purred, pressing soft kisses to her inner thigh. Lola's legs began to shake and she tried to close her thighs, but he pressed his palms to her, keeping her open. "You stay open for me. You understand?"

"Yes." That one-syllable word held so much meaning to him. So much trust and need.

Looking up at her, Javi licked from her ass all the way to her clit as he let the sweet taste of her fill his mouth. She was tangy and sweet, a perfect combination. The first stroke of his tongue caused her to claw her nails into the bedding.

So she was extra sensitive. Good to know.

With the second stroke, her thighs tightened around his head, unable to stay in place. He chuckled softly into her pussy, not bothering to push her thighs back down. He liked the proximity and full access this gave him.

Javi moved to suck her clit into his mouth, his tongue teasing the already swollen nub. One finger traced the outside of her lips before parting them and pressing deep inside. She was tight, but that didn't stop her from clamping down around him. When he curled his finger inside of her, she let out a piercing scream.

"Javi! Fuck!" She groaned, reaching up to play with her beautiful tits, pinching and twisting her nipples.

"So fucking perfect." His hot breath hit her core and he watched as her entire body shuddered for him. Knowing she needed another one, Javi pushed in a second finger, moving them in and out at a steady pace. His tongue worked on her clit mercilessly.

"Javi, I'm close. Fuck...Oh god!" Her sweet cries did nothing to derail the pleasure he continued to give her. He wouldn't stop until she came undone around him. His licking, teasing, and fingers didn't cease, even as her cries and pleas grew louder. He almost felt bad for the neighbors, but not enough to quit what he was doing.

A few moments later, Lola's orgasm exploded through her, filling the room with her tangy sweetness. Javi cursed under his breath, lapping at her pussy until he forced himself to pull back.

"We're not done," he growled and crawled up her body. "That didn't even begin to take the edge off. It only fueled my addiction to you. Do you see how much you affect me?" he asked and guided his cock through her folds, only teasing. Always teasing because her cries of pleasure tasted like sweet nectar.

Lola was a writhing mess underneath him and he liked

seeing her so open and vulnerable with him. "I don't want to wait," she whined, reaching for his cock to bring it to her entrance.

"So needy," he tsked, which earned him a searing kiss to his lips. Lola pulled him down until their mouths connected. He knew she tasted herself on his lips and that made it even more erotic.

Knowing he couldn't hold back for much longer, Javi reached for the small bag on the bedside table that held condoms. He didn't know what made him decide to put them into his bag before he left home, but he was incredibly thankful he did.

With ease, he opened the foil and slid the condom down his cock. As much as he wanted to one day give Camilia siblings, he doubted knocking up Lola now would be the wisest idea. They needed to establish their complicated relationship first.

"I'm not going easy on you. I know you can take it." She had once and he was certain she could again. It was the last warning he gave her before he thrusted inside of her, filling Lola up to the hilt. They moaned in unison, Lola's legs came up and wrapped around his torso. He dropped his arms to either side of her head, curls framing her face on the pillow.

Javi was lost in his pleasure. Lola scratched down his back as he moved inside of her, listening to their bodies move together. He had been so close to coming multiple times and wouldn't last long in this position.

Each thrust sent their bodies crashing together. If Lola needed him to take off some steam from her less-than-impressive family interactions, he would be here to fuck her until she forgot everything but his name.

Reaching down between them, he let his thumb find her

clit again. The small moans of satisfaction only increased when he found the right speed.

"I'm not going to last much longer, Lola. You're fucking incredible." He kept reiterating the fact in hopes of counteracting the negativity her family fed her. He was only one man, but perhaps his words would help. Even if it was just a little.

"Come with me, Javi. Let me see you lose yourself inside me," Lola panted, her legs tensing and he knew she was going to orgasm again soon. It was his goal to pump out all the orgasms he could until she was putty in his hands.

Each stroke brought him closer and closer to the edge. It wasn't until she tightened around him and moaned his name that he finally found his first release of the day, hoping many more would follow after. He came with Lola not far behind him.

Satisfaction and smugness ran through his body. He felt like a king who came back to his quarters after finding the prettiest girl at the ball. Gently, he pulled out of Lola and discarded his condom, before laying on his back next to her.

Neither one of them spoke for a while and he hoped that didn't mean she was having second thoughts. Just as he was about to open his mouth and ask her if everything was okay, Lola rolled over until she was straddling him. A large smirk played across his features and she ran her hand down her chest.

"I hope you aren't tired." She pouted and damn if his cock didn't twitch in anticipation. It was confirmed, Lola would be the death of him and his cock. "Because I'm not done with you."

He liked the sound of that and rolled his hips underneath her. A sultry moan left her lips. "And what else does my lovely date have planned for us?"

To answer his own question: a lot. Lola had a lot in store

for them and he was too eager to be the willing participant. "How about I show you?" She smirked and did just that.

Lola

There were good ways to spend one's evening and then there was a gorgeous man on his knees in the shower eating your pussy for the third time that night good. How she even held herself up at this point was some kind of sex witchery that Lola didn't understand. Lola knew Javi was good in bed from their one brief night together, but she felt cheated after learning how much of a machine he was.

Orgasms never came as bountiful or quickly from anyone else. Even her small pink vibrator was getting a run for its money. Javi was just so...eager and left her a blissed-out mess, reeking of sex. It was a good fucking scent too.

A delicious ache formed between her thighs and tomorrow she would feel him with each movement. She would carry that around like her own beautiful secret, knowing what they did together in this room. If she thought too hard about it, the guilt and confusion would come and Lola didn't want anything to dampen this moment. It simply deserved to be.

Javi must have noticed the ever-changing emotions on her

face and insisted they take a shower. The thought of warm water on her muscles felt good, but she didn't know if she'd be able to keep herself standing when she felt like a sack of potatoes.

The shower started innocently enough with a few touches and caresses. Javi offered to wash her hair and she let him. The next thing she knew, Lola was bracing herself against the wall and Javi had dropped to his knees. His fucking knees! As if she was a damn Khaleesi from *Game of Thrones* and he was swearing his loyalty by eating her out.

With her back pressed firmly against the shower wall and one leg draped over his shoulder, Lola gasped. Her nipples grew hard and she began to absentmindedly play with them, adding more pleasure.

"Javi I can't..." she whined again, but those words did not stop her from riding his far too pretty face with wild abandon.

"You can. I know you can come for me one more time." His naughty tongue found her clit, sending jolts of pleasure straight through her body.

How the fuck was she ready to come again? It shouldn't be possible and yet Javi managed to pull them from her as if he alone held the key to unlocking her orgasms. Damn him and his sinful tongue and thick dick. Until him, she had not known that she could finish by penetration alone.

She was learning so much.

Another tantalizing flick of his tongue had her coming undone in his arms once again. Before she fell on her ass, Javi grabbed her hips, holding her as he leisurely pulled away from between her thighs, wearing her juices on his lips. The bastard dared to smile at her. He was far too smug for what he had done and honestly, she couldn't say she blamed him. He deserved his cocky attitude, at least for tonight.

"Let's get you to bed," Javi murmured once he stood up. They spent time cleaning off the rest of their bodies and giggling like teenagers in puppy love. If she stopped and thought about what they did and how her emotions were changing by the second, she knew the panic would set in.

"I'll keep you up. Come," Javi insisted. She wanted to point out that she did, indeed, come a lot and doubted she would ever come again thanks to him. But no words formed. Instead, she nodded and reached out to him.

With ease, Javi leaned down and scooped her up. Was it insanely attractive that he could scoop her up as if she were a real bag of potatoes? Absolutely. She wouldn't make the mistake of saying she was too heavy again...though the spanking was nice.

Javi was a good man. He was attentive and caring and Lola wanted nothing more than to be next to him for as long as time would allow. But...there were still things she needed to fix about herself before she allowed someone into her life again.

Not to mention that so much money was on the line for Javi right now and although she knew for a fact he didn't spend the last few hours giving her mind-blowing orgasms because she was paying him, she also knew that created a gray area for them as well. No good relationship started out as fake and turned into something real.

But could it?

All of those things were pushed aside when Javi helped her out of the shower and into the bed. "Do you need anything?" His voice was like a gentle caress on her skin.

Next to her bedside table was her water bottle full of cold water—which she remembered to fill after a break between sex sessions two and three—and a half-eaten bag of Doritos. They had expelled many calories and tomorrow her body would demand nourishment, but she didn't want to leave the comforts of their room or have room service bother them. She'd deal with her hunger needs in the morning.

"I'm okay. Hold me?" It came out as more of a question than a command. The bed dipped next to her before Javi's warm, naked body pressed up against hers, pulling her to his chest.

Cuddling felt more intimate than the marathon of sex they just had. Perhaps it was because she was baring herself to him in a different way and letting her guard down. She hadn't done that for a while, scared that any new person in her life would find a way to disappoint her. She was still waiting for the other shoe to drop because what she felt for Javi had to have an expiration date.

Unless...there didn't have to be.

His arms provided the sense of safety she needed tonight to keep the doubts and regrets at bay. She couldn't regret what they did today, but she would need to clarify what they were to each other. This was so much more than cute touches and secret glances, this was...something she wasn't yet comfortable describing.

A part of her was scared to develop anything further with Javi. Was she truly ready to put herself out there again? Javi made her feel like the most interesting person on earth, but was that enough?

But another part of her was scared because she had once thought Archie would never hurt her. The two men couldn't be more different, but putting her heart out on the line again came at a huge cost and she didn't think she was ready to pay it yet.

"Sleep well, Lola," Javi said, pulling her out of her opposing thoughts. His breathing slowed and she felt the soft rise and fall of his chest. Tonight had been amazing, even if the aftermath was scary. The negative thoughts tried to penetrate her mind, but she kept them at bay. Tomorrow she could worry about their future and feel her feelings. Tonight she would let the ignorance comfort her and think of Javi's arms around her.

Within a few minutes, Lola fell into a dreamless sleep.

CHAPTER 29

The soft thrumming of a guitar filled the air, breaking the silence of the morning. Lola squirmed in his arms, whining at the sudden intrusion of sound. At first, his sleepy brain conjured up an image of a mariachi band playing outside as if they were sent by their neighbors to congratulate them on their marathon of sex.

When the sound abruptly cut off only to start back up again, Javi realized his phone was going off. His body was wound tightly around Lola's, so extricating his limbs from hers was no easy task, especially because he didn't want to wake her up. He had shown little to no mercy to her yesterday and she needed the rest.

After exiting the bed and hoping he didn't jostle her too much, Javi grabbed his phone. The screen lit up with an incoming call and Ofelia's picture popped up. His stomach dropped as dread and dad guilt threatened to consume him. When he agreed to be Lola's date, he had made a promise to Camilia that he would call her every single day. And he had not lived up to that promise. The past few days came and went without a single call or text.

He wouldn't be winning a best dad award anytime soon.

Grabbing a shirt and sweats from the floor, Javi got dressed at record speed and made his way outside onto the patio balcony in an effort to not disturb Lola's sleeping form. Right before his phone cut off, he answered it. His sister's frown greeted him. "You too busy to speak with your own family?" Her tone bordered on annoyance and his sister hardly ever lost his cool with him.

It was his stupid fault. He hadn't been thinking about anything other than his feelings and the strong pull he felt toward Lola. While he was selfishly taking care of his own needs, he left Camilia to fend for herself with Ofelia. Being away for an entire week was going to be hard on her and yet he had done nothing to make it easier.

"Shit—I'm sorry, Ofi. How is she? Is everything alright? Do I need to come home?" His words were a jumbled mess and he tried to peer around Ofelia's head, hoping to catch a glimpse of his daughter.

"No, no. None of that." She sighed and ran a hand through her hair. "Sorry, Mav's back at training today and I'm alone with the kids. I called papá for backup because Arturo is going to drive me to drink. This morning he thought it would be a good idea to wake me up by dropping a sopping wet towel on me and proceed to belly flop on my face."

Despite his tense mood only moments ago, Javi couldn't help but laugh. Arturo was a rambunctious kid, but apparently so was Maverick at this age. He also made a mental note to buy his sister dinner and books for having to take care of two kids. That sounded like a handful, especially when they were two and six.

"But Camilia has been asking about you. She wants to talk; do you have time?" she asked, and Javi saw his sister move through the house toward the room she had set up for Camilia.

"I have time. I'm so sorry again, Ofi. I should have been checking in."

Ofelia waved away his apology. "Honestly, it's fine. Camilia is doing great, but I know she will appreciate talking to you. Hey, Camilia." Ofelia smiled, no longer looking at Javi but over the phone to where his daughter must be. "Papá is on the phone. Are you ready to talk?"

There was some shuffling and a black screen before a rosy-cheeked little girl popped up. Her beautiful curls were pulled back into a high-top ponytail with a few unruly strands crowning her face. She had on her favorite hoodie he had gotten at a gas station a few months ago with a unicorn riding a bike. The biggest smile greeted him, slamming in the knife of guilt. His sweet girl didn't hold grudges, but he couldn't shake the feeling of fucking up.

"Mija, how are you? Papá misses you so much." A strange lump formed in his throat, but he coughed it away.

"I miss you too. This much!" she said, dropping the phone on her bed and holding her arms out wide. "But tía Ofi is taking us to the movies today. After Arturo has a nap or else he will be a grumpy monster like tío." Javi heard Ofelia laugh outside the camera.

"That sounds like a lot of fun. And abuelo is going too?"

"Oh yes. And it's my job to keep him from snoring in the movies." She giggled and launched into her plan of how she was going to make that happen. While she spoke, Javi listened and nodded his head when appropriate. Inwardly, he wrestled with his guilt of missing out on these small moments, even though there would be plenty more.

Camilia then spoke to him about school and how she was doing with her sight words. How she almost had all of them correct, but still needed to work on a few. Ofelia made sure to read to her every night and Camilia retold the stories they read. Javi couldn't help but smile when his daughter mentioned *The Giving Tree*. He pictured Lola rolling her eyes and explaining how problematic the book was. Still, he wondered if Camilia would ever ask Lola to read it to her.

It terrified him how easily he could picture Lola in his life. Would she be okay with starting a relationship with a man who already had a child? And why the hell was he even thinking about any of this now? Deep down, in the pits of his lonely heart, Javi knew exactly why he could only think of a future with Lola.

How he didn't want any other man to have her.

She was his and his alone.

Perhaps not yet, but she would be soon. If he could sort out his damn feelings.

"Oh, papá, tía wants to talk to you," Camilia said, pulling his thoughts back toward his daughter.

His face relaxed and he smiled at her. "Okay, mija. Tomorrow is the wedding, so I might not be able to call you, but I'll send pictures."

"Oh! Bring home cake!" she said and suddenly disappeared, tossing the phone to Ofelia. The sound of her small feet hitting the floor and running off filled his speaker, leaving the siblings alone.

"And she's gone now. I think she heard the door open and ran to her abuelo. Do you have a minute though? I wanted to talk to you about something. Nothing bad!" she clarified, which was good because he didn't think he had the capacity for anything bad.

When he nodded his head to signal for her to continue, Ofelia started in on her news. "So I've been absolutely killing it being a stay-at-home mom, but I do miss cheer. I called Willow —she says hi by the way—and she suggested I apply as a part-time coach at the cheer clinic Camilia goes to."

Willow was Ofelia's best friend who lived back in Texas. She had visited a handful of times and stayed most of the summer at their house while her husband traveled for work and she was off for summer break. Teacher perks.

"I just got a callback and will be starting next week!" Ofelia squealed. Her excitement was contagious and he was so happy for her. Ofelia had given up a lot of things when she moved from Texas but was eager to be closer to family. She had chosen to be a stay-at-home mom and from what Javi gathered, she had not regretted this decision. But getting back into something so deeply rooted in her soul would be a good thing.

"Congratulations, hermana. You're going to be so good at that. Is Arturo going to go to work with you?"

"Oh yes, he's big enough to run around and play. And Maverick will be home to watch him at other times. Papá offered too, but he's a handful so I would rather he didn't have to take on the responsibility.

"But, the reason I'm telling you this is because Camilia gets a discount on cheer. I think it will apply to your next payment. I can ask them when I take her tonight for practice. Did you want me to go ahead and take care of the bill?"

She said the last bit as nonchalantly as she could. It was no secret he got bent out of shape when talk of money was involved. He hated that he was like this, but having struggled most of his life with paying off bills, debts, and now cheer practice, it was a point of stress for Javi.

Last month had been hellacious with very little work and

worse pay than normal. It was one of the reasons why he wanted to go independent, now that he had worked up a decent clientele. He was behind on his phone bill and a credit card bill and would have been able to afford both if he didn't have to pay for cheer. Camilia loved cheer though. It was in her blood like it was in Ofelia's blood and he would be damned if he made her suffer because he couldn't pay the damn bills.

He had swallowed his pride last month and asked Ofelia to help. She had been all too eager and offered to pay until his new business was off the ground, but he refused for now, hoping that this month brought a more prosperous income. And it did.

But it all hinged on Lola. He was taking so much money from her. Money she was willing to give for his work and pretending to be her boyfriend, but sometime between then and now the lines of faking began to blur.

There was nothing fake about his real feelings for her. The way his heart swelled at the sight of her. How he wanted to see her roll his eyes at him if he said something she didn't agree with or thought was cheesy. The way her cheeks would turn red when she was shy or turned on.

Fuck, things had spiraled so quickly and his heart was leading his actions these days.

"I wrote a check. It's in my bedroom on the bedside table. You can take that," he answered after a minute.

"Javi, I really don't mind—"

"I got this, Ofi. I got this." He worked hard to keep his tone neutral, not wanting to snap at her nor wanting to divulge where he got the money. It would be too complicated and he wanted to sort out his feelings first.

Ofelia bit her lip and looked like she wanted to argue, but

soon nodded, letting it go. "Okay, but I'm still going to see if the discount starts this week."

"Sure, that would be very helpful. Thank you."

Ofelia seemed happy with his response and nodded. She then told him about a few things they had done while he was away and from the sounds of it, Camilia was having an amazing time with her tía. Ofelia pried into how his week was going and he gave a brief run down, not going deep into Lola's family because that wasn't his story to tell.

When he finally got her off the phone, an hour had passed and with it, a new uneasy feeling settled over him. Ofelia bringing up the cheer bill reminded him just how much Lola was changing his life, not just emotionally but financially too. If he were a better man, he would tell her he just couldn't accept the money. She didn't need to pay him for dating her when he wanted to date her for real. The money would always be between them.

They still had a few more days together and he hoped within that time he could sort through his feelings and make a better and more informed decision about his money dilemma. For now, he had a woman waiting in bed for him and he wanted to soak up every last minute he had with her.

He just hated feeling like there was an hourglass counting down their final minutes.

CHAPTER 30

Lola

Sleep claimed Lola's body last night like a ship in a calm sea, rocking her gently until darkness overtook her. The entire night she slept in Javi's arms and the presence of another person against her back brought more comfort than she anticipated. The hold this man had on her was alarming, but she wasn't yet ready to sever the fragile tethers connecting them.

When she finally managed to rouse herself the next morning, two things hit her instantly. Firstly, the delicious ache between her legs which reminded her of yesterday's activities. She had never had so many orgasms back-to-back and she was sure Javi ruined her sex life completely. How was she to come ever again for any other partner? Just the thought of another man in bed who wasn't Javi left an ache deep inside her chest.

Secondly, Javi was gone. The space he had occupied last night lay cold. The familiar brown, tattooed arms that once squeezed her to his chest were gone, leaving her empty in a dark room. Lola lifted her head off her pillow, trying to locate him.

Images of their first night rushed back to her and the memory of waking up to an empty room after a night of passion.

This time was different, and she didn't think Javi would leave her high and dry. He wasn't that kind of man, but she hated the sliver of fear coursing through her body at the thought of the possibility of him leaving. A small part of her brain whispered that he was only with her for the money, but that was her anxiety talking.

But where the fuck was Javi?

She pushed herself into a sitting position on the bed, her muscles screaming in protest. Lola made a mental note to do yoga later today to ease the soreness. She had seen a spacious gym on the first floor and could utilize the space for stretching.

A hushed voice sounded from outside, grabbing her attention. Through the thick curtains keeping the sun at bay, she saw tousled black hair sticking up at odd ends. A smile crossed her face at the thought of her hands gripping those strands.

Javi's posture was rigid at first, as if bracing himself for an argument. She watched in silence as his body went from a defensive stance into a more relaxed posture. She couldn't see his face, but she imagined him smiling at his phone. Only one person made him melt like that.

Camilia.

Fuck, she had been so consumed with her selfish desires that she hadn't stopped and considered his daughter. How could she be okay with keeping him away from his sweet little girl, especially knowing what happened to her mother? She had only met Camilia briefly, but it was easy to tell how much Javi loved her. Being away from her had to be difficult, and she hadn't considered the sacrifices he was making.

Lost in an internal battle, she barely registered the sliding glass door opening. Javi stood in rumpled sweats and a wrinkled shirt that hung loose around his torso. He shouldn't look as good as he did, but Lola had the impression he would look good in a trash bag.

"Hey, I hope I didn't wake you," he said as a way of greeting.

Javi had woken something up in her, but not in the way he thought. These last twenty-four hours had been the best of her life. If she were being honest with herself, the past few weeks she had been able to spend with Javi were easily becoming core memories for her.

If she wasn't so chicken shit, perhaps she could call this feeling for what it was. Love was a funny thing. It demanded so much from a person and consumed their lives, but it could also be broken in an instant and feel like it was never there at all. Only the lingering pains served as a reminder.

Not that she loved Javi. Probably. Maybe. It was just that this feeling growing inside of her felt a lot like it and that scared the absolute shit out of her. He had a whole-ass family to think about and money troubles, since he had agreed to take her up on this wild offer. Not that money was a big deal to her, but it was possible she had actually bought his affection and their relationship was built upon a pillar of lies.

"No, I didn't even hear you leave," she said, which wasn't a lie. She had woken up on her own and then eavesdropped on the entire conversation which sent her into a panic about taking a father away from his daughter.

Javi, oblivious to her internal struggle, nodded before rejoining her in bed. He took up the spot behind her once again and pulled her into his arms, nuzzling her neck. "Please tell me we can stay in bed all day again."

She wanted to. Like, really and truly wanted nothing more than to have this man ravage her body again. But today would be busy with last-minute preparations for the wedding. If she looked at her phone now, she was certain she'd find a list of things she needed to do today. She was but a servant to be bossed around by her mother.

"Judging from your lack of response, I'm certain you're about to tell me you are going to drop everything so I can feast upon you until we are both satisfied and wallowing in our combined pleasure," Javi said.

It was the furthest thing from her mind, which made her bark out a laugh. She tried to hide it with her hand as if covering her mouth would somehow make the sound disappear but to no avail. "Haven't you feasted enough?"

His eyes darkened with wicked intent and she knew what he was going to say before he even spoke. "Absolutely not. I could never be satisfied after a single night with you."

"Greedy boy." She smiled despite herself. Just a few minutes ago she was worried about taking up his time and set on creating distance between them, but now she was considering his invitation to spread her legs and feast.

No, she couldn't allow that. Not now. The distraction of the wedding would be good enough to keep their horniness at bay.

"We need to feast, but not on each other." She swore Javi muttered something about that being "dumb," but she pretended like she didn't hear him. "There's a cafe on the first floor where we can go for breakfast. And then I'll probably need to run some errands for my sister. You are free to relax since I doubt you'll want to join Archie and his prissy-ass friends in whatever they have planned today."

The look of his pure disgust was all she needed to see to know he had zero interest in hanging with Archie. Not that she could blame him. Archie was a pompous asshole and he and his so-called "friends" would probably find a pretentious bar and talk about how great they were. It didn't seem like Javi's scene.

"Do you want me to help with the errands?" Javi asked instead.

"No, I'm sure it won't be anything exciting and I'll have to deal with my mom and sister a lot. It would be easier—"

"If I wasn't there." She hated the dejection in his voice, but she also didn't know what to say. It would be harder if he were and it wasn't as if she needed him for support since her mother and sister's focus wouldn't be on her. Plus, a little time apart so she could sort through the tangle of emotions wouldn't be a bad thing.

"We can spend this evening together. Maybe we can have dinner tonight?" she asked, hoping her tone was light. The disappointment was evident in his features and it nearly made her cave, but then Javi's mood changed in a blink of an eye and he smiled.

"Sure. We can do it tonight. Let me get dressed and we can head down for breakfast before you go."

He didn't wait for her reply. He kissed her cheek once more and untangled himself from her. He disappeared into the bathroom, leaving her with unwanted uncertainty and the need to distract her ever-changing thoughts.

Once the door was closed, Lola jumped out of bed to find her clothes. She decided on jeans with a fitted, but breathable seafoam-green blouse and sensible booties so her feet wouldn't be hurting by the end of the day.

Lola then checked her phone, only to see her mother's list of tasks for her today. The first thing on the list was to arrange rides for the bridesmaids from the airport to the hotel. Why they couldn't do it themselves was beyond her, but she learned long ago it was better to simply do, rather than argue.

Her duties also included picking up Marisol's shoes from the store, checking in with catering, and picking up the wedding rings from her mother's suite to keep them safe until their big day tomorrow.

She had just finished going over her list and transferring it to the notes section of her phone when Javi emerged from the bathroom, smelling of citrus and pine cones. "Ready to eat?"

"Very." Her stomach growled on command and she reached for her purse, following Javi out the door. Today would be full of unwanted tasks, but at least she would be alone and able to think straight for the first time in weeks. Javi had a hold on her emotions and she was starting to fear for her own heart.

BREAKFAST HAD BEEN RELATIVELY QUIET, but not uncomfortably so. Neither one of them seemed to be looking forward to the day and she felt bad for leaving Javi alone. He was a grown man, capable of taking care of himself, but she still felt responsible for his entertainment.

In the end, Javi had decided he was going to explore the hotel and find something to bring back for Camilia.

Lola took the time for herself to grab another coffee and scroll through her list one last time to make sure she knew exactly what needed to be done. The idea of facing Luciana and Marisol's ire if she fucked up was the only motivation she needed to march her ass out of the hotel.

At least that was what she was planning on doing, until she collided with a hard body rounding the corner at the same time she did. The impact sent her back a few steps before she could right herself.

"Oh, I'm so sorry—" Her words cut off as her brain registered the man standing in front of her.

Archie.

She had done a good job of avoiding him this entire week, only seeing him when she saw the rest of her family, and had planned to keep it that way. But of course, the universe had other plans for her.

Like her, Archie was alone. Unlike her, he looked more put together after the head-on collision than she did. She pressed her mouth into a tight line. The only positive thing was that he didn't appear any happier to see her than she was to see him.

As far as Lola was concerned, she had two options. She could either walk past him and pretend as if they never saw each other, or she can reach deep into the depths of her soul to start a conversation. She knew which one she wanted to do, but she also didn't want Archie thinking he had gotten the better of her.

"Archie—hi." Her voice was higher than she would have liked, showing just how anxious she was.

Archie arched a brow and the corners of his lips pulled up into a smile, clearly amused. "Lola. I have to say, I'm surprised you're here."

"In the lobby?"

"No, in Colorado. At the wedding. I didn't think you would come." He laughed as if he had just finished telling a joke. "I mean, I just know how hard the breakup was on you and I wondered if coming here would make you sad all over again."

It took a Herculean effort to bite back the retort on the tip of the tongue. To yell and scream at him for being a pompous jerk and always making her feel small and insignificant. Yet she knew that was the exact reaction Archie was expecting from her, to blow up and cause a scene. Another scandal, courtesy of Lola.

Instead, she tried to keep her voice calm as she spoke. "Why would I be mad that you dumped me for my sister?"

"Well, you can't help who you fall in love with. And we gave you the courtesy of ending things before we began dating. I knew you would need time to process things." Archie reached out and placed a hand on her shoulder as if to comfort her.

Lola recoiled from his touch. Was he seriously insinuating that she should be grateful that Archie hadn't *cheated* on her with her sister, as if that was not the bare fucking minimum in any relationship? She didn't buy his declaration of love for her sister though. Men like Archie only ever loved themselves.

"Anyway," he said, clearly bored of this conversation. That made two of them. "This man you brought to my wedding. Who is he?"

"I've already introduced him, if you cared to listen. His name is Javi."

"And he's your...?"

"Boyfriend," she supplied, with more confidence than she felt.

"Oh." That one syllable made her tense. It wasn't just an innocent acceptance. No, Archie was deliberately holding his words back, forcing her to ask him what he meant by that.

And because Lola was a glutton for punishment, she asked, "Oh? Do you have something to say?"

"Just that you tend to dive into things without thinking them through all the way."

Lola felt her jaw drop. What right did Archie have to tell her she recklessly made decisions? "How dare you—"

"Does he know you have money?" he asked, his question rendering her immobile. He must have seen the anger in her gaze because he put his hands up to subdue her. "Guys like him prey on lonely, wealthy girls looking for companionship."

This time when she spoke, she couldn't keep the anger out of her voice. "What do you mean 'guys like him?'"

Archie paled, for once looking slightly uncomfortable. But only for a moment before he schooled his expression back into his normal cocky demeanor. "You know the ones. Guys with tattoos who don't know how to conduct themselves in public. Guys like *him*," he repeated.

It was one thing to say something nasty about her, but quite another to say anything bad about Javi. She took a step forward, invading his space. She watched as Archie straightened, puffing out his chest as if to intimidate her.

"Let's be real fucking clear, Archie. I don't give a shit what you think about me. I stopped caring a long time ago, once I learned what a pathetic excuse of a man you are. But say one more disparaging thing about Javi and I'll kick you so hard in your balls, doctors will never be able to recover them."

A beat of silence hung between them as she stared Archie down. He was the first to fold by looking away and clearing his throat. "No need for such dramatics, Lola. I'm simply a concerned friend who knows you and how you jump into things without thinking."

"You don't know a damn thing about me," she spat.

Except he did. He knew some things about her. He had been a crappy boyfriend, but they did spend a lot of time together while they were dating. He was bound to pick up some of her traits.

Was she really that impulsive and not thinking things through?

Well, she was quick to jump into a relationship with Archie. Looking back, there had been so many red flags and yet she chose to ignore all of them. She couldn't help but think about her abrupt move from Florida back to California to open up a bookstore, something she knew virtually nothing about. Then again agreeing to jump into a fake-dating scenario, not allowing herself to dwell on everything that could go wrong.

Fuck. She couldn't help but think Archie might be right.

Not wanting to have this personal crisis in front of a man she held no love for, Lola stepped back. "For the record, I'm glad you broke my heart because it made me realize how much I was settling for a man that wasn't worth my time. I just feel sorry for my sister because even though we may not be close, I still think Marisol deserves better and I hope one day she realizes that too."

She had said her peace and didn't need to hear any futile rebuttal Archie might have. She left him scowling after her, not once looking back as she walked away. It was what she always needed to do and even though it was six months late, she felt lighter with each step. She felt like her Archie chapter had finally come to an end.

Yet as she walked away, she couldn't help but think about Archie's words as doubts about all her recent choices began to creep in despite her best efforts to keep them at bay.

CHAPTER 31

Javi

Much like breakfast, dinner was quiet that evening. Javi kept glancing up from his chicken Alfredo to study Lola. Ever since they walked into the restaurant—the same one from the disaster dinner with her family—something had been off with Lola, but he couldn't quite figure out what it was. He didn't want to push her either, since the weary look on her face indicated she had a hard day of errands.

Lola had hardly touched her meal. She spent most of the time moving her shrimp from one side of the plate to the other, only eating about a third of her meal. Javi frowned. He hated seeing her so disconnected and not knowing the reason why.

Javi let his fork drop on his plate, the soft thunk of metal on porcelain drew Lola's attention. She glanced up with heavy lashes and her posture stiffened. It was as if she had forgotten he was there.

"I'm sorry—"

"What's wrong?"

They spoke at the same time and Lola, for the first time

that night, cracked a sheepish smile. She finally put down the fork, ignoring her neglected meal. "It's just been a long day."

"Did something happen?" It was a gentle nudge because he didn't want to push her if she was not ready to talk about it. Not knowing would slowly eat away at him, but he wanted to respect her privacy as much as possible.

"I...ran into Archie today. Alone." Her voice was barely more than a whisper, but Javi heard it as loud as if she were speaking into a megaphone. His body grew hot and his leg began to bounce with the new energy coursing through his body.

In the back of his mind, he had wondered if this scenario might happen, though he routinely pushed it out of his mind. He planned on accompanying Lola wherever she went, but she had insisted on running errands by herself. Maybe he should have pushed harder to go with her.

"What did he say?" Each word was a struggle to get out. He didn't *want* to know, but he needed to hear regardless.

Most likely sensing his internal struggle, Lola quickly continued. "It wasn't bad. I mean, it definitely wasn't pleasant, he was being his normal dickish self, but it wasn't anything I couldn't handle.

"I got to stand up for myself, something I should have done in the first place. I might have threatened bodily harm and told him that I thought Marisol deserved better than him."

Despite the agitation building in his body, he let out a breathy laugh. "That's my girl. He deserves to be put in his place."

"Yeah, he did." Her smile slowly faltered as she grew pensive. "But he said a few things that really got me thinking. I guess it's just messing with me."

And just like that, the anger came back at full force. How

anyone could find that man even remotely likable was beyond him. He hardly knew Marisol and from their brief interactions, he couldn't say he was her biggest fan, but not even she deserved a lowlife like Archie. He was sleazy and looking for people and things that fit his image.

"Whatever he said was bullshit, you know that, right?" Javi didn't even need to know what he said. Whatever came out of that man's mouth only proved to serve his best interest.

"Yeah, but—"

"No, there's no 'but' about it. He wanted to get under your skin and that's exactly what he did. Don't give him that power over you."

Lola pursed her lips into a tight line, eyeing him like she didn't know whether to snap at him or pull him in for a kiss. He hoped for the latter.

She did neither of those things.

Instead, she let out a deep breath and sank back against her chair. "This isn't about me giving him power or anything. I just can't help but feel that there was a part of what he said that is closer to the truth than I realized."

"And what is that?" Javi tried to keep his tone even. He didn't want to take out his anger on her. She didn't deserve his anger, that was solely reserved for Archie. What Lola needed was for him to just listen and that was what he planned on doing.

"That, well..." She trailed off, hesitating. After a pregnant pause where Javi thought he would have to ask her again, Lola continued. "He said I jump into things without thinking them through. That I'm reckless."

Unable to help himself, Javi scoffed. "Oh, that's rich coming from him. The man who jumped into a relationship right after he broke your heart. Men like Archie aren't happy until they instill doubt in those around them. I'm sorry you had to deal with him alone, preciosa, but I'm proud of you for standing up for yourself."

Javi wanted his words to be a comfort for her, to let her know that this one interaction shouldn't shake her confidence. Though he wasn't sure if he was doing a good job at that because Lola averted her gaze from him, still locked in a battle with her own thoughts.

"Lola," he started, reaching across the table for her hand. Before he could make contact, she jerked her hand back as if she had just been burned. Confusion and hurt rippled through him as he slowly pulled back. A look of regret passed through Lola's eyes, but she didn't try to take his hand back.

"Sorry, I guess I just have a lot on my mind right now," she said and to his dismay, Lola stood up. "I'm just tired. I'm going back to our room to lie down."

"Lola—"

"Can you just charge our dinner to our room? And get to-go boxes? Maybe I'll be hungry later." Once again, she did not look in his direction as she leaned down to gather her purse.

"Sure, but—"

"Thank you. I just need to rest." She cut him off again, not willing to hear what he had to say. Lola finally met his gaze and took a step back. She plastered on a smile that he saw right through.

"I'll be up soon and maybe we can watch a movie," he suggested, trying for an olive branch.

Lola averted her gaze and started backing up. "Not tonight. I just want to go to sleep. I'll see you in a bit," she said and then beelined for the door, leaving Javi alone.

A sense of anxiousness and dread filled the pit of his stomach at the thought of Lola pulling away from him. He didn't like it and wanted to soothe whatever fears that man put into her head. But for now, he let her go so he could finish off his dinner alone.

Tomorrow was the wedding. He just hoped he could last through it long enough to get Lola alone at the reception.

CHAPTER 32

Lola

The large suite felt smaller than the last time she had been in here, but that was because four extra women occupied the room. None of whom she recognized at all, not even after an hour of doom scrolling through her sister's socials.

Marisol had plenty of pictures, but mostly of herself, the food she probably only took two bites of, and some of her and Archie. All of those looked posed and awkward. There may have been something akin to lust on their features, but love? No, she couldn't say she saw that.

Lola was noisy by nature and probably a detective in a former life, so she had no qualms Googling the ever-loving shit out of the three bridesmaids while the hairdresser worked on their hair. It didn't take too much digging after she found a tagged photo on her sister's Instagram of a charity event.

The three women stood next to Marisol in the photo, all smiling for the camera. None of their smiles reached their eyes, but rather looked like they were practiced from countless other events.

At first glance, the photo looked like four friends having fun and enjoying the event, but upon further speculation—meaning Lola zoomed in to analyze every angle—their rigid postures and how they angled themselves to be almost touching, but not quite, showed the truth. None of the women looked excited to be there but knew how to wear a mask when cameras were around.

The women belonged in the same social circle as her parents and sister. They were here for appearances only. Though she couldn't say for certain these women—who she believed were named Ashlyn, Vanessa, and Eliza—didn't care for her sister, judging by the lingering silence in the room, she could surmise they were here out of obligation. Just like Marisol would be at their weddings.

Everything was for show.

If she didn't know any better, Lola would think they were getting ready for a funeral. The navy dresses her sister insisted they all wear looked black in the shadows. The mood in the room didn't indicate a blushing bride about to be reunited with her one true love. It felt more like a sterilized hospital room. The only one fluttering around the room working herself up into a stupor was her mother.

"No, no, no. The hair is supposed to be an updo. None of this curling nonsense," her mom spat at the poor woman hired to do their hair. If she had to bet, she would guess the hairdresser gravely regretted taking this job. No amount of payment was worth this nonsense.

She listened to the woman calmly explain the styling process to her mother when Lola's phone buzzed.

She looked down at the phone glowing in her lap and saw that she had another text from Javi. Shame and guilt fought for dominance in her belly at his name. When they parted last night, she had left Javi all alone at their table. There was something different in their dinner date that time, something that felt suffocating when it should have brought comfort. She couldn't pinpoint the exact moment her lust turned to love for a man she paid to date her, but she knew the moment she was in over her head.

The fire burning between them had become an inferno and the only way to put out the flames was to act on the passion. That, she didn't regret. She regretted losing touch with reality and falling hard for a man she had no business being with. Not when she was still so conflicted over her own feelings. This had to be a sign that she wasn't ready to jump into a relationship yet.

She had jumped into a relationship with Archie and it bit her in the ass. Perhaps it had always been a ploy to get with Marisol. The pretty one. The one that would look good at his side at events.

And maybe there was love between them, even if they showed their love differently than her, she still did not feel like this was the happy ever after everyone raved about. It felt much more like a business exchange. Exactly what she was doing with Javi right now.

> Your father offered to take me golfing three
> times in the last thirty minutes. Does that
> mean I'm part of the family?

Despite her traitorous feelings, she smiled. Oh, how she wished that to be true, but it was becoming more apparent that her own feelings couldn't be trusted.

Another text came in.

> I miss you, preciosa.

Another dagger straight to the heart.

Lola had only seen Javi in passing this morning. She had woken up before him, with Javi sleeping on the far side of the bed. Quietly, so as not to disturb him, she tiptoed into the bathroom. Five minutes later she heard a loud banging on the suite door and peeked out to see who it was.

Javi had wrangled himself out of bed, looking disheveled, and opened the door only to see her father standing on the other side. She choked on the toothbrush in her mouth, gaining both of the men's attention.

Her father had been on his way to Archie's room, and he wanted to extend an invite to Javi. Poor Javi had looked like a frightened lamb caught in between two wolves. Either he went with her father and left her to her own devices or he stayed and potentially made her father angry.

Lola knew she needed to decide for him. Even if it wasn't what he wanted to hear.

With her being away with Marisol and her bridal party, it seemed only fitting that Javi joined the men. And as she predicted, he wasn't thrilled with the prospect, but he had agreed nonetheless.

He had given her a swift peck on the cheek—an appropriate response with her father in the room—before leaving. That was the last interaction she had with him and since then, he had texted multiple times to update her on his endeavors with "stuck-up, rich, white people," as he put it.

Lola had read every message, but not replied. She only hated herself a little for leaving him on read, but she just didn't know how to wrangle her feelings into words yet. Besides, if he asked about it later, she could say she was busy. In a little over an hour she would see him anyway. She didn't think she was prepared to handle Javi dressed up for a wedding yet. She could only imagine how handsome he looked in a suit.

"Dolores! Do you have the rings?" Her mother's voice broke through her thoughts, indicating this had not been the first time she had asked Lola this question.

Rummaging around in her white clutch, she pulled out the small black box. "All safe," she assured, having picked up the rings earlier this morning. She had stored them away, knowing her mother would ask her dozens of times if they were safe.

"Ah, perfect. And you'll give them to cousin Luis when we arrive at the venue? Not a moment sooner. I don't need the boy losing these rings. They cost us a fortune." About that, Lola had no doubt. She didn't remind her mother that she wasn't stupid and wouldn't be giving anything to five-year-old cousin Luis until the very last possible second.

"And my shoes? You picked them up for me yesterday, right? Please tell me you grabbed my shoes from your room." Marisol piped up, looking in the mirror to see her. Her hair was finally becoming the updo her mother wanted and she looked gorgeous, even more so than usual.

"I grabbed your shoes from my room," Lola repeated like the obedient sister she was. "You look beautiful, Marisol." Despite the coldness between them, she still felt the need to say it. All brides should hear it on their wedding day, shouldn't they?

The dress was a tiered ball gown with a plunging neckline, making Marisol look ethereal. Her bodice was covered with lace, spanning down to the skirt of the gown. Small, intricate flower designs adorned the bottom half of her dress, making her look like she just walked off the set of a romance movie.

"Of course she looks beautiful. My girl is beauty incarnate," her mother replied before Marisol could, leaning in to kiss her cheek fondly. She had seen her mother do this before, but it still surprised her every time she showed her sister any affection. The most Lola got was a side hug or a tap on the shoulder, but those were infrequent.

The rest of the hour came and went like a bird passing through the sky. Lola finished applying makeup and helped Vanessa with hers as well since the hairstylist—who was also the makeup artist—had spent far too long on the bride and left everyone else scrambling.

Once again, not her fault.

After intense scrutiny from her mother and being told to fix a smudge of lipstick, Luciana was happy with everyone's appearance. The hairdresser left, and Lola swore she saw steam behind her at how fast she left the room.

"It's time to get married, my baby girl!" Deep within her heart, her mother conjured up a few tears for Marisol who seemed put off by them. What should have been a joyous moment just seemed like a normal Friday. If anyone else noticed the less-than-stellar vibe pumping through the room, they didn't comment.

"Dolores, let's go. We have our jobs to do," her mother said, making a beeline to the door, expecting her daughter to follow. With one last half smile geared toward her sister, Lola left the room. They had a wedding to start and there was a beautiful man waiting among the guests for her to face.

CHAPTER 33

Javi

Lola was avoiding him.

Javi tried not to let that affect him while he was getting ready with Travis, listening to him talk about the different golf courses he had visited last year. He did his best to conjure up the ability to care, even though he didn't give two shits about golf and the only thing on his mind was Lola. She clearly saw his texts but was making the conscious choice not to respond.

She could be busy. It was wedding day after all, and Archie was in the other room, taking a round of shots with his groomsmen, all clad in shades of white. He had the feeling they had all belonged to the same fraternity in college. Javi hadn't gone to college and most certainly never belonged in a fraternity, so he was sorely out of place.

He hadn't wanted to go, but he couldn't tell Lola's father no. Especially when Lola all but pushed him into his eager arms. Something was bothering her and he wanted to know what.

Despite her not answering, Javi continued to text her

unabashedly. She was going to hear from him, even if she didn't respond because he needed her to know he was thinking about her.

He texted her when Travis asked him to go golfing with him. Then again to send a sneaky photo of Archie and his basic-ass friends discussing some boring policy in regard to their business. He sent her another message when they were on their way to the venue.

Since Javi wasn't in the ceremony, he didn't have to spend any more time with Archie. Not that the time they spent together mattered much. Archie never acknowledged him when he walked in with Travis and Javi hadn't gone out of his way to congratulate him. Travis also never pushed Javi to talk with Archie, and Javi appreciated that.

They didn't have to go far for the wedding. The top floor of the hotel—which could only be accessed by a special code given to guests—felt like stepping onto the first pages of a fairy tale storybook. The room was decorated in splashes of green and silver. The altar in the center of the room was raised with an arch made of greenery and twine covering most of the platform. Rows of benches that looked like they were sculpted from tree trunks lined the rest of the room with a sheer white runner going in between. If he had to guess, the room would hold close to two hundred people. Judging by the number of people here, Javi assumed the place would fill up soon.

The theme and decor were not what Javi expected for Marisol. He had pictured sleek corners, white and cream color arrangements, and flowers that looked to be grown in shops and not in the wild. Though if she was playing up the fairy tale theme because she viewed herself as the princess of the family, she accomplished that.

Not wanting to mingle with guests who made his yearly

salary by simply coughing in the right direction, Javi took a seat in the back. There was still no sign of Lola, but he hadn't expected to see her yet. Though he wanted to catch a glimpse of her soon to see her dressed in her figure-hugging dress, hair and make-up done, looking like the most beautiful woman in the room. While everyone would have eyes on the bride, his would be on Lola the entire time.

As he waited for the guests to filter in and the wedding to start, Javi's mind wandered. He thought of Camilia. He missed her little hugs and the way she would crawl into his bed each morning to cuddle before they had to leave for school or make breakfast.

He thought of the work that still needs to be done on Phoenix. He hadn't heard much from his crew and when he checked in yesterday, one of his lead men sent him progress photos of the shelves. They looked damn good and they weren't even finished. He hadn't seen all the progress in person yet, so he was itching to get back to the store.

Naturally, his mind circled back around to Lola. The way her body moved against his when they made love. For that's what it was. Sometime throughout the night, it had changed from a need to feel one another and get off as quickly as possible, to something that meant more than either was willing to admit. But Javi could admit it now.

He loved Lola Roberts.

The revelation should frighten him. Should have made him fall back into his insecurities and doubts about money. How he was juggling time between being the perfect father and a loving partner, but those fears seemed so trivial now. There was a solution there and he was certain he would find it, but he didn't want to do it alone. He wanted Lola by his side and he hadn't been the best at telling her that.

Maybe that's why she was avoiding him. They hadn't yet had time to talk about how their fake dating turned real so fast. He should be there to help her through her insecurities and fuck out any doubts she might have about their relationship because he wasn't going anywhere. Lola was his.

The opening chords of a familiar hymn started to play. Javi looked up to find Archie and his men at the altar. When did that happen? The grand doors opened up and everyone's heads swiveled around as the first bridesmaid walked in, holding an elegant bouquet of white flowers.

Two other women he did not recognize followed after, making their way toward the bride's side of the altar. The music quieted some as the last bridesmaid walked out. The navy-blue gown hugged her curves like a glove. He loved her body, loved the way it felt underneath him or snuggled up against him. Her dark, caramel hair was pinned in the back with loose strands framing her face. Her eyes had a smokey look, making them look sultry. Despite all the eyes on her, she kept her chin up, looking fucking breathtaking as she commanded the aisle.

Lola was a sight to behold.

Long after Lola went to stand in her spot by the other bridesmaids, Javi didn't look away. He didn't look away when Marisol walked in and made her way up next to Archie. He didn't look away when vows were exchanged and rings were put on fingers. Lola's eyes kept scanning the room as if feeling his stare. It wasn't until the officiant pronounced Marisol and Archie man and wife that Lola's brown eyes meet his.

He locked in on her, the intensity of his stare making her squirm under the heat. It was as if they were the only two people in the room and at a wedding neither of them particularly wanted to be at.

Javi kept her stare even after the bride and groom walked back down the aisle, hand in hand, on their way to the reception. People next to him murmured their apologies as they scooted by him to leave, but Javi stayed in place until Lola descended the dais. His girl looked ready to flee, but he wouldn't allow her to escape him again, not with this new burning need growing inside of him.

Before Lola could dash for the exit, Javi was out of his seat and fighting his way through the crowd. When he was close, he reached out with his hand before she was lost to him, grabbing her wrist and pulling her against him.

Lola didn't struggle, but she bit her bottom lip, looking up at him as if he were about to punish her for misbehaving. And damn if that didn't send a jolt straight to his cock.

He was tempted to do just that.

"You've been avoiding me, preciosa."

There was no use in lying; they both knew it to be true, but she still tried. "I've been busy, Javi. I'm not avoiding you."

"You're pushing me away." And he didn't understand why.

Lola sighed, casting a look over her shoulder to see that the other bridesmaids had left. "I'm not doing that either. Listen, can we do this later? We both need to go to the reception and I need to make sure my mother doesn't have a fit if I'm late. I promise we can talk then."

Promises could be broken. He knew that from experience. He needed more leverage. Something to get him by until they spoke later. "Kiss me, Lola."

"What?" The stunned look on her face made him smile. She was so damn sexy when she was confused.

"I said, kiss me. Let's seal our promise with a kiss."

"Javi—"

"Kiss me." The command in his tone sent shivers through

Lola's body. His girl liked his dominance and he was using that in his favor.

She hesitated, but only for a moment before she tilted her head back and waited for him to close the distance. He gladly did. The kiss was different from the bedroom kisses that resulted in them taking off their clothes and falling into bed. This one was searing and full of unsaid words. He felt Lola relax against him, allowing him to hold her for just a second.

After a minute, Lola was the one to break the kiss as she pulled back, her lipstick slightly askew. He probably sported his own red lips from her and made a mental note to wash that away in the bathroom.

"I'll talk to you in a bit. Let me get everyone settled at the reception and I promise I'm yours."

She didn't know just how badly he wanted those words to be true. Not trusting his voice, he nodded once. Lola offered him one last tight smile before turning away from him and following the rest of the wedding party out of the venue.

If he had to wait a little bit longer for his girl, then so be it. But one way or another, he was going to show Lola just how right they were together.

Lola

The reception took place in the hotel's upstairs courtyard and by the time Lola caught an elevator up, the party was in full swing. Tables were positioned at the edges of the courtyard, spectacular place settings beckoning guests to enjoy their meals. The DJ set up in one corner, rocking instrumental music of popular songs while he waited for all the guests to arrive. A few feet down, waiters in fancy black suits bustled in and out of the kitchen, setting up the first round of appetizers.

What caught Lola's attention was the open bar nestled between shrubbery with nobody yet in line. She braved the cool evening air and headed outside. Her lips still tingled from Javi's searing kiss and his dominant command. It was evident that avoiding him wouldn't work and trying to weave through her feelings right now was out of the question.

What she needed was liquid courage.

"What can I get you, ma'am?" the pretty, young woman behind the bar asked her. Lola took quick inventory of the bottles she had displayed behind her before settling on something that would give her the courage she needed.

"Bone-dry martini, please."

The bartender smirked. "A girl ready to party. I like it." She started to make Lola's drink. "Hoping to find a lonely groomsman to take home?" she asked.

Despite herself, Lola snorted. If only that were her problem. "More like, I need the courage to talk to the one I brought with me."

"Oh no. Sticky situation?" she asked, showing genuine sympathy.

"I guess you can say that. He's perfect and I'm...intimidated. You know how things can feel too good to be true?"

"And you find out it was indeed, too good to be true?"

"Exactly!" Lola exclaimed as if the bartender got a particularly hard test question right. "And I think it's better to protect my heart now before it inevitably gets crushed."

"Preach sister. Protect your heart first. Here's your martini," she said and handed over the glass. "For what it's worth, you seem like a smart woman, so I'm sure you'll figure it out."

Who knew she needed such a pep talk from a strange bartender? What she wanted was to call Mona, but her friend was busy overseeing her bookstore and running the bakery, so that call would have to wait. All she had were insights from a friendly bartender and her muddled thoughts.

"Thank you. I'll be back for another one soon," she said, earning a thumbs up from the woman who moved on to the next person in line.

Before she faced Javi, she needed to check in with her mother. Finding her through the throngs of people hadn't been easy, especially since Luciana wasn't answering her phone.

She finally found her mother by the catering table, barking orders at the hardworking waiters.

"Mother, do you need me to do anything?" She came up behind Luciana placing a hand on her shoulder.

Luciana turned her head away from the poor man trying to serve up the appetizers to look over her daughter. She felt the woman's judgment as she took her daughter in. "I see you decided against the shapewear I bought you." Her mother's words cut deeply. If it wasn't a comment about her chosen profession then it was about her weight. Luciana hated how comfortable Lola was in her skin and tried to knock her down a peg at any opportunity she got.

"You saw me while we were getting ready and didn't mention it then. I don't understand why you feel the need to bring it up now."

"Well, I had hoped you would come to your senses, but I was wrong."

Ignoring that bitchy comment, Lola tried again. "Do you need me to do anything?" The patience in her voice should have made her a saint.

"Dolores, must I tell you everything? This is your sister's wedding! Her big day. You should be making sure everything is going according to plan. We need to make this perfect for your sister; she deserves it."

Lola had to grit her teeth. Deep down, she knew her mother was stressed and when Luciana was stressed, her cattiness came out tenfold. Anyone unfortunate enough to be in the way would be open for criticism and Lola was an easy punching bag for her. That didn't excuse her mother's behavior but helped explain it a bit.

"I'm trying to make it the best day of her life, but everything seems to be running smoothly. If there's nothing you need my help with, then I'll make sure everyone is enjoying themselves."

At this point, her mother was back to barking orders at the wait staff, so Lola knew she lost her. "See to that," her mother said off-handedly, signaling she was done with the conversation.

Lola sipped her drink, trying to forget her mother's cruel comments. The dry martini burned going down her throat but also eased the budding anger and panic building inside of her right now.

It was too soon to go for round two of the martini, but not too soon to reach for the glass of champagne one of the waiters served. If it was a different person serving her a drink, it was like the first one never happened. Right?

A loud commotion brought her attention toward the entrance of the courtyard. People began to crowd together in groups, clapping and cheering. It wasn't until she saw glimpses of a snow-white dress that she realized the bride and groom had made it.

The group of people parted for the happy couple. Genuine smiles plastered Archie and Marisol's faces and a ping of jealousy worked its way through her body. Not jealous of Marisol marrying her ex, but the fact that she found someone to spend the rest of her days with. Lola still wasn't convinced that their love ran deep, but hoped her sister truly found love and happiness with Archie. Not for Archie's sake, but because Marisol deserved someone who would truly love her. Maybe it would mellow her out.

The music changed to a slower tune, making her think of far-off places and love that ran deeper than surface level. They were a sight to behold as Archie and Marisol took the floor, commanding it as if they danced together every night.

Dampness coated her cheeks and it took Lola a second to realize she was crying. Why the hell was she crying? Seeing them together shouldn't have made her feel like this. Perhaps this was what healing was. Finally letting go of anger that had weighed her down for so long.

Lola wasn't and would never be the type of girl Archie would come to love and Archie would never be the man of her dreams. Marisol was better suited to that role, but it had taken her until this moment to fully see that. The two of them fit together in a way she never would and she hoped she was seeing genuine happiness on both of their faces. Marisol was just so hard to read sometimes.

"Tissue?" The sound of a deep voice next to her made Lola jump. She had been far too caught up in her thoughts to notice Javi approaching. She gave him a puzzled look, but before she could ask, he shrugged. "When you have a daughter, you learn to carry all sorts of things in your pockets. I have chocolate too, if you're interested."

Actually yes, she was very interested in the chocolate and told him as much. He dug in his pocket before holding out a mini chocolate bar. She needed something in her stomach besides alcohol—which she was already feeling.

"Thanks," she muttered around the first bite.

"No problem. Did you want to sit down?"

She shook her head. Her body was abuzz with newfound energy and sitting down would cause her nervous energy to manifest in leg shakes and overthinking.

"No, how about we dance." She didn't phrase it as a question. She was going to dance whether Javi wanted to join her or not. The first song between husband and wife had come to an end and the music had changed to a more upbeat tune that demanded to be danced to.

Lola took a sip of the champagne before joining the rest of the crowd on the dance floor. She turned her head to see Javi had followed her and she bit back a smile. Her body began to move to the beat, her hips swaying as she backed up against Javi. From this angle, her hips pressed right up against him.

Lola heard an intake of breath and rewarded herself with another sip of champagne. Two large hands landed on her hips, anchoring them together. "Lola..."

Her name was a warning on his lips, but she didn't know what for. With her free hand, the one not holding the champagne glass, she reached around, snaking her arm around his neck. Javi cursed in Spanish and she giggled. "Are you okay back there?"

"I'm more than okay, but why do I have the feeling you are trying to distract me?" Even as he said it, she felt his hips against her ass. Just a touch from this man left her a wanton, needy woman incapable of speech.

"Distraction? From what?" The alcohol was clouding her mind but also made her brave. Before he could answer, Lola untangled herself from him and turned in his arms. Her lips met his with frenzied passion. She moved against him, demanding more from the kiss than what he was giving her.

"Lola..." He tried to protest, but she didn't want to hear it. She didn't want this moment to end and fade like everything else good in her life. She didn't want to think, only feel.

"Javi, please." What she was begging for, she didn't quite know. Instead, she pressed herself closer to him, as close as two people could be with clothes on. She didn't care that they were standing in the middle of a dancing crowd or that anyone could spot them in this compromising position because she frankly didn't care.

"Lola—" Struggle played across Javi's face. Heat coursed

through their bodies and she knew a part of him wanted her, but the part of him hesitating seemed to be winning. She couldn't have that, not now. Maybe not until they were done with their wedding week adventures.

Lola leaned in to kiss him again, but Javi backed up, putting a few inches between them. The hurt on her face softened his features, but only slightly. He remained firm, keeping her at arm's length. Her boozy brain wasn't too pleased with this.

"We need to talk, Lola. Now."

CHAPTER 35

Javi

Lola stumbled when Javi gently took her by the arm and led her away from prying eyes. More than once he had to catch her before she fell on her face, but instead of getting mad or embarrassed, Lola laughed. It was like trying to lead around a toddler who just had their fill of all the sugary snacks inside the house.

Javi had never seen Lola so...out of place. He knew it was from the alcohol making its way through her system, but he had not been prepared for tipsy Lola. And for what? To talk to him? God, he hoped not. He was kicking himself for not being able to see her pain and worry earlier. Maybe he could have helped prevent this.

Still, it wasn't all his fault. Lola had been acting strange around him and hadn't been subtle about it either. If something was bothering her, why didn't she come to him? They could have talked it through like grown-ass adults in grown-ass situationships did.

Javi pulled them to a private nook between the elevators and the entrance to the courtyard. The main party was still in full swing and the only people over here were waiting for the next available elevator, paying them no mind. He pushed Lola up against the wall and not in the sexy way he had done the other night. No, this was to keep her upright so she didn't fall on her ass.

"You got me alone. Has that been your secret plan all along?" Lola giggled, sloppily leaning forward to wrap her arms around his neck. In the span of the two minutes it took to steady her and lead her away from the dance floor, Lola's drunkenness hit a whole new level. She didn't appear to be aware of what she was saying anymore and that frightened Javi. He had wanted her attention, but not like this.

Fuck. She was making this more complicated than it needed to be.

"How much have you had to drink?" That was apparently the wrong fucking thing to say because Lola's easygoing smile faded. She narrowed her eyes, lips turning into a deep frown.

"Are you shaming me for drinking, Javi?" Her voice had gone unusually low, sending his body into alert mode.

"No, I'm not, but—"

Just like that, the anger was erased as if it had never been there at all. "Good." She giggled and leaned up to kiss him. He tasted the alcohol on her lips and groaned. His dumb brain wanted more. To press up against her until she was writhing with need for him. But she was fucking drunk and he would never take advantage of her in this state.

He came here to talk, not to fuck.

With great difficulty, Javi untangled himself from her. Lola whimpered, sticking out her bottom lip in a pout. "Do you not want to kiss me?"

"Not when you are too drunk to think rationally," he said, unwavering. Javi sucked in a deep breath to calm down his racing heart before stepping back to put more distance between them.

He hated the pain flashing through her eyes and every part of his body screamed to take her back into his arms. There she would be safe. But that wasn't true, was it? If he held her now, he'd be inclined to forget everything he wanted to say. Everything he needed to tell her.

"Lola, I can't do this anymore. I can't continue when I don't know where we stand." The moment the words were out of his mouth, he knew he fucked up.

Lola balled her hands into fists at her side, her earlier swaying no longer seemed to hinder her balance anymore. "Oh, you can't do this anymore? And what exactly is that, Javi? You can't *do* me anymore?" The anger in Lola's voice carried, and a few guests waiting for the elevator turned to look at them.

"Fuck, no, Lola, that's not what I'm saying. I'm saying I don't like this lie we've made up. I knew what I was getting myself into, but I didn't expect to fall for you the way I did."

"Fall for me?" She huffed, once again doing nothing to hide her voice. He thanked God they were out of most of the public's eye, but he wished she would lower her voice to not warrant unwanted attention.

"Is that so hard to see, Lola? Is it so impossible that during our time together I have fallen in love with you?"

"Don't say that!" she growled, tears springing to her eyes. She put her hands over her ears as if she could block out his words. "Don't fucking say that if you don't mean it!"

"Don't say what? That I care for you? That I want to talk about what's happening between us because I know you feel it too? Tell me, Lola, what is it you don't want to talk about? Because everything I'm saying is *real*."

She was getting more agitated by the moment and he was

pushing her to the brink of explosion, but he couldn't stop. Not now when he was finally getting through to her. He would have preferred it if she wasn't drunk and near tears, but he didn't know if he'd have the opportunity again.

"Lola, please. I want to know where we stand. That's all I'm asking. Let's go back to our room and we can—"

"We can, what?" The tears started to run freely this time and Javi desperately wanted to understand what she was feeling, but she wasn't giving him anything other than drunk anger. He refused to believe these were her real thoughts, he knew his girl and she liked to talk things out. That was exactly what he was trying to do.

"So we can go back and we can fuck and pretend like this never happened?" she continued.

"No, that's not what I'm saying."

"Oh, so now you don't want to fuck me? You didn't have a problem with that the last time you had me in bed!"

"Fuck, Lola, what the hell is wrong with you? Are you not listening to a damn word I'm saying?!"

"If I gave you more money on top of the fucking two hundred thousand dollars I'm giving you, would you fuck me then? It's just a job to you, isn't it?"

Her words rang around him like an ominous finale. The curtains had closed on the tragedy, but something wasn't quite finished. There was more to be said, but emotions were high and running rampant. It would have been kinder if she punched him in the face repeatedly until he passed out.

After all, hadn't he been worried about the same things? He knew the damn money would play a negative role in this, but it wasn't fair to say everything he was feeling and the night they spent together was because of the money.

"Lola…"

He didn't know what to fucking say. His words were not coming and he didn't know how to make this right. He fixed and repaired things for a living, but when it came to his relationships, he was hopeless.

Lola opened her mouth to say something, but her body froze and her mouth fell open in a silent scream. She wasn't looking at him anymore, but rather at what was behind him. Dread washed over him and he didn't want to turn around to see what left Lola as pale as a ghost.

Despite everything screaming at him not to, Javi slowly turned around. Standing there, not even five feet away, was Luciana Roberts. Judging from the pinched expression on her face, she had heard everything. And she was pissed.

CHAPTER 36

Lola

Never in Lola's twenty-plus years of life had she ever sobered up as quickly as she did right now, seeing her mother staring at her. It reminded her of those old cartoons when a character got angry and steam poured from their ears. That was her mom to a T and she braced herself for the onslaught of disappointment about to leave her mother's mouth.

"Dolores, what did you do?" Her mother's voice held no emotion, just a forced patience she had only ever heard once in her life when she was caught skipping class to smoke in the bathroom in middle school with a couple of girls from her science class.

Her mom had been livid then but kept her face neutral the entire time she spoke to the principal. Luciana knew how to keep up an appearance when the time called for it, especially when it would reflect badly upon her. The moment they got into the privacy of their car her mother let her have it. How ashamed she was of her behavior and how those poor decisions could add up. How would that make the family look if she continued to make bad decisions? She had a reputation to uphold and people in their small, posh community talked.

Lola thought her reaction had been over the top then, since she was not the first, nor the last, spoiled rich kid to try smoking at school. She was just unfortunate to be a dumbass who skipped with friends that had the same class. She didn't know how skipping one science class would doom her entire family's wine legacy, but she didn't try to argue with her mother. Even then, she knew it would be a lost cause.

But something like this? Hearing her daughter pay someone two hundred thousand dollars to attend a wedding and pretend to be their fake boyfriend would rate astronomically higher than skipping a class and smoking in middle school.

"Mom, it's not—"

"Don't you dare tell me it's not what I think. Because from my viewpoint, it looks as if I overheard a loud conversation between you and this...*man*," —she spat the word like poison from her mouth— "involving sex and money. Are you hiring an escort service for your sister's wedding?"

The words were said in a hushed tone to not let any passersby hear their damning conversation. The softer tones did nothing to hide the vitriol behind her words. Despite the tension lingering between them, she couldn't help the laugh bubbling out of her throat. She half blamed the alcohol for her outbursts. Luciana pursed her lips together, clearly not amused by the situation.

"He's not my escort," she managed to stammer out between fits of giggles. It was wildly inappropriate to laugh at this moment and yet she couldn't make herself stop.

"Keep your voice down." She huffed, reaching for Lola's hand and pulling her into a room only a few feet away from them. She hadn't noticed it was there, probably because her drunk mind was processing extra slowly. Movement sounded from behind her and she knew Javi was following, she just didn't know if that was a good or bad thing yet.

The door shut behind Javi with a resounding thud and they were left in a small room, barely larger than a janitorial closet. The light flickered on and off, highlighting the animosity brewing in the room. Her mother finally let her go, turning and muttering something in Spanish Lola couldn't understand.

If she didn't know her mother was pissed before, she knew now. She never talked in Spanish. Ever. Honestly, Lola barely remembered her mother knew Spanish. It was a testament to how angry she was when she unassimilated herself.

"Now, let's try this again. Did you or did you not hire an escort to pretend to be your date on your sister's big day?" She emphasized as if Lola did not understand what a wedding was or its significance.

"I didn't hire an escort." Her mother visibly relaxed until Lola went on. "But I did pay Javi to be here."

"Dolores!" her mother shouted, throwing her hands up in exasperation. "What the hell were you thinking?" Now she had her mother cussing. Pretty soon Lola would have her mother in the hospital with a stress-induced heart attack.

"It's not Lola's fault. I wouldn't have agreed if I didn't want to come," Javi, who she had forgotten was there, spoke up.

The redness in her mom's face reached new levels and Lola was quick to intervene. "I don't need you standing up for me, Javi. I got this. This isn't anyone's fault but my own."

Javi looked ready to argue. He opened his mouth and then seemed to think better of it. He cleared his throat, stuffing his hands into his pants pockets. Only the slightest nod of his head was all the assurance she was given, but a part of her was disappointed he didn't try to fight harder for her. Which was a shitty thing to say after the hell she had put him through.

Too many secrets had piled up and not just from this wedding. They weighed heavily on her shoulders and she couldn't carry them around anymore. So she started to tell her mother everything. How this all started with getting the invitation in the mail and knowing she couldn't face this wedding alone. How she had met Javi previously—though she did not explain how they knew each other—and how she hired him to remodel Phoenix. How they came to a mutual agreement on the remodel and the wedding.

"Javi isn't an escort. He's my friend, who also happens to be remodeling my bookstore. I couldn't do this alone. I can't be here and pretend it's not weird or ignore the silent judgment from everyone in the room, knowing Archie broke up with me for Marisol. How it could have been me up there instead of her."

She knew now she never wanted it to be her, but that didn't make the situation any less awkward or the looks any less unpleasant. All she wanted was for her mother to acknowledge this was a weird situation and that her feelings were valid. Perhaps even mention how proud she was of Lola for going through with being in the wedding despite all of those things.

But that was not the mom she was given. No, the woman she was given was looking at her without an ounce of sympathy. Only disgust and anger reflected in her features and the last bit of hope she had for their relationship crumbled. Luciana would never be the mother she needed and Lola would never be the ideal daughter. She saw that now. After years of trying to keep the peace, she couldn't keep doing this anymore. For once, she wanted her mother to fight for their relationship.

It was an eye-opening experience and not one she wanted to have while drunk and uncertain about where she stood with Javi.

"You are sabotaging your sister's wedding for your selfish reasons, Dolores. I knew there might be problems with you considering your history with Archie, and I was prepared to deal with them anyway I could. That's why I kept you so busy in hopes that it would keep you distracted. That was a mistake and I should have checked in on who you would be bringing as your so-called date."

The words cut like daggers through her heart, but her mom wasn't finished. "If anyone finds out what you did, our family will be dealing with cleaning up your mess of a scandal when we should be celebrating your sister's happy day. She is going to be devastated when she finds out her sister tried to sabotage her wedding."

"Scandal? Sabotage?" This woman really thought they were the Clintons and not another wealthy family in America. A bitter laugh escaped her lips as she shook her head in disbelief. "I was trying to survive a fucking visit with this family! I was trying to protect my mental health because no one else would."

"Oh, it's always this same old excuse. When will you give up this idea that you have such a cruel family? When all we want is the best for you."

"You don't know what's best for me and you never have! You only care about your image and I'm too emotional or too fat to fit into whatever impossible box you've built for me. Well, guess what, Mother? I'm so fucking done with trying to please you. I'm done trying to measure up to this impossible standard you have for me because I never will. And you will never change."

Luciana looked taken aback by her words. She had never seen her mother look so thoroughly chastised and at a loss for words. "What are you saying, Dolores? Speak frankly."

"I thought I was speaking frankly. But since you can't see through your own prejudices, I'll say it again. I'm done. Done with you and trying to salvage a relationship that was never good in the first place. I'm done being disappointed by you at every turn and I care about myself too much to continue to place myself under your scrutiny. I'm done with you, Mom. And I hope like hell you get the help you need."

"Dolores!" The complete shock in her mother's voice nearly made her come crawling back and beg her for forgiveness. But she needed to stand her ground for the ten-year-old little girl who never had the strength or the means to walk away. She needed to do this for the woman she had become and who still struggled with the need to have the mother she deserved.

Lola walked right out of the small room, leaving behind a lifetime of pent-up aggression and trauma. With each step, she became a little lighter on her feet, but she couldn't help but mourn the loss of a mother who was still very much alive, just one who didn't deserve her.

As she walked, soft footfalls followed her back to her room.

CHAPTER 37

Javi

She did it. Lola fucking did it. If he hadn't seen his girl stand up for herself with his own two eyes, he doubted he would have believed it otherwise. Not because she wasn't capable, he knew she had it in her, but because he never suspected it to be during her sister's wedding, in a tiny room barely bigger than a closet.

The look on Luciana's face as Lola stormed out of the room was priceless. Her mother's mouth hung open as if stuck on the last word she said. There was a faint twitch in her eye, the only sign she had not processed what happened. In truth, Javi hadn't yet processed it either.

Then, as if a light had been switched on in her mind, Luciana's mouth clamped shut. The fury and rage brewing inside of her turned toward Javi.

"You should be ashamed of yourself! You should—" she started, but Javi didn't bother waiting around to be the recipient of her ire. With each second that passed, Lola got farther and farther away from him.

By the time he made it out of the room and rounded the

corner, the elevator was closing on a determined-looking Lola. He jammed his finger against the button and almost immediately the elevator opened…just not the one with Lola inside.

Before anyone else could follow him, he pressed the close door button on the elevator, quickly followed by his floor level. The damn elevator took its time descending before it finally reached his level. The doors had barely started to open when Javi squeezed his way out, catching sight of the navy-blue dress Lola was in.

She was only a few feet ahead of him, head down as she made a beeline to their room. "Lola, wait!" he called after her, willing his legs to move faster.

"Not now, Javi," she murmured, fumbling with the key to unlock their door. She found it and pressed the plastic against the reader. Once it turned red, Lola pushed her way inside with Javi at her heels.

"If not now, when?" he insisted, letting the door fall closed behind him. Lola did not stop her speed walking into the room, but instead tossed her clutch onto the bed and vigorously started taking off her jewelry.

"I don't know!" The frustration unleashed in her voice made him pause. He stood a few feet behind her, but didn't dare move any closer. She rounded on him in an instant, chest heaving and looked moments away from crying. Yet, her jaw was clenched and she remained unwavering despite the showdown with her mother.

"I know you want to talk about what just happened and I know you want to talk about us, but I don't have any more to give anyone right now. Please, I want to be left alone."

No, he didn't want to leave this alone and let it get swept under the rug to be forgotten. He wanted to address it now while it was still fresh on their minds. He didn't care that emotions were running high. It was all the more reason to talk about this now.

"I'm not going to leave you alone, Lola. Don't you understand that? You want space? Fine, I can give you space, but I'm not leaving you. You're going to talk to me and we are going to work this out together. But don't you dare think you are pushing me away."

The words seemed to hang between them, but neither made an effort to fill the silence. What could he say that he hadn't already? She was cutting herself off from him and he was holding on to the fraying tether still connecting them. He wasn't prepared to let go unless she asked him to walk out of her life. Even then he would still fight.

After an uncomfortably long pause, Lola sighed in resignation. She turned back to the mirror and started removing bobby pins from her hair. "I just need time," she said at last.

It wasn't the answer he wanted and didn't help ease the unsteady feelings growing inside of him, but he nodded. He wasn't sure what he was supposed to do, so he continued to stand awkwardly as he watched her unpin her hair until it fell in tight curls around her face.

"I'm going to shower and then we can head to bed. I'll sleep on the couch tonight," she said, gathering her things up for the bathroom and heading in without a look back.

There was no way in hell he was going to let her take the couch and the moment she closed the door, he grabbed a pillow off the bed and tossed it onto the couch. He pretended it didn't sting to have been kicked out of bed with her, but he was at capacity with lying to himself.

While she showered, he changed out of the too expensive tux he rented for this occasion and changed into sweats and a plain T-shirt. With nothing else to do, he planted himself right on the couch and waited for her to get out. After a few minutes, Javi turned on the TV to drown out the voices in his head and to distract his wandering mind.

An hour passed, or maybe two, Javi lost all concept of time as he desperately tried to shut his brain off by watching some documentary about coral reefs, when Lola finally stepped out of the bathroom. The steam from the room followed after her as she walked, sending the smell of clean laundry and lavender to his senses.

She was dressed in a silk tank top and shorts set, giving him ample skin to look at. He couldn't enjoy her body on display, he was too nervous watching her work her way around the room, grabbing her brush to comb her hair, and moisturizer to apply to her face.

The silence was torture.

As if sensing his eyes on her, Lola turned to look at him once she was done towel-drying her hair. "I managed to change our flight to tomorrow at noon." Her words stunned him. He believed they had more time reserved at the hotel and he had hoped that would allow them to talk. But apparently, that was no longer an option.

"I'm ready to go home. I just need to be back somewhere I feel more comfortable, doing my daily routines," she said, answering his unasked question. "And no, I'm not ready to talk. I know I'm being an asshole, but please, let me deal with one problem at a time."

Problem. So he was a problem now? As much as he tried not to take it personally, he couldn't help but take offense to her words. Maybe he wasn't as prepared for the conversation as he thought he was.

"So, that's it? We are going to pretend as if nothing

happened?" His words came out harsher than he intended, but he couldn't help it.

He heard Lola's intake of breath the moment before she turned off the lights. "I just need time," she said again, though it sounded flimsy this time. A mere ghost of a promise that would never see the light of day. "But...thank you for being there with me during that. I needed your strength."

"Nah, preciosa. You didn't need me at all. That was all you and I'm so proud of you."

You don't need me at all. The words played like a mantra in his mind and he only hoped they didn't come to be realized.

Lola didn't reply and he didn't expect her to. He listened to her breathing and turning in bed, trying to find a comfortable position. His mind was wide awake as he replayed these last two days. Lola had never seemed further away from him than she did at that moment.

Javi didn't sleep much that night, fearing what the morning would bring.

CHAPTER 38

Lola

Before the sun had the chance to fully rise, creating pockets of light that brought with it new hopes for the day, Lola awoke. The only hope she had today was to board the plane without a panic attack and not think about yesterday's fight with her mom until she was home. She just had to survive a little bit longer.

Sleep had not come easily for her; she had tossed and turned most of the night. More than once she had woken up and noticed a light from the other side of the room. Apparently she hadn't been the only one that sleep eluded, for she caught Javi on his phone a few times throughout the night.

When she decided laying around in a lonely bed was no longer an option, Lola rolled out and was surprised to find Javi sitting up. He had dark circles underneath his red-rimmed eyes and his clothes were rumpled from the couch. Their eyes met momentarily and she detected a spark of light inside him. When she didn't address him, the light was smothered out and he looked resigned to the silent treatment.

She needed to talk to him; she wasn't being fair by holding

back her concerns. But the truth was, her mind was a minefield of chaos right now and any wrong step would push her over the edge. There was still so much she needed to untangle and the truth of the matter was she couldn't think clearly when she was around him.

Her body and heart wanted Javi more than they have ever wanted anything else, but she had been led astray before. She needed her brain to be in on this too and right now, it was in overdrive mode.

They gathered their things in silence, moving past one another to reach for the items they needed to pack away in their suitcases. Lola had sent a quick text message to her father, asking him to meet her downstairs in ten minutes. Thankfully he was also an early riser and responded immediately that he was getting dressed and would be there soon.

All that was left to do was to gather up her bathroom belongings. She had managed to pack most of her makeup last night, so she just had her shampoos and other toiletries to pack. All of Javi's things were gone from the bathroom when she entered and she couldn't describe the emptiness she felt by not seeing his things next to hers. She was sleep deprived. There was no other reason to be sad over missing toiletries.

By the time she was finished gathering up the last of her things and zipping up her suitcase, Javi was waiting for her at the door. Without asking, he took her bags from her and she let him. "A car is upfront. Do you mind waiting for me out there? I'll just be a minute; I want to say goodbye to my dad."

Javi stared at her and she felt naked under his gaze. It wasn't a piercing hot gaze that eye fucked her. That would have been easier and much preferred over this. No, this gaze was staring straight into her soul, as if seeking hidden truths she wasn't yet ready to give.

The words he seemed to want to say played on his lips, but instead of speaking them, Javi nodded. "Of course." That's it. No preciosa, no kiss, no nothing. He left without another word. Just like she wanted.

And yet it didn't make her feel any better.

Because she was a coward, she waited until Javi stepped onto an elevator before she left the room, letting the door shut on their shortened week. She didn't have to wait long for another elevator and rode it down to the first floor. Just as the doors opened, her father stepped out from the opposite side and beamed at her. His sweet smile nearly brought tears to her eyes. How sad that an ounce of kindness would bring her to her knees.

She met her father in the middle of the lobby, happily accepting his embrace that he always gave her so freely. She knew her father's love never came with strings and it was easy to seek him out for comfort. His biggest fault was his compliance and ignorance of her treatment.

"Hey, sweetheart. Is everything alright? Your mom came back to the room last night in quite the mood. Do you know what that's about?" her father asked once they broke apart.

So her mother hadn't told her father what happened, which surprised her. She didn't think her mother would pass up her chance to belittle her.

"We fought. She's not happy with me. And I left Marisol's reception early." There was no use in lying and her father didn't appear surprised.

"You know your mother. She's a tough woman to please. I'm sure whatever it is, she will get over it soon."

"That's the thing. I'm tired of waiting around for her to get over it. I can't live like that and I'm so tired of the way she treats me, dad." She sighed, shaking her head. "I'm sorry, I know this will cause more problems, but Javi and I are leaving right now."

"Right now?" Her father's eyes widened. The shock on his face was almost comical, but only because he was so deceived by his ignorance. "But tonight is your sister's dinner party. I'm sure your mother would want you there. Let me talk to her."

It was too late for talking. At least the type of talking he wanted to do. Lola needed action because she had been talked to enough of her life and with no actions, their words meant nothing. "I'm sorry, but I'm going. Please give Marisol my best." Though she doubted her sister would care much. Not with her mother's claws dug so deeply into her.

"Dolores, please. Tell me what happened. Let me try to fix this," her father pleaded and the tears she had tried desperately to hold back began to roll down her brown cheeks. "Oh, sweetheart. Please don't cry. What can I do?"

"Nothing." The words were barely a whisper and the smile on her lips didn't meet her eyes. "I'll call you when I'm home. I love you, Dad," she said and stood on her tiptoes to give him one last kiss.

Her father called her name once more, but Lola was already waking away. Away from the lifelong trauma of her mother and into the car where Javi waited for her. Javi, who she still had no idea how he fit into her life when everything seemed to be falling apart.

To top everything off, the plane ride home was filled with aggressive turbulence that had Lola nearly in Javi's lap, hyperventilating. Despite the wall she had built between them, Lola gladly accepted Javi's comfort on the flight home.

Numerous times throughout the flight, the contents of her hastily eaten breakfast threatened to come up. She managed to keep it down though out of sheer spite.

When they landed, she was tempted to join in with the other passengers clapping. She never understood why people—specifically white passengers—clapped when landing and had always made fun of her father each time he did the same thing, but now she was joining them. Motion sickness was no joke and even as they deboarded she still felt unsteady on her feet.

Luckily the nausea went away by the time they reached the baggage claim. She felt Javi's warm presence next to her and despite their cuddling on the plane—which was only to ease her nerves and nothing else—they hadn't said much to each other. A heaviness settled between them and she knew he was waiting for her to be the one who broke it.

Unfortunately, all she provided was more disappointment when she took out her phone and took it off airplane mode, letting the notifications sweep in. She had a few from Mona, asking why she was coming home early and how they needed to talk. None from her mother or her sister, but one from her father asking if she made it home safe.

She sent a text to him to let him know she had arrived back in California before putting her phone away. If he replied, she wasn't yet ready to deal with any more questions or pleas to make up with her mother. The fight with her mother, funnily enough, was the only thing she didn't regret from her time at the wedding.

As distracted as she was, she wasn't surprised that she didn't notice Javi moving to grab her bags until he returned, rolling them up to her feet. "Thank you," she murmured, taking the handle from him.

"Do you need help getting to your car?" His voice was

detached, nothing at all like the friendly version she had been spoiled with over these last few weeks.

She opened her mouth to say she didn't when a loud, high-pitched voice screamed behind them. "Papá!"

Both she and Javi whipped their heads around at the same time, seeing a sprinting six-year-old coming to them at full speed. "I thought you drove yourself here." Lola's words came out far more accusatory than she meant them. It wasn't as if Javi deliberately invited his cute daughter here to trap her to talk about her feelings.

"I did...I only told them I was coming home early and..." But he wasn't looking at Lola or paying her any mind. He moved from behind her and crouched down to catch Camilia as she catapulted across the tiles into his arms. She slammed into her father's chest, nearly knocking Javi to the ground. He steadied himself though, wrapping his arms tightly around his baby girl and peppering her happy face with kisses.

"I missed you so much!" She giggled before launching into a long story about everything she did with her tía while they were gone, going into great detail about a painting activity she and her cousin did.

An approaching figure laughed, her curly hair bouncing with each step. On her hip she carried a very tired toddler who Lola believed to be named Arturo. "She wanted to surprise you," Ofelia said to her brother before bringing her gaze up to meet Lola's. "Lola, hi! Did you have a good trip?"

There was no way she was going to get into all the nuances of her trip in the middle of the airport, so she smiled. "We had a good time, but I'm so thankful to be home. I missed my bed."

She laughed at that, obviously buying her half-truths. "Believe me, I know a little about that. When Arturo and I travel with Maverick, I miss my bed and his toddler bed so much. Love my little man, but he's the worst bed buddy. Between him and his father starfishing across the bed, I barely fit."

"Is he traveling now for work? His season starts soon, doesn't it?"

Ofelia nodded. "It does and he had to leave this weekend for various press conferences, so it was just the three of us." She smiled down at Camilia. Javi stood up, holding his daughter in his arms.

"I was thinking we could go out to lunch. Lola, would you join us? I would love to hear about the wedding if you're up for it," Ofelia asked, not realizing the weird position she had put Lola in.

Since she was a people pleaser by nature, she was inclined to say yes so as not to cause conflict or disappointment, even though she wanted nothing more than to go home and lie in her bed, watching her favorite shows on Netflix for hours.

Clearly seeing the panic and indecision on her face, Javi jumped in because of course he did. He was too damn good. "Lola is tired. I think she wants to go home."

"Awe, but next time you'll come, right Ms. Lola?" Camilia piped up, speaking to her for the first time.

Her rigid posture eased some at the sound of the little girl's voice. She still thought back to the fun day they shared at the bookstore while her father was working. Camilia was sweet and a little Javi in so many ways. She was kind and inquisitive. Plus she was interested in reading and any kids who loved reading were perfect in her books.

"Next time," she assured, earning a cheer from Camilia. Though when the next time would be, Lola had no idea.

"Hey, amore, can you go with tía for a moment so papá can

say goodbye to Lola?" Javi asked, putting her back on the ground.

Ofelia jumped in, evidently understanding they needed a moment to say goodbye. "Let's go look at the gift shop we passed on the way in. Maybe we can find something to bring back to abuelo."

The idea of shopping sparked an interest in Camilia because she nodded and waved goodbye. "Bye, Ms. Lola. See you soon," she said cutely before following Ofelia off to the gift shop, leaving her and Javi alone to deal with their mess.

When they were left alone, it took a moment for either of them to talk, but instead of letting Javi fill the silence, she took initiative. "Thank you for giving me an out. Your family is lovely and I wouldn't have minded, but I just want to get home."

"I know you do. You have a lot on your mind right now."

It wasn't a question and he didn't say it as such, but she nodded anyway. "Right. So..." She had never had any problems talking to him before, but each time she opened her mouth, she felt like she was sliding a dagger a little bit deeper into his heart. "Can we meet at the shop on Monday? I can give you the last of your payment and we could...talk."

"About the money, Lola, I've been thinking and—"

Before he could finish that sentence, Lola put her hand up to silence it. "Monday, please. We can talk about it then."

Although he didn't look happy, he tensed his jaw and nodded. "Fine. Monday."

"Thank you." Although it was cruel, she leaned up to press one last lingering kiss on his lips. She wanted to remember the taste of him now that she was sober and not trying to throw herself on him. Javi reciprocated and she felt the hope behind his kiss.

She just needed a little time to figure out her feelings. Archie said she jumped into things without thinking them through and that was partly true. Some time apart from Javi would hopefully give her the answers she needed.

When she finally pulled back, the hope instantly vanished from his eyes. Something in her expression must have given her away. "I'll see you on Monday," she murmured, licking her lips to taste the last bit of him. Then she grabbed her suitcase and headed to the car without looking back.

CHAPTER 39

Lola

Monday brought with it a mix of emotions that felt like riding a seesaw up and down. The "up" was arriving at Phoenix for the first time since traveling and walking inside with Mona to see her built-ins. She invited her best friend along since they had so much to catch up on and Mona had been here throughout the process.

Which brought her to the "down." In a little under an hour, she was going to be breaking the hearts of two people. Which seemed self-sabotaging and dramatic—she tried talking herself out of this numerous times—but she always fell back on the same conclusion. She couldn't start a real relationship with Javi because, ironically enough, she didn't want to hurt him. Or herself. Jumping into another big life decision without thinking it through was not what she needed at the moment. Her focus needed to be on opening Phoenix Books.

After all, what type of relationship started as a lie? A paid lie at that. A small part of her still could not wrap her head around the fact that Javi liked her for her and not the large check he was on his way to pick up. She didn't know how she would survive the next few weeks seeing him work in her shop but not being able to have him.

Those were problems for future Lola. Current Lola was about to see her shop. Mona parked her car behind the store and cut the engine. "You ready, Lo-Lo? Because your mind is about to be blown." Mona grinned and got out of the car.

Lola's chest was abuzz with nervous energy. "So ready. I still can't believe you didn't send me any photos of the progress, you bitch."

That only earned a laugh from her friend who took the spare key out of her pocket and unlocked the back of the door. "Yeah, yeah, I'm a bitch. At least I'm not the dumb-ass who is about to throw away a perfectly fine man for reasons I don't quite understand."

Ouch. She flinched at her words. Harsh...but accurate.

This morning, Mona had picked her up for breakfast. They went to her bakery and Mattea had a spread of various pastries and juices set out for them to eat. She knew the instant Mona shut the door behind her that both women were going to demand answers about her trip and the reason she came back early and cranky.

There was no hesitation as she sat down and subsequently poured her heart out to them. She told them about the disastrous encounters with her mother, the way Javi stood up for her, the amazing night they spent together, the final fight with her mother, and her reasons to leave early.

Mona, ever the inquisitive, still didn't understand why she planned on ending her situationship with Javi if she felt this strongly about him. It was a fair question, but not one she could easily answer.

She was trying to figure out a lot of things. The relationship fallout with her mother and how it would affect her family. She was trying to sort through her feelings for Javi and it was hard enough when they were forced to spend so much time together in close proximity. And she was also desperately trying to heal from the jabs her mother had thrown at her over the years and unlearn them.

Like she had kept saying before, she needed time and space.

Mattea and Mona had looked at one another, sharing a silent conversation Lola was not part of. None of them tried to coax her one way or another or tell her what she was doing was wrong, but she still saw the hesitancy in their eyes.

"Are you sure you really want to cut Javi off? Just like that?" Mona had asked her.

She wasn't sure and that was the problem. She didn't know what she wanted; all she knew was that Archie's words were fucking with her brain and making her second-guess every decision.

"I think it might be the best choice for now," she had said.

After that, they dropped the subject of her trip and she caught up with what had been going on while she was gone.

And now she was finally at her shop, ready to walk in for the first time. Excitement vibrated through her and she all but pushed past Mona as soon as she got the door opened. "Damn, eager much?" Mona laughed, following after her. "Be careful, I think there might still be supplies out and I don't want you stepping on something and breaking your ass."

"I'm not going to break my ass."

"Not if I can help it!" Came her echoing reply, followed by laughter.

Lola felt the air leave her lungs as soon as she made her way out of the back and into the main room of her shop. All the old brown, decrepit bookcases had been taken down and hauled out of the room. It opened up the room and made it appear bigger than it was. All along the walls were beautifully placed white shelves. Though unfinished, Lola could picture the end product and the books that would soon line each row.

The coffee area, which also served as a checkout, had been stripped of all the old furniture and appliances. Two new, sleek, pink counters stood in its place. They were L-shaped with a small opening for Lola to move in and out of when needed. She shrieked, unable to hide her excitement.

"Mona, have you seen this?!" she yelled though she knew the answer. Her friend had been here the entire week, so of course she saw the pastel pink counter.

"Doesn't it look good? I gotta admit, I was a hater until I saw it in person, but it's so *you* and adds a pop of color. Did you check out the floors yet?"

The last time she had been here, Javi's men were about to start on the floors which made her get her ass in gear and pack all the books. It had been the day Javi brought Camilia. There weren't many worth saving and she had ended up donating many of the books to the library in town, but still had enough to fill the entire back office.

Lola looked down. What was once a reddish, brown wood flooring was now stained a cloudy gray. The color complimented her color scheme perfectly and made the room feel more elegant. "I'm dying! What the fuck, this is perfect."

"And it's not done yet," Mona said, placing her hands on the pink counter before pushing herself up to sit atop it. She crossed her arms over her chest, surveying the room. "It's coming along amazingly though. Your man and his crew do a good job."

Lola's smile vanished and the excitement became tainted with something ugly and uncertain. "He's not my man," she said feebly, but she wasn't sure who she was trying to convince.

"Right," Mona said, the tone in her voice telling Lola that she didn't believe her. "Well, good luck telling him that when he gets here. Do you want me to stay?"

She should say no and maybe it would be easier if Mona was in the car, waiting for her. But she wanted to have a backup in case her emotions got the best of her.

"Stay. Please."

Mona's features softened and she nodded. The lump working its way up Lola's throat subsided, knowing her friend would be there. It felt a lot like relief.

Relief was short-lived though because a moment later, she heard someone knocking on the front door of the store, and her whole body tightened. "I'll get it," Mona said, probably seeing the terror in Lola's expression. She pushed herself off the counter and went to let Javi inside.

Lola waited with bated breath, bracing her body for the fallout that was bound to happen. She heard her heart pounding loudly in her ears. She watched as Mona unlocked the door and swung it open. Lola braced herself, pretending she was ready to see Javi.

However, standing behind the door wasn't Javi as she suspected. Her entire body sagged forward and her face was a picture of shock. "Ofelia?" she asked, not understanding why Ofelia was here instead of her brother.

The pretty woman offered an apologetic smile. "Hi, Lola. I came here on Javi's behalf. Something came up."

"Is everything okay?" Her mind went to the worst scenarios possible. Did he hate her? Did something happen to Camilia?

"Yes, or...I believe it is. He was pretty vague on the details. He said he needed to run an errand," she admitted and stepped inside. Mona let the door close behind her. "Hi, I'm Ofelia. Javi's sister." She offered her hand to Mona.

"Monique. Nice to meet you." She greeted but was unable to hide the skepticism in her expression. Mona kept looking at her as if she had an explanation for why Javi wasn't her, as if she knew the reason.

But she did, didn't she? It was avoidance. Javi was avoiding her and she couldn't blame him. She hadn't given him much hope that she wished to continue this relationship and it was selfish, but she had wanted to see him today. If it was to be the last day they had the opportunity to speak about matters outside of the job, then she wanted this final moment together.

Being stood up by a man you planned on ending a situationship with sucked ass. It felt incomplete, like she couldn't say the last things that were left unsaid. Now they would forever live rent-free in her mind.

"Look, I know you weren't expecting me," Ofelia started, clearly sensing the confusion and tension in the room. "But... last night Javi came clean to me."

All the color drained from Lola's face. She couldn't imagine what Ofelia must think of her right now. Somehow knowing she knew about their arrangement was worse than Javi not showing up.

"I have to admit I was surprised by what he said. Not the fake dating part, but that he agreed to take such a large payout. My brother's prideful and doesn't like to admit he's struggling. I try to help him as much as I can, but he hates when I offer. I'm trying to respect his boundaries, but it's so hard when he's suffering. You know?

"Anyway, I'm here to tell you he said he didn't want to accept the rest of the payment. Just enough to cover expenses and pay his men."

Lola had suspected as much and was ready to argue the point that Javi earned the money fairly and should be compensated. But apparently, Ofelia was thinking the same thing. "But my brother can be an idiot, so I'm here to accept it and make sure he gets it. If you are still offering. At the very least, he can put the money away for Camilia for when she's older."

"Of course. The money is his to do with what he pleases," she said, fishing in her jeans pocket to pull out the check with the remaining balance she offered to Javi.

Tears began to pool in the corner of her eyes and she had to rapidly blink them away before they could fall. This felt like the final piece of Javi and once she gave that away, they had nothing tethering them together. Sure, he would still be working in the shop to get it prepared for the grand opening, but she wouldn't be his and they wouldn't have time alone.

"Can you tell him something for me?" Lola asked, handing Ofelia the check. Immediately she safely put it away in her purse. When she nodded, Lola continued. "Just that I'm sorry. And...no—just that. I'm sorry."

She had a whole speech prepared, but it didn't seem right anymore. Not when the message would be delivered by someone else.

Ofelia's kind eyes shined with sympathy. "Lola, for what it's worth, I don't think my brother is ignoring you. He's not that type of man. And even if you claim the situation between the both of you was fake, I saw the way my brother looked at you. He hasn't stared at anyone like that since Estella."

Hearing Javi's former girlfriend mentioned surprised her. She wasn't trying to be his new Estella, but maybe she had played her part a little too well and tricked them both.

"I guess what I'm trying to say is that I know my brother. Don't be surprised if he finds ways to stay in your life. He's a private person and doesn't let many people in, but he's different around you. More...alive." She sighed and finished her explanation with a shrug. "Anyway, thank you. And if it's okay, I was hoping I could still come to the opening?"

"Of course you can. I would love it." Lola was surprised by how true those words were.

Ofelia beamed. "Good. Then I better go. This place looks amazing. I can't wait to see the final product." Ofelia hesitated, but then hugged Lola. She was so surprised that she didn't think she managed to hug back, but when Ofelia pulled away, she didn't seem upset about it.

"I'll see you soon," she said and then waved goodbye to Mona. Lola watched as she walked away, opening the front door and leaving the shop. When the door shut, the reality of what happened settled over Lola, leaving her empty and thinking she had just made the worst decision of her life.

CHAPTER 40

Javi

The moment Javi left the airport a plan had started brewing in his mind. He understood Lola needed time to sort out her feelings, which Javi could respect...even if he was impatient as hell about it. There was no doubt in his mind that she cared for him, even if she was too afraid to admit it right now. That didn't mean he had to deny the love he felt for her and he was showing his love by giving her what she asked for.

Space.

But space didn't mean he had to sit down and twiddle his thumbs until she realized his feelings. Hell no. Instead, he had things he needed to do and spent the past week since returning back from Colorado getting things in order.

A small part of him feared he was overstepping, but on the other hand, he had not been the one to request the meet-up he was driving to. He saw it as an opportunity and not one he planned on losing, even if that meant Lola would hate him forever. It was a risk he was willing to take if that made just one person understand the hell she put up with for so many years.

That would change today.

Camilia sat in the back seat of his truck, kicking her legs absentmindedly and watching the world pass them by as he drove. He opted not to leave her with Ofelia today since she had already done him a favor by meeting Lola. Every time he thought of Lola seeing his sister walk in instead of him, it sent a longing pain through his chest. This feeling was temporary and he would make her understand why he had not been there. In time.

No, he brought Camilia along for two reasons. One, he had missed his princess after nearly a week away. He hadn't realized how much that would affect him until he returned and had her in his arms again. And secondly, they needed to talk.

Nearly all her life, it had only ever been the two of them. She had been too young to remember Estella, but she knew Estella had been her mommy and that she was no longer with them. Never in her short life had he brought another woman over or introduced her to anyone out of fear the relationship wouldn't work out, leaving Camilia attached to yet another ghost.

He couldn't do that to her.

But he also had come to realize he would start dating again. Hopefully Lola, if his plan all went accordingly, but at the very least to someone in the future. He didn't want to be alone his whole life and he did want to have more kids one day.

"Mija, can we talk for a second? About something important."

From the rearview mirror, he saw Camilia swivel her head toward the front. She nodded, but it still took him another moment to get his thoughts together. He wanted to make sure he said this in a way a six-year-old would understand.

"So, you know how much I love you, right?" he asked.

Camilia nodded, holding her arms far apart to indicate "this much." "Exactly. Well, one day papá wants to find a partner to love that much too."

Camilia tilted her head to the side as if digesting the information. "Like a girlfriend?" she asked, stunning the ever-loving shit out of him.

He nearly jerked his car to the side of the road as he momentarily turned back to look at her. Overprotective-dad mode activated. "How do you know about girlfriends and boyfriends?"

His daughter giggled, finding his flustered mood comical. "I know things, papá. Girlfriends and boyfriends are people you hug and play Lava at recess with. Duh," she said like it was common knowledge.

"Right. Well for adults, a girlfriend is someone you love dearly and want to spend your life with. How would you feel if one day papá introduced you to a woman he loved?"

"Would she be my new mamá?"

Javi had expected this question, but it still knocked the wind out of him. He had to walk a fine line between respecting Estella's memory and also preparing Camilia for the new mother-like figure that would hopefully come into her life.

"Well, let's think of her as a bonus mamá. Your mamá Estella will always be your mother and even though she isn't here, she still loves you and is always watching over you. Anyone I want to spend the rest of my life with is someone you are going to have to like too since she will be in your life." He hoped he made some semblance of sense trying to navigate these new unfamiliar waters.

"Would she read books with me and make cupcakes? Oh, like Ms. Lola! Lola should be your girlfriend, papá. She makes funny voices when she reads—like tía does."

It was getting harder to concentrate on the road with new reasons to fall deeper in love with Lola. Camilia had loved their time reading together while he worked in her shop, a situation he had not meant to put either of his girls in, but it turned out well in the end.

But on the off-chance that he was ruining his relationship with Lola, Javi didn't entertain the idea with Camilia just yet. It was good to know she wouldn't mind it though. "I'm glad you're okay with me one day bringing home a girlfriend. Just know, you always have a say, okay? You are my princesa. My number one. Always remember that, okay?"

"Okay, papá. I love you."

"And I love you."

The conversation had left him feeling lighter. The inevitable conversation had started to feel like an anchor weighing him down and now he was finally free of it. He should have known Camilia would have reacted so well. She was much more mature than he gave her credit for.

The rest of the ride to lunch, Javi learned all about what Camilia was learning in school and how she doesn't like her music teacher because she yells a lot. And then, because no car ride was complete without a little karaoke, they sang Camilia's favorite songs at the top of their lungs.

When they arrived at the restaurant, a popular Mexican place that served California's version of Mexican food, Javi got out of his car to help Camilia out.

"Who are we meeting, papá?" Camilia asked, making sure to grab her purple purse that had her coloring book and markers inside.

Javi hesitated before answering. "A...friend." Friend was a stretch, but he had liked the man enough during their brief moments together. It still had come as a shock when the unfamiliar number popped up on his phone. He almost didn't answer it but changed his mind at the last minute.

And he was glad he did. Equally glad that he managed to trade numbers after a rather serious golf discussion.

Taking Camilia's hand in his, he led her through the parking lot and inside the building. They were ahead of the lunch rush, so the restaurant wasn't full yet. He checked the tables, seeing if he could see a familiar face looking back at him.

"Javi," a deep voice called from behind him.

Standing at the entrance of the old restaurant stood Travis Roberts looking like he stepped out of a golf magazine shoot. He was dressed in khaki pants and a blue polo he had tucked in. The man's eyes went to Camilia and his extroverted girl waved happily.

Travis's features softened. "And who is this pretty girl?"

"Mr. Roberts—"

"Call me Travis, please."

"Travis, this is my daughter Camilia. Camilia, this is Lola's papá," he said, introducing the two.

"I like your daughter. She's nice," Camilia said in a way of greeting.

The man laughed, crouching down to get at eye level with her. "I like her too. And if Lola likes you, you must be one special girl."

"I think so. I get all A's and B's at school and I know how to spell Mississippi."

"Well, you are practically a genius then!" Travis grinned and pushed himself up. His smile faded, but the kindness in his eyes did not. "Thank you for meeting with me. I'm...well frankly Javi, I'm worried about my daughter. As a father, you must know you hurt when your kids are hurting."

Javi knew that feeling all too well. Perhaps it was why he

agreed to meet with him in the first place. But also, Lola deserved a cheerleader and he had been around his fair share of cheerleaders—thanks to his sister—to be one for Lola.

"I can only tell you what I've observed, but after this, you are going to have to show up for Lola. Not just some of the time. All of the time. She deserves that. Hell, she deserves so much more than what you have allowed to happen all her life."

For a moment, Javi thought he might have gone too far. Color rushed to Travis's cheeks and his jaw clenched. Javi wasn't here to sugarcoat anything and he told Travis as much on the phone. He agreed then, but had his mind changed since?

After a beat, Travis let out a resigned sigh and nodded. "I see. Well, we should find a table. I figure we have a lot to talk about. I like that you don't hold back. It's a good quality in a man," he said and signaled the hostess. When he turned back to Javi, before they were seated, he said, "I want you to tell me what happened at the wedding and I don't want you to sugar-coat a damn thing. It's time I see what I've been allowing to happen for so long."

Javi hoped this was a step in the right direction and the beginning of the healing process for Lola. Without another word, he followed Travis to their table.

CHAPTER 41

Lola

THREE WEEKS LATER

Dreams tended to start as nothing more than a seed. With the right fertilizer, a good amount of water, and a little sun, a flower could bloom out of nowhere. That was how Lola felt standing in the middle of Phoenix today, seeing her bookstore come to life. It had started as nothing more than a vague idea. A "what if" that reshaped her whole trajectory.

And now it was complete.

The once-dated bookstore had gotten a major facelift. Out were the old-school browns and beiges and in were the pinks, whites, and grays of her new color palette. The room was more vibrant and open with floor-to-ceiling bookcases. Each section was marked by genre, spanning from romances, to memoirs, to fantasy, with everything in between.

Throughout the large room, various table displays were set up to grab readers' attention. Mona had helped her last night to finish the displays before the big day. Her favorite they had come up with was a book display titled "Not Your Average Romances," where they placed Latinx and BIPOC selections because if there was one thing Lola was doing, it was diversifying.

Off to the side was another small room with the perfect reading nook. When she had worked here all those years ago, Mrs. Sanderson had used it as storage, wasting precious space. She had always pictured an area for kids, full of bright colors and diverse books that reflected all types of children and families. This was the only space that didn't follow the main color scheme.

A huge rainbow stretched from one end of the wall to the large window. The other walls were off-white, but the rest of the space was an explosion of color. Multicolored bookcases that reached up to her were pushed up against one wall, displaying board books at the bottom and picture books above them.

A larger set of bookcases were placed across the room for older readers who were just starting chapter books and middle-grade books. Her young adult section was within the main room because she didn't want the older kids and adults who read young adult books to have to step through crawling toddlers.

Lola took it all in, the fresh coat of paint, the smell of old and new books, and the sound of the coffeepot making a fresh brew. Serenity like she had never felt before washed over her as she took a moment to think of all she had accomplished. It was so easy to get lost in the hustle and bustle of the daily tasks of a small business owner that it was hard to remember the incredible job she was doing.

Yet, even through the pride and happiness, she could not deny the sadness creeping inside her each time she thought too hard about the last few weeks. Seeing Javi every day and not being able to talk to him had been brutal. It wasn't for lack of trying either.

After the shock of seeing Ofelia three weeks ago instead of Javi, a feeling of wrongness lingered within her. She had been set on ending things between them, but the more she thought about her life and what she wanted out of it, the bleaker it seemed without Javi. Which was fucking scary, considering he seemed to be ignoring her.

The first time he had come in to work on the shop after the wedding, Lola had planned to talk to him. But then she had gotten lost in cataloging books and ordering new ones for the shop that by the time she finished, Javi was gone.

So she tried the next day, but the damn man hadn't been there. According to his crew, he was busy getting more supplies they needed and would be back later. Which would have been fine if Lola hadn't had to go to the bakery to help Mona out while Mattea was home with the flu. She couldn't tell her best friend no, especially after everything she had done for Lola while she was at the wedding.

The third time she tried to corner him ended unsuccessfully and made her look like she was hovering over his crew, waiting for them to make a mistake. Javi had been skillful at avoiding her and hadn't even tried to talk to her.

She had asked for space.

He had given her that.

But space fucking sucked and she regretted that with all her heart. But she also knew when she was being ignored and let down easily. She didn't try to talk to Javi after that, but that didn't stop her from looking at the man. Drooling over him as he worked because there was just something about a sweaty man building a bookstore that did it for her.

A small part of her, though the likelihood of it happening

was zero to none, hoped Javi would show up to her grand opening. She was just setting herself up to be disappointed, but here she was—a delusional idiot.

"Hey, you doing okay?" Mattea's voice cut through her thoughts and she looked up. She felt something wet on her cheek and went to wipe it away. That's when she realized she was crying. When did that happen?

She grabbed a tissue from the whale holder it was in and dabbed at her eyes. "I'm okay. These are happy tears." Mostly. "I've been thinking about this day a lot, you know? And now it's here."

It felt significant in a way she had not planned for. Like she was taking back pieces of herself that her mom had tried, and failed, to rid her of. It was empowering to finally do something for herself and not worry about the repercussions. It had been a spur-of-the-moment choice that had completely changed her life for the better.

"I get it. Did Mona ever tell you how much I sobbed when I held the keys to the bakery? Not even opened or anything, just holding the keys." Mattea smiled, leaning against the doorframe as she played with one of her braids.

"We had just gotten engaged and you know Mona, she can't do anything half-assed. She knew I wanted to open a bakery. Girl barely had any of my desserts, but she had enough faith in me to forgo the ring and buy me the bakery. I was shocked and cried immediately. It felt so surreal. Like this thing that had been in your head for so long was finally tangible."

"Do you still feel that way? About your bakery?"

"Every single day. Every single damn day I thank my lucky stars for Mona and the bakery. Always feels like I'm living in a dream world."

The women shared a knowing smile before Mattea laughed

and pulled her in for a hug. "Today is your day, miss. You get to enjoy it."

"Ten minutes!" Mona yelled, barging into the room carrying a whole tray of assorted donuts. "You know you got a line forming outside, right?"

"What? Seriously?!" Lola gasped, all but sprinting to look out the window at the front of the store. Sure enough, a line of at least a dozen people waited. They were all different ages, but all here for the same reason: the books.

"I have another box of treats in the car. I think we might need them." Mona said.

"Are you sure you and Mattea can afford to be here? Neither one of you need to be in the store?" Lola had pulled them away from the bakery so many times throughout the process, but neither woman complained.

Mattea waved her concern away. "Justina can handle it. She's been begging us to give her more responsibilities at the bakery. She knows she can call if she needs help." Justina was Mattea's nineteen-year-old niece who had been working since she was sixteen. "Besides, I have a feeling we are going to be very busy today. All hands on deck."

"And now we are down to six minutes," Mona called, obviously taking up the job as a talking clock. "Imma get the last box of desserts," she said and made a beeline for the back door.

"Tell me where you want me to go," Mattea said like a soldier waiting for orders.

"Uhm...do you mind running the cafe? We are only selling a few items and all of them are programmed into that fancy cash register. Mona and I can take care of the checkout counter."

"Don't forget to walk around and mingle. Building a community is important. Mona can handle the cash register so you can make your rounds. Trust me, you are going to want to meet and talk to your first-time customers."

"Ugh, seriously Mattea, I don't know what I would do without you." Lola couldn't stress enough how thankful she was for her chosen family. The support and love radiating off her friends had given her the strength she needed to get through these last few weeks.

"You would do just fine, though perhaps have a little less fun." She winked, just as the back door flew open again and Mona came in carrying the pastries they would be selling in the cafe.

"Three minutes," Mona sang, stacking the delicious-smelling desserts away.

Lola took a moment to breathe before making a final walk through the store, making sure everything was in its proper place.

"Two minutes."

She plugged her phone in, connecting it to the speakers to play instrumental music throughout the store.

"One minute."

Heart pounding out of her chest, she swept the room with her eyes as if something would jump out at her. Nothing did.

"And...you're open, babe!" Mona's giddy self appeared beside her. She bumped her hip against hers. "Go open the door and let's get started."

Inwardly, Lola was freaking the fuck out, and outwardly... well she probably looked like she was freaking the fuck out. Mona had to give her a gentle push to get her feet moving. The crowd had only grown in size and watched her with eager eyes from outside.

With a small, awkward wave to her first-time customers, Lola unlocked the doors. She opened up to the public for the first time and was greeted by a chorus of claps and excited cheers.

Ah, she loved book lovers.

"Welcome to the grand reopening of Phoenix Books. We have free donuts, so make sure you grab one on the way in. Our cafe is open and everything is ten percent off today. Now—" She stepped aside, unblocking the entrance.

The first few customers went inside, a few stopping to congratulate her or tell her how excited they are for the reopening. The shop began to fill up quickly, but no one seemed to mind the crowd. Sounds of laughter and excited chatter drowned out the music, but it was a much better sound in her opinion.

Lola's cheeks hurt from smiling so much and as the last person strolled into the store, she got ready to follow them in when she heard her name called. She turned around to see a familiar family and her heart squeezed tightly for a moment. Ofelia and her husband Maverick approached with Camilia and Arturo holding hands.

But just the four of them. No sign of Javi.

That hurt more than it should. She had thought maybe he would be here since he had known how much this moment meant to her. Maybe he would...

No. She had hesitated too long when it came to Javi and she was getting what she deserved.

Even though it hurt, she smiled through the pain. Ofelia had still come like she promised and brought her family.

"I'm so glad you all could make it!" Which was the truth. Lola leaned down to get eye level with Arturo and Camilia. "Are you ready to see all the books?"

"Yes! Ms. Lola, can you read me one? I like your funny voices." Camilia smiled.

"I read too!" Arturo said excitedly.

Lola was overwhelmed by all the cuteness. "I think we can arrange that. I have to make a few rounds, but before you leave, we can read a book of your choosing." The cute cheers from the cousins made her laugh. "Off you both go. There are donuts on the table."

"Donuts? Say less." Maverick grinned and walked inside to find said treats. Ofelia rolled her eyes, but Lola didn't miss the fondness in her features when she looked at her husband.

"I swear that man is a giant toddler sometimes. Anyway, we don't want to keep you. Besides, we will see you later tonight." Her eyes sparkled with mischief and she ushered the cousins in before Lola could ask what she meant by that statement.

What the hell was happening tonight?

Before she could contemplate it more, an elderly woman approached her and asked about book recommendations for her grandson. She soon got lost in helping her customers, manning the second cashier when they had a steady flow of customers, and managing to sneak in one quick storytime that was meant to be for Camilia and Arturo but ended up being for quite a few kids.

After her impromptu storytime and the morning rush of customers, Lola finally had a second to tidy up a few displays needing her attention. The bell to the front door chimed and she looked up to greet her new customer. "Welcome to Phoenix Boo—"

She abruptly cut herself off, blinking once and then twice to make sure her mind wasn't playing tricks on her. Because there was no way her father had just walked through the door. More shocking than that, and even more unbelievable, he wasn't alone.

Marisol had come too.

All of the words she had ever learned in her life magically vanished, leaving her gaping as she struggled to come to terms with what she was seeing.

"You didn't think we would miss your grand opening, did you?" Her father's boisterous laughter echoed around her. Marisol remained quiet, but for once didn't look disgusted to be around her. She seemed...almost shy. And that was not the Marisol she knew.

"I, uhm, actually did." She didn't have her father and estranged sister showing up to her store opening on her bingo card. Must have missed that one. "I just...You've never...I'm sorry. I'm really surprised. That's all."

"We had to find out the opening date from a friend."

A friend? What friend was communicating with her father?

"I'm not missing my daughter's opening of her own business. What kind of father would I be? I brought your sister for support as well." He smiled and patted Marisol's back.

Brought or forced? She didn't voice that question but wondered all the same. Marisol had yet to say anything, but she saw her biting her lip as if holding back words she wanted to share.

She also noted her mother wasn't present, which didn't surprise her in the least. It still stung though. What surprised her was that Archie wasn't there with his new wife.

"Where's Archie?" she asked, despite herself.

Marisol and her father looked at each other before Marisol shrugged. "Not here," was all she supplied and Lola made a mental note to ask about that later.

"This must be a bit of a shock and I hope us coming isn't upsetting you," her father spoke and for the first time in her life, he seemed nervous.

Was she upset? No, not really. It felt...nice. Weird and a little awkward, but nice. So many questions ran through her mind and she wanted to ask them all, but now wasn't the time for a family meeting.

"I'm glad you're here. Do you, erm, want me to show you both around?" she asked, suddenly feeling self-conscious. The bookstore was an extension of her and if they didn't like it, she wouldn't be able to feel like they didn't like a part of her.

"We will request a private tour later. Right now, we are here for support. Put us to work," her father said and she couldn't have been more stunned if the books started to fly off the shelf.

"You want to help?" She couldn't keep the skepticism out of her voice. Had her sister ever worked a day in her life?

"If you'll have us," Marisol said softly.

"I—yeah, okay. Sure. Do you know how to make coffee?"

"No."

Lola laughed. "Doesn't matter. Mattea will teach you. I'm sure she could use the help. And Dad, if you wanted to help run the other cash register, I would appreciate it."

Her father saluted her. "You got it, kiddo."

"Not that I'm not grateful, but I'm very confused as to why you are both here. You've never—" She cut herself off. She was going to say they never showed an interest before, but didn't want a fight.

Her father seemed to understand what she was implying and his features softened. "Yeah, I know this seems out of character. And we fully plan on having this conversation, but let's save it until after you close. You have a steady stream of customers and I don't see that stopping any time soon. Is that okay?"

As curious as she was, it was for the best to save this conversation for later. Right now, the only thing that mattered was their willingness to help. If today's opening showed her anything, it was that she needed to hire employees, stat. Something she hadn't thought about and wished she had planned better.

Luckily, her friends and family picked up the slack.

"Sure, sounds good to me. You ready to work?" She grinned, taking some much-needed pleasure in seeing her sister do mundane tasks.

With a single nod and a quick hug from her father, the two of them went straight to work. It was bizarre and unbelievable to see her father and sister jump right into action without complaint, but she couldn't deny the pride she felt seeing them.

So many questions ran through her mind and she wanted answers to all of them. The conversation would be hard, but long overdue. For now, she just needed to focus on her store and keep the momentum going.

She still couldn't help but wish Javi was there to see her first day.

Lola

The rest of the day went by in a blur of books and smiling faces. Lola was sure her face was set in a permanent smile from talking to her customers and helping book lovers find their next story. She barely had any time to pee or eat, though she did scarf down one of Mattea's pastries in the back room.

By the end of the day, she didn't even care that her feet throbbed from running around the store. She was still on cloud nine. Since this morning, they had a steady stream of customers. The bell above the door chimed so many times that she knew she would be dreaming about it tonight.

Yet, each time the bell rang a small part of her was holding out for Javi to be there, smiling at her in a way that made her warm and gooey all over. Her father and sister had come, so it didn't seem too far-fetched.

But he never showed.

The last hour before they closed, things started to slow down and Mona had said she and Mattea needed to go. She was vague on the details but assured her she would catch up with her soon. Lola wasn't the only one dying to understand why her dad and Marisol were here.

It still felt so surreal. The two of them worked hard to help her throughout the store and never once complained. Even when Marisol spilled coffee on her blouse. Her sister shrugged. *Shrugged!* And carried on as if nothing had happened. Lola kept waiting for the second shoe to drop; for something drastic or terrible to happen. It said a lot about her relationship with her family when she expected things to fail.

To their credit, they had stayed within their positions all day. Never once slowing down, besides the occasional quick bathroom break. When it was time to close the store, all three of them sagged in relief. The adrenaline had finally worn off and it was as if their bodies finally realized how tired they were.

"That's it. Day one done," she called out, sitting down for the first time that day. The moment she was off her feet, she groaned.

A moment later the chairs opposite her at the cafe table were occupied by her father and Marisol. Her dad wore an expression she had desperately missed coming from him. Pride. He was proud of her. "I've never had so many paper cuts in my life." He laughed.

"I don't think I have fingerprints anymore. I think they have been permanently burned off." Marisol inspected her hands and then rubbed them against her dark jeans. Marisol looked so...normal. Lola felt as if she stepped into an episode of *The Twilight Zone* and she would soon wake up to realize she slept through her first opening.

Lola was half tempted to pinch herself, but she refrained. Only just.

"I'm so proud of you, kiddo." The pride on her father's face was evident once again. "I always knew you were tenacious. Always knew you had it in you, but seeing you achieve your dreams is an entirely different ballgame. You shined today."

I'm so proud of you.

How long had she yearned for her family to give her the recognition she had always craved? Hearing those words as a child would have healed a part of her still desperately trying to please a family who never quite accepted her the way she was.

The only exception had been her father but he had always been complacent in the way she was treated. That shit hurt too and he needed to know.

It was as if a fire was lit inside of her, giving her the strength and grit she needed to reclaim pieces of herself. "Yeah, I did. Didn't I?" The abrupt change in her caught the attention of both of them. "I appreciate your assistance today and the money you put aside for me to do this. I realize how privileged I am to have never gone without and for you to trust me enough to never question the ways I spend my money."

"But?"

There was always a but, wasn't there? Her father had heard it in her words. Marisol tensed, bracing herself for what was to come. She slipped back into the haughty expression she normally wore. It took until now to realize blocking her emotions was Marisol's way of coping.

"But that doesn't excuse the way Mom has treated me all of these years. The way you have treated me, Marisol." For a brief second, Marisol's eyes widened before her mask of indifference took over. But Lola wasn't going to let her hide today.

"You are my sister and all I ever wanted was a relationship with you. We had one once, but then Mom got her claws into you. You were always her favorite and you claimed that spot ruthlessly. You went along with the backhanded insults and never once stood up on my behalf. None of this even begins to cover the betrayal I felt when you started dating Archie almost immediately after we broke up!"

As she spoke, her anger mounted. She was surprised her eyes weren't watery with tears because when she got passionate about something her emotions would overwhelm her and she would end up crying. But not today. Too much had to be said.

"Lola, what the hell did you want me to do? We hardly talked and it wasn't as if you answered any of my calls. You only ever answered for Mom or Dad. Never me," Marisol argued, her voice shaking on the last words.

"So it's my fault you started dating Archie? It's my fault you treated me like shit since I didn't pick up the damn phone to talk to you?"

"No, I'm not saying that!"

"Then what the hell are you saying?"

"Girls." Their father stepped in, but Lola's ire found him next.

"And you"—she pointed a finger at him—"only stood up for me when you got tired of the bickering. You allowed the comments about my weight, appearance, and ambitions as long as it didn't interfere with your perfect family photo. News flash, Dad. It was never perfect!"

Suffocating silence followed her words as they stewed in their thoughts. She searched their features, finding shame and hurt in their eyes. It was something they needed to feel, just for a second, to realize how in the wrong they were.

After a few more seconds, Lola was ready to break the silence, but Marisol's whimpering caught her attention. When she looked back at her sister, she realized Marisol was crying. "Marisol?" Her voice softened somewhat but was tinged with apprehension.

"I'm sorry. Fuck, I hate crying." Their dad reached into his pocket and pulled out a tissue before handing it to Marisol. She dabbed at her eyes, careful of her makeup. Lola couldn't remember the last time she saw her sister cry.

"When Dad called me last week and said we needed to check in on you, I admit, I wanted no part of it. I didn't know how me being here would help you at all. As I said, we don't talk." Before Lola could protest, Marisol put her hand up, silencing her. "And that's largely my fault. It was so much easier to go along with Mom than be the person she pestered."

"I wouldn't call putting me on a diet as an eight-year-old 'pester.' Or shaming me for not fitting in perfectly with this facade she wanted to share with the world 'pestering,'" Lola protested.

To her credit, Marisol looked embarrassed by her words. "Right. Sorry. You've always been better at words than me. What I'm saying is I knew Mom treated you differently than me. I took advantage of that because I could. It became such a part of me that half the time I didn't realize what I was doing. I didn't think my words hurt you because I had become so desensitized toward you."

"You learned all of this in a week, have you?" Lola muttered, doing her best not to roll her eyes. Marisol was trying and it was more than she had ever done before.

"No. I guess I started noticing the differences once I got engaged to Archie. Mom was so excited for me in a way she had never been for you when the two of you were dating. The wedding brought out the worst in her...in us."

"I..." Lola sighed, pinching the bridge of her nose. She tried to remember the breathing techniques to calm her racing heart and took a minute to count each breath before she started again. "I guess I don't understand what changed. Why you care."

"For so long I always thought you were the problem. That the Mom I got was the same Mom you got, but you pushed her away and deliberately did things to piss her off. After the wedding, once everything settled down, I had time to think. That's when Dad called and I realized I've wasted so much time being mad at nothing. It scared me when you cut Mom off because...believe it or not, I don't want you to cut *me* off."

That revelation stunned her. Never would she have thought that Marisol would be so scared of getting cut off by Lola. Marisol's words from earlier rang through her mind and made her reflect on how she treated her sister.

How many times had Marisol called her only for Lola to immediately put it to voicemail? How many unanswered texts had she left unread?

It wasn't an excuse for her behavior. Not at all. But it did provide some insight.

"I guess it's hard for me to realize we had two very different moms growing up. I couldn't fathom how you could feel so much hatred toward her, but...I'm starting to understand."

"To be clear, I don't hate Mom," Lola said. As much as her mother hurt her, she didn't hate her. Some part understood her need to fit into the society she married into and present this perfect family to the world. She wasn't only a woman, she was a Mexican woman and she had to fight tooth and nail to earn any ounce of respect.

However, her mother needed to work on her own trauma and stop projecting it onto Lola. If she didn't see a counselor, she wasn't sure she ever would. As hard as it was, Lola needed to keep herself safe, and cutting off someone so toxic was the first step.

"And neither do we," her father said. "But we also don't like how she's been treating you. And you're right. I have been pretty ignorant in that way. I thought eventually you two would get along. Your mother can be overbearing, but I didn't see how much she affected you."

Her dad reached over the table and grasped her hand. "Your mother knows we are here and that she was not allowed to join us. Obviously, she isn't happy about it, but she brought this upon herself. That being said, if you would like time away from your sister and me too...well, we would understand."

Did she want that? Maybe she would have wanted her sister gone once, but now? Lola turned back to Marisol. "Just one thing. Why didn't you tell me about Archie? I never understood why you started dating him when you knew I dated him first."

Marisol's cheeks reddened. "Archie had wiggled his way into our family, but especially with Mom. She always made comments about how it was so surprising that Archie and I weren't the ones together. It was constant and got to the point where I just couldn't ignore her anymore. The night Archie broke up with you, he came by the house to inform our parents. Except Dad wasn't home, it was only Mom."

During their relationship, Archie had formed a strong relationship with her parents. She knew now it was because her parents had money and status, and that was the only thing Archie had even been attracted to.

"When he asked to take me on a date a few days later, I said yes because I felt like I didn't have a choice. I didn't know it would lead to him declaring we were dating and I definitely didn't know that it would lead me to marrying him." Marisol's eyes filled with tears, and she looked at Lola as if pleading for her to understand.

Lola had spent so long being mad at Marisol, hating her for being the perfect daughter, without really realizing her sister was hurting too. Only in a different way. Marisol had to live up to the perfection their mother set for them every single day. She always went along with whatever their mother said because it was easier just to do as Luciana asked than deal with the fallout from disappointing her.

For the first time in her life, Lola felt like she actually understood her sister and her heart hurt for her.

She reached out and took Marisol's hand in hers. "Marisol?" She spoke gently, meeting the eyes of the sister she was just starting to understand. "Do you love Archie?"

"No!" Her body began to shudder with the sobs working their way through her. "No, I can't stand that man. I only married him because I just wanted to keep everyone happy but I didn't because I hurt you and continued to hurt you. Lola, I'm so sorry. So damn sorry."

Lola couldn't stop her own tears as she got out of her seat and wrapped her arms around Marisol. They needed this moment, needed to break down and see each other at their lowest to truly understand one another.

Her heart hurt for Marisol and the pressure she was under every day trying to remain the perfect daughter. Hurt for herself for living all these years thinking she didn't have a sister that loved her.

Marisol soon pulled away, eyes puffy from crying and hair disheveled. "Archie isn't here because I didn't want him here. I was too scared to say that before, but I'm not anymore. Not after hearing you stand up to Mom...it made me feel like maybe I can do the same."

There was so much to unpack there and Lola wanted to dive into it all eventually. Marisol shouldn't have to stay married to that prick if she didn't want to be. She wanted to say as much, until she felt a large hand rubbing her back. It took her a moment to realize it was her father. His face was splotchy and red, obviously hurting as well.

"This doesn't begin to right the wrongs we've done. This doesn't excuse the way Marisol treated you or the way I always tried to diminish the situation. But what I can say is that we will try our hardest to make it up to you, if you let us."

Lola rubbed her eyes, slowly untangling herself from her sister. There was still a lot they needed to address, but this felt like a step in the right direction. Now it was up to her and she had to make the decision whether or not she wanted them in her life.

She had acted on fear and let others' opinions influence her decisions. It had cost her the man she loved. She didn't want to do that again, but things needed to change.

"Until I'm ready, I don't want to be around Mom. She has to deal with her shit before we can think about talking and I don't want either of you pressuring me into talking to her. If that means I miss a few family functions, then so be it. But I will not be made to feel bad about it anymore.

"It's going to take some time for us to heal our relationships. If you're serious about wanting to be in my life, then there's a whole lot of stuff we have to work through as well. So be prepared for tough conversations.

"If you can agree to this, then I see no reason you both can't stay in my life." Lola watched Marisol visibly relax and her father nodding his head enthusiastically. Their willingness to try spoke volumes.

"There is nothing more I want than to support my girls. Through your bookstore endeavors"—he smiled at Lola—"and a potential divorce." The last part was spoken to Marisol.

"No matter how different you both are, I love you equally and am so proud of you both," he said fondly, reaching out for both their hands. "Our Dolores has a backbone on her. Not everyone can stand up to your mother and leave the room a victor."

The nervous energy between them evaporated as Lola snorted. "I don't know if I would say victor. I'm sure she exaggerated some of the details."

"Your mother wasn't the one to tell us about the fight."

"Then who..."

Before she could finish her sentence, a familiar face popped up in her mind. The only other person who was there that night. Who saw everything.

Javi.

The amused expression her father wore said he knew she answered her question. "That's a fine young man you have there. His daughter is adorable. They both speak highly of you."

Javi had gone and talked to her father without her knowing. Knowing him, he did it because he knew she had wasted her last bits of strength on her mom and she doubted she would ever have the courage to speak so freely to her father, much less her sister.

If it weren't for him, she would have never had this moment. Even when she tried to push him away, he still made sure her voice was heard.

"Dad spoke highly about him. I didn't get a chance to talk to him at the wedding, but I'm hoping I can soon," her sister said, the words still sounding foreign, probably to both their ears. Kindness and connection didn't come easily in their bond and it would feel strange for a while.

"I don't think that's going to happen." Marisol's smile

faltered at Lola's words. "We aren't together. And it's my fault. I took something Archie said to heart, about me being recklessly impulsive, and I let my doubts cloud my judgment."

She hated admitting her failure and she didn't know when the pain of losing Javi would ever heal. Her feelings had been real. The amazing sex had been real. All of it was the most intense love she had ever experienced and it scared the hell out of her. Instead of facing her fears, she chose to lose it all.

"Nonsense. That boy loves you. No one would meet with a woman's father to berate them for how they treated her if they weren't madly in love."

"Madly in love." She scoffed, unable to keep the bitterness out of her own words. She wasn't sure if she was angry with herself or irrationally angry at Javi for making her fall in love with him. "I can assure you, that is not the case."

"Then you'd be very wrong, preciosa."

Lola had never jumped out of a chair so quickly, whirling around to make sure her mind wasn't playing tricks on her. That the man standing before her was the same man who haunted her dreams night after night. She didn't know how he got in, didn't know why he was here, but he was not a figment of her imagination.

Standing in front of her, dressed in dark denim jeans and his usual black T-shirt, stood Javi. And in his hands, he was holding two things: a greasy bag of food and an old copy of *The Giving Tree*.

Lola opened her mouth, but the only thing that escaped her lips was a sob.

CHAPTER 43

Javi

Three weeks. That was how long it took for every piece of the puzzle to fit together to create this moment right here. Javi would not soon forget the look in Lola's eyes when she turned around and saw him standing only a few feet behind her. Her eyes were blown wide and her lips didn't know whether to smile or scowl at him. There seemed to be a raging war inside her, probably wondering if she wanted to hug him or cast him out.

There was a chance he only made things worse between them. If she rejected him again, he would have to give her up. He knew when he was fighting a losing battle, but he hadn't failed yet.

Three weeks ago, Javi met Travis for lunch. Out of concern for his daughter, he wanted to reach out to someone who knew what was going on because Lola tended to bottle up her emotions and not feel them until they became overwhelming.

Javi only spoke about the incident he saw between her mother and Lola at the wedding. There was far more that needed to be said, but it wasn't his story to tell. This was how they came to an agreement that Travis would leave Lola alone long enough for her to focus on the shop and come support her on opening day.

Bringing Marisol had never been part of the plan, so it was a pleasant surprise to see her at the shop as well. It made sense though, given their troubled history. Perhaps she was there to patch things up with her sister. The only person missing from the scene was Luciana.

Good.

Travis broke the silence and stood up. "Well, I think it's time for Marisol and me to go." Lola didn't so much as turn around to acknowledge him. "We will see you later for the—"

"Yes—" Javi cut him off, not wanting to spoil the other surprise he had waiting for her. A surprise that was contingent upon her response to him being here.

"Right. We will just see our way out." He winked at him and offered his arm to Marisol. As they walked out, he noticed Marisol's gentle squeeze of Lola's shoulder and the way Lola relaxed her body.

Soon the door closed, leaving the two of them in absolute silence for the first time in three weeks.

"This was you? All of this was you?" So his girl found her voice. Her ever-changing emotions made him want to take all the doubts away. "But how? And what the fuck, Javi? You've been avoiding me for three weeks and now you come in here holding"—she gestured down to the book she hated, causing Javi's lip to quirk up in a smirk—"that damned book and food? Like that's going to fix everything?"

He flinched at her statement. The past three weeks hadn't been easy. More than once he had been tempted to seek her out, just as she did for him. Each time he came up short though. There was still much left unsaid between them, but he didn't want to add any extra stress as she prepared for her opening. Javi had things to prepare for as well and they all revolved around her.

They both needed time apart to find their way back together.

Lola stared at him expectantly, waiting for a response. He took a step forward and her body gave an involuntary shudder, giving away that she was affected by his proximity.

"No, I don't think this will fix everything," he said, putting the book and food on the table. From his experience, food did wonders to calm the most strenuous situations. Ofelia said it was better than flowers, so he took her word for it.

"Javi, did you talk to my dad? What did you tell him? You don't have to continue to stick up for me."

"You still don't get it, do you?" Javi laughed, which only made Lola purse her pouty lips together in anger. "I admit, talking to your father may have been a mistake. I don't regret telling him what happened, but I should have asked your permission first. I'm sorry."

Lola remained stoic, not answering him with words. The slightest nod of her head told him to continue. "He came to me as a father and asked what I would do if my daughter was hurting. So I told him. I said nothing on this earth would stop me from making it right. I wouldn't let my own stubbornness or pride force me to miss out on the best thing to have ever happened to me."

He thought of Camilia and the lengths he would go to for his daughter. Travis was struggling to find his footing and Javi had attempted to give him advice, not knowing what he would do with it, but hoping he'd make the right decision.

Showing up and admitting you were part of the problem was a good first move in his book.

Lola sucked her bottom lip between her teeth. "And my sister? Did you talk to her too?"

"No, I think that might have been your father. He seemed determined to fix a sibling relationship he had a part in breaking. But it's up to you on what you want to do." Not that he needed to tell her this, she had done a good job of standing her ground like she rightfully deserved.

Yet she still didn't seem at ease with him in the room and he was starting to second-guess his plan. "Listen, I'm sorry about talking to your dad—"

"No. Surprisingly, I'm not mad about that." Lola admitted, cutting him off. "I know you did it for me. I'm mostly mad at myself." Her voice came out so small, cracking on the last few words.

Every muscle in Javi's body tensed. "Why are you mad at yourself? You didn't do anything."

"And that is exactly the problem. I shouldn't have let my doubts take over and push you away. I should have fought harder for us and when I was finally ready, I thought you wanted nothing to do with me anymore. Which is, once again, my fault."

"Fuck, this isn't going like I planned." Javi ran a hand through his hair and for the first time, he felt shy around her. He hated that she had thought she lost him and felt guilty.

"How was it supposed to go?" Lola asked softly. When he looked up, he saw that she was only a breath away from him. He needed her in his arms. Except he needed to get out what he had to say before he made the situation any worse.

"I was going to show you the book." He gestured toward his old copy of *The Giving Tree.*

Lola made an adorable, scrunched face that was supposed

to convey her anger but just made him want to kiss the wrinkle in her brow.

"You got me the book I hated?" she asked skeptically. "That was your grand plan?"

"No, it's not for you, it's for your store. And I have been thinking about this book a lot. How could anyone hate a seemingly innocent book? And I think it's because you are the tree."

Lola blinked once. "I'm...a tree?"

"Yes." He cleared his throat, thinking back to his sister's analysis of the book. It sounded so smart when she said it, being a former English teacher and all, but he didn't think he could mimic her words but hoped they made sense.

"You have given up so much of yourself to others to keep the peace. Your heart is the best thing about you and you never expect anything in return. When someone shows a genuine interest in you, it scares you because you've had to live in a flight or fight mode for a long-ass time. I understand the need for caution, but I don't want you to continue to give your time and heart away while gaining nothing in return."

"Like the tree."

"Like the tree," Javi repeated and this time cupped Lola's face in his hands. Their eyes met and he searched hers, finding something akin to hope in her expression. It gave him the confidence he needed to continue.

"Lola, I know you wanted time and I gave you that. If you ask me to leave now, I will. But not without telling you what you mean to me. It stopped being about the money the second I took you out on our first date. You remember how nervous I was?"

Lola shook her head the best she could with him holding her. "You looked so confident when we went to the bingo hall."

"I'm glad it came across like that, but I was nervous as hell.

It had been so long since I wanted to impress anyone and I wanted to make you smile. I wanted to hear you laugh and I lived for the moments you smacked my arm when you got excited.

"Falling in love with you was easy. I think I loved you the moment I saw you reading with Camilia because that was the first time my daughter ever gravitated to another person that wasn't family. My feelings only grew stronger during our week in Colorado and I wanted to tell you so many times I loved you, but I never knew if it was the right time until it was too late."

Tears rolled down Lola's cheeks now, leaving tracks where her makeup had once been. Even a crying mess, his girl was the most beautiful in the world. Javi was surprised to feel his own eyes burned with unshed tears.

"Lola, I love you. I'm a single dad who works too damn hard and I'm sure I have a lot of other things against me. But I'm hoping you can look past that and consider being mine—"

"Yes!" Lola didn't let him finish his speech before she threw herself into his arms. "I want you. I want your stubborn, workaholic ass coming home to me. I want to read with you and Camilia every night. I want you, Javi and I know you and Camilia are a package deal. If you'll both have me, I want it too."

Nothing could convey the way her words made him feel. No words captured this feeling of rightness that engulfed him the moment she agreed to be his. He let his actions do the talking for him and he swooped down to capture her lips in a heated kiss. He was met with the same intensity he was giving.

"I can't believe your big gesture is bringing that damn book here and comparing me to a tree." Lola giggled, pulling back slightly to speak. Her lips still brushed against his when she spoke.

"I brought tostadas too."

"Fuck, that's so hot."

Javi laughed and backed her up against the counter, caging her in with his body. He saw the moment the humor left her eyes, replaced by desire. He felt his body heat at the thought of her and how long it had been since he last made his girl come.

He needed to remedy that. Even if he still had one last surprise for her. That could wait until later.

"I want you, Lola," he said, his voice growing gruff. His knee nudged its way between her thighs and she spread for him. "Preciosa, I need you now." He needed to feel himself inside of her, remember how her pussy gripped his cock. He wanted it hard and fast, to claim her properly.

Lola whimpered and her hands flew to her jeans. They were far enough into the store that no one walking by would see them. Not that he cared about that right now.

Lola peeled off her skin-tight jeans, scrunching them up on the floor before kicking them away. Part of him wished they were back at his home or hers, but right now he just needed to feel their bodies connect. Judging by the hunger in Lola's eyes, she needed that too.

Javi reached into his pocket to grab his wallet. He had a condom in there, but Lola stopped him. "I can't wait. I started taking the pill shortly after we left Colorado. Please, Javi." The sweet sounds of her begging made his cock stiff. Fuck, he needed her now.

"Are you wet for me, Lola?" he asked, moving his hands between her thighs. He felt the dampness seeping through her panties and knew she was aching for him even before he pushed a finger into her. He moaned, feeling her wetness on his finger.

Then he made sure she was watching before he slid his finger back out and brought it to his lips. He sucked his finger into his mouth, tasting her eagerness.

"Fuck," Lola gasped.

Javi wasted no time unzipping his jeans and pushing them down until he freed his erection. The look of raw need and desire Lola gave him was nearly enough to make him come on the spot. He didn't think he'd ever get sick of that look.

"Counter. Now," he said in a caveman-like voice, only capable of one-word sentences.

Lola braced her hands on the counter behind her and Javi helped lift her. He pulled her right to the edge, making a mental note to personally clean the counter with bleach later.

"Tell me what you want," Javi said, spreading her thighs again and rubbing his erection through her folds.

Lola gave a shuddering breath. "You. Your cock. Javi, *please*."

As much as he liked to hear her beg, he was desperate for her. Javi yanked her forward, pushing his hips up and disappearing inside of her. They both moaned in unison, Lola's arms wrapping around his neck.

There was nothing gentle in the way he fucked Lola. It was a sheer, carnal need. He felt her tightening around him, driving him to the brink of orgasm each time. Lola pulled him closer by wrapping her legs around his waist, pushing him deeper inside of her.

Mine. Each thrust seemed to say and Lola's gasping breath told him she was getting close. His hand flew to her clit, his thumb rubbing circles around the bundle of nerves.

"Javi!" she cried out. "I'm close."

He was too. He didn't stop his merciless thrusting, his back and arm muscles flexing. They reached orgasm together. Their cries of pleasure echoed around them in the empty store. Javi panted, lowering his forehead against hers.

The only sounds around them were the sounds of cars passing by on the street. He felt like he was in a cocoon of warmth and love and they were on the cusp of creating something great together.

"I love you too, Javi," Lola said after a moment, once her chest stopped heaving. "I don't think I said that before, but I do. And I'm sorry it took me so long to realize that."

"I would have waited for you for as long as you needed," Javi said, meeting her gaze. "Don't apologize. You needed to do this on your own time. So did I."

"Thank you for being patient with me." Lola nuzzled him, shifting her body so he moved inside of her involuntarily, eliciting a groan from him.

"I think you should take me home," Lola purred. The woman was going to be the death of him and send him straight to the grave. She rolled her hips and Javi felt himself getting hard again.

"Fuck Lola, you make saying no incredibly hard," he groaned.

"Then don't say no." Lola giggled, tightening her legs around him.

Javi wanted to give in. He wanted nothing more than to take her on every available surface, but they had people waiting for them. It had taken a lot to organize and many people were expecting them to show.

"There's one more surprise," he said and Lola stopped.

A giddy smile spread across her lips. "What is it?"

"We have to go."

"Well, color me intrigued." She giggled and finally released him. Javi pulled out of her with a grunt. "Just give me a minute to...erm." She looked down at their mixed pleasure dripping down her thighs. "Clean up. Then we can go?"

Tucking himself back into his pants, Javi nodded. "Truck's out back, ready to go when you are." With that, Javi kissed her and smacked her beautiful ass as she walked by. As much as he wanted more of her, he was excited about the next surprise.

Lola

As much as she enjoyed going to bingo for their first date, Lola had to wonder why Javi was pulling up outside it now. The thought of going back to his home and celebrating her opening privately was tempting. Her thighs were still slightly sore from the frenzied fucking from earlier and she wanted more.

"Love, as tempting as this is, are you positive you wouldn't rather go...oh, I don't know, to my bed?" Lola asked.

Javi smirked and cut the engine off, parking outside the building. "That will happen later, but I brought you here to tell you about the money you paid me."

Confusion settled over Lola as she cocked her head to the side. "It doesn't matter, Javi. I already said the money is yours and I wanted you to spend it however you wanted—"

"I know, but just let me get this out." Javi's stricken face gave her pause and she nodded for him to continue. "I was able to give each of my men bonuses for their hard work on your bookstore. Some of the money went to bills that, regrettably, I was late on, and a good portion was set aside for Camilia when she gets older. However, the rest went into making tonight possible."

"I...don't understand. Did you buy out all the bingo cards so we'd win for sure?"

Javi barked out a laugh and reached over to undo her seatbelt. "No, but good idea. I'll remember that for next time." He offered her a wink before undoing his belt and slipping out of the car.

Now she was more confused than ever but let Javi help her out of his truck. "So, why are we here then?" She didn't want to sound ungrateful, she just wanted to know what secret he had up his sleeve.

Javi was practically bouncing with excitement but kept his mouth shut. Instead, he led her inside the front door to the check-in part of the bingo hall. No one was manning the booth which she thought was odd. "How do we..."

Her question died on her lips the moment Javi ushered her through the welcome room and into the main part of the building. Beautiful and colorful decorations still adorned the walls and ceilings, but only this time it was accompanied by a large banner reading, "Congratulations, Lola!" in a beautiful, cursive script.

Balloons in various colors of pink, white, and gray were interspersed with the normal decorations of the room and while it should have clashed, it only added to the beauty. Each table had what looked to be bouquets made entirely out of books.

Yet none of that was the most impressive part of the surprise. Standing in the room were familiar faces beaming and clapping for her. Amongst the sea of faces were Mattea and Mona, wearing something different than they had earlier. They had known this the whole time? And kept it a secret? That was almost more surprising than the actual party.

Ofelia and Maverick were there too, holding their son Arturo who seemed dazed but was clapping along anyway since everyone else was.

Her father's face caught her attention next. Among everyone in the room, his bellows of joy rang loudest of all. Mostly because her father was naturally loud and used to speaking over people at business meetings. Next to him was Marisol, changed from her coffee-stained blouse.

A few other familiar faces were there as well. Crew members who she had gotten to know during construction and what was probably their family. A swirl of pink and silver came charging straight toward her, colliding with her and Javi's thighs. A smiling Camilia looked up, a gleeful expression on her face as she yelled, "Surprise!" Then softer, only speaking to her father, "Did I do it right?"

Javi's laugh echoed around her and he nodded. "Yes, mija, you did good."

So many emotions fought for dominance inside her. Shock, disbelief, and a growing warmth that could only be described as love.

"Do you, uh, like it?" For the second time today, Lola noticed the nervousness in his posture. The way he slid his hands into his pockets, shoulders curving forward as if bracing for an unfavorable response. "I don't know if surprises are your thing. Probably should have asked. You must be tired—"

"Javi?"

"Yeah?"

"Shut up and kiss me."

He expelled a deep breath, shoulders sagging in relief. The

smile she had come to love so much returned as the anxious-ness wore off. "Gladly."

Brazenly, he took her into his arms and claimed her mouth with his. The hollers and whistles around them didn't seem to deter Javi. Not only did he privately claim her, but this was him publicly declaring their love in front of family and friends. Her heart threatened to burst at the seams with the outpouring of love she felt in the room.

When they broke apart, happy tears ran down her cheeks. Three weeks ago she had gone through the motions of day-to-day living and part of her was excited for Phoenix to open. But her heart had been broken as she thought of everything she had sacrificed to get to that spot. A life with Javi and contact with her family.

So much had changed in one night. More than she could have anticipated and it would take her some time to come to terms with it all. One thing was for certain. She had a family now. One that she chose for herself. And it started with the man standing next to her and the little girl still holding on to their legs.

This was home.

"Lo-Lo! Get in here, bit—girl," Mona censored awkwardly, seeing as there were children in the room. "And let's drink to a successful opening!

"What do you say, preciosa? Ready to revel in your accom-plishments?" Javi grinned, leaning down to pick Camilia up. He then offered Lola his hand. A few short seconds later, Camilia offered hers with a toothy smile.

There was still a lot that needed to be done. She had to hire full-time employees for her store. The bond between her and her family only had a Band-Aid on it, and there were still a lot of tough conversations that needed to be had. She also needed to process what it would be like to be a prominent figure in Camilia's life and how best to go about it.

But all of these things would take time and patience. They didn't have to be sorted out today and instead, she could enjoy the moment. As Javi said, she deserved to revel in her accomplishments and enjoy the night with the people she loved and admired.

Her people.

With a full heart and a smile stretching wide across her face, Lola took Javi's hand. "I'll follow you both." And she would. Always.

Epilogue

TWO YEARS LATER

The smell of fresh cilantro and cumin wafting from the kitchen made Lola's stomach growl, even though she had been grazing all morning. She couldn't help it, she seemed to always be in a snacky mood these days, and with Ofelia cooking in the other room, her snack threshold all but tripled.

"Ofelia, please tell me what I can help you with." Lola entered the kitchen slowly, knowing any sudden movement would gain her ire. As of this morning, her sister-in-law had already shooed all the men out of the kitchen. Normally she was the first to have them help cook, but since it was Father's Day, they had all collectively decided to give them one day off.

"Sure, can you take the bottle out of the warmer and give it to Mav? I hear Violeta crying and I know it's because she's hungry." Ofelia barely looked up from the pot as she added extra seasoning. Lola's mouth watered at the thought of the menudo she was making.

"Oh, I'll do it, tía." Camilia smiled, hopping off the

counter where she had been supervising Marisol cutting up the veggies for the salsa. When she passed Lola, she winked, giddy with the secret the two of them shared.

"Thank you, mija," Ofelia called as Camilia skipped out of the room. Violeta was the newest member of their ever-growing family, just shy of a year old. She was an adorable little girl with the biggest brown eyes and tight curls that Ofelia had styled into tiny pigtails.

"Lola, can you make the salsa? Yours always tastes so much better than mine." The slight whine in her sister's voice made her laugh. Marisol was many things, but a chef, she was not. She was much more accustomed to other people cooking for her, but Lola gave her credit for trying. Honestly, she was just proud she hadn't sliced off a thumb yet.

"Yeah, just hand me your knife and move out of the way." She laughed and Marisol all but collapsed in relief when Lola took over.

Over the past two years, they had worked hard on mending their broken relationship. Marisol had a lot of trauma to work through along with her divorce from Archie. Some days were better than others and they still went through periods of arguing, but they were trying. It amazed Lola how much she learned about her sister over the years and she loved finding things in common.

Surprisingly enough, they were both huge fans of rage rooms, as suggested by a therapist they saw together once a month. He had thought this would be a good way for the women to get their frustrations out. There was nothing more satisfying than breaking porcelain plates or hitting an old TV with a baseball bat.

She only wished she found a similar outlet with her

mother. Their relationship hadn't progressed as much as Lola had hoped. It had taken her a year to even sit down with her mother and talk to her about the pain she'd caused her. Luciana had listened to her daughter, but they were still trying to find ways to reconnect. Right now, their meetings only consisted of large family gatherings and the occasional phone call.

The last time Lola had been on the phone with her mother, three months ago, Luciana had stated she had finally found a therapist that she liked. According to her father, said therapist cost him an arm and a leg, but he thought every penny was well worth it.

It gave Lola hope for the future.

"Technically, I don't have to cook since I'm not married or have children," Marisol said, leaning back against the counter.

"Yeah, but you have a father we are celebrating today," Lola insisted.

"Oh, right." Sometimes her sister was still so caught up in herself that she tended to forget those around her. Lola had long ago stopped being insulted by that. Her sister didn't do it on purpose and she was actively trying to be less self-centered.

It was still a work in progress.

For the next twenty minutes, Lola listened to whatever Ofelia needed her to do to prepare the lunch for the dads. With Camilia and Arturo's help, the three of them got the dining room table set. Ofelia was the only one to have a table that expanded big enough to accommodate the family.

"Boys! It's time to eat," Ofelia called, carrying the large pot of menudo out while Marisol brought out a few other dishes Ofelia had somehow been able to make. That woman was a master in the kitchen and she didn't know how Maverick didn't gain a million pounds with her food. Probably due to his intense baseball fitness regime.

One by one, the men of the family began to amble in. As expected, her father was the first one since he was Ofelia's biggest fan when it came to her cooking. Her mother had come down with the flu and opted to stay home, which was fine by Lola. It gave her one less thing to worry about.

Next came Maverick with his father-in-law Ruben, discussing baseball stats she never quite understood. Maverick held Violeta in his arms, which made Lola smile. He hardly ever put that girl down.

Finally, her husband walked through the door, eyes scanning the room until they landed on her. The smile he reserved only for her spread across his features and butterflies formed in her belly. She didn't think she would ever get used to that smile. The way he looked at her with all the love and adoration in this world.

"Where are we sitting, Mrs. Mendez?" he purred into her ear, wrapping his arms around her torso. A giggle left her lips when he started to nuzzle and kiss her neck.

Their wedding had been small and intimate. Only a few of their closest friends and some family were allowed to come. Mona had officiated their wedding in a ceremony that took place in Ofelia's backyard. Camilia had been their flower girl and Arturo their ring bearer. It was what they both had wanted. She couldn't believe that had only been five months ago. She felt like she lived a whole lifetime in those five months while simultaneously thinking it was going by too quickly.

"Camilia already called dibs on the middle," Lola warned and gestured to the three seats in front of them. Camilia found her way to hers and eagerly patted the spots next to her.

The last person to sit was Ofelia. As soon as she did, she gestured for everyone to eat. No one hesitated and began to fill their bowls and bellies up.

They didn't often get together. Everyone's schedules clashed, which only allowed for meets ups once in a while. Lola never had a big family and she had not realized how much she wanted one until Javi's family took her in. Two years ago, if someone would have said they would all be sitting down together, sharing a meal on Father's Day, Lola would have laughed in their face.

Yet here they all sat talking about everything from Maverick's games to the small, mundane family moments. Arturo would be starting kindergarten next month, going to the same school as Camilia. Camilia told everyone all about the third-grade teachers and which one she wanted, to which Lola's father said he would write a strongly worded letter to the principal to assure that would happen.

Lola would have to make sure he didn't.

By the time they finished eating, two hours had flown by. Camilia twisted in her seat to get Lola's attention. "Mamá Lola, is it present time yet?"

Mamá.

She was still getting used to that. It had shocked the hell out of her when she said it the first time a day after Lola got engaged to Javi. They had only one conversation prior where Lola sat with Camilia and talked to her about how she was allowed to call Lola whatever she was comfortable with. In no way would Lola ever pressure her. She understood and they hadn't talked about it since until she called her mamá for the first time.

"I think it is." She grinned and Camilia squealed. The little girl was bouncing out of her chair. "Remember what to do?" she whispered, just loud enough for her to hear.

Camilia nodded before running off. Javi raised his brow in confusion and Lola waved him off. He would see soon enough. A few minutes later Camilia came back with a small square-shaped box and a zipped-up jacket.

"You cold, Cam? I can go turn the air up," Maverick offered, but Camilia shook her head adamantly.

"I'm okay!" She plopped back onto her seat, keeping the present in front of her. "You can't open yours until last, papá."

"Then I will start." Travis grinned, looking between Marisol and Lola. "C'mon. What did you get your old man, don't be shy."

The sisters rolled their eyes simultaneously but laughed. If there was one thing that their father loved—other than Ofelia's cooking—was presents.

Marisol had been in charge of the present this year and handed him a neatly wrapped box. He tore into it like an over-excited toddler on Christmas. Seconds later he pulled out what appeared to be a scrapbook.

"I felt like it was time you needed some updated pictures. The grandkids are in it too," Marisol explained. Though Arturo and Violeta weren't technically his grandkids, Travis spoiled them like they were. The adoring smile on their father's face told them he appreciated the gift.

They went around the table, letting each dad open his gifts. Ruben got a new BBQ set from Javi and Ofelia. Camilia made him a cute card with a picture of both of them on it. Then it was Maverick's turn. Ofelia had gotten him new running shoes for training days and the kids—with Ofelia's help—made him a mini book for all the reasons they loved him.

It was all very sweet, but the closer they got to Javi opening his present, the more Lola grew nervous. Which was a crazy thing to feel, but her nerves had been all over the place for weeks. Her heart beat so loud in her chest that she was certain everyone heard it.

"It's your turn, papá." Besides Lola, Camilia was the only other person who knew. Lola had made an appointment at the doctor's after two days of what she thought was a stomach bug. Camilia had gone along with her since Javi was working and had heard the news with her.

They both cried. And laughed. Then promised to keep it a secret until today.

Javi unwrapped the present and it felt like the world slowed down. Lola was certain she was shaking. There was only so much longer she could keep it together.

Javi tore off the remaining paper and opened the lid to the box. Folded neatly inside was a gray shirt with the words "World's Best Dad" in red across the chest. He leaned down and pressed a sweet kiss to the top of Camilia's forehead.

"Thank you, mija. I love it."

"There's more!" Lola blurted out, far too loudly. The room, who had been talking among each other, all stopped and looked over toward them. The blush crawled up the back of her neck, coloring her cheeks.

Javi looked back at the seemingly empty box. She watched as he went from smiling, to complete confusion. Her heart beat faster as he picked up the box, bringing it closer to his face so he could make sense of the taped photos Lola had placed at the bottom. She saw the moment the realization hit and his head snapped to her so quickly, she was surprised he didn't get whiplash.

"Lola. Are you serious?" His words did not indicate how

he felt. Was he mad? Fuck, should she have done this in private when their whole damn family wasn't watching?

Before she could say anything, Camilia stood up on her chair and unzipped the jacket she wore to expose her shirt that read "Big Sister."

"Mamá Lola is having a baby!"

Chaos. The whole room exploded with excitement and she was rushed by Ofelia. "I knew it! I had this feeling."

"My baby is having a baby!" She heard her father exclaim, his deep laughter filling the room. Even Marisol came and hugged her and wished her congratulations.

Javi had not moved from his spot, looking down at the sonograms she taped to the bottom of the box. "Please say something," Lola whispered, the tightness in her belly growing by the second. She didn't think anyone noticed his lack of response yet, they were all too busy trying to guess when the baby would be due.

"Javi..." she said his name again, reaching for his hand to try and stir any response out of him. Her eyes flooded with unshed tears and she was seconds from losing it until she saw his first teardrop.

Javi was crying.

She had never seen him cry ever. She lost the battle with her emotions and couldn't keep back her tears. "Please tell me you're happy. Or mad. Or...something!" she demanded.

The shrillness of her voice snapped Javi out of whatever trance he had been in and back toward Lola. His eyes were red rimmed, but she let out a breath of relief when a smile began to form.

"Preciosa, you're pregnant?" he asked again, still in a state of disbelief. He turned toward Camilia. "And you knew?"

"Yup, and I kept it secret. I told you I can keep secrets," she said proudly.

"I'm twelve weeks today. Still early on, but the doctor said the baby is healthy and that—" But she didn't get to finish. Javi was out of his chair and pulling Lola out of hers too, kissing the words out of her.

Her body sagged in relief against his. Javi cradled her face between his hands as he pulled back to look at her—all of her, stopping at her belly. "Lola, you've just made me the happiest man in the world."

"Really?" She was on the verge of becoming a puddle of tears but was trying desperately to keep herself together for just a moment longer.

"Really. You have given me the best gift I could have asked for."

"I...I guess you can finally add on to the house like...like you've been trying to...do," she said in between sobs.

Javi laughed, leaning down to kiss her tears away. From the corner of her eye, she saw Camilia move closer and wrap her small arms around Lola. "No crying, Mamá Lola. Not good for the baby," she muttered, causing an unexpected laugh to burst through her.

"Exactly, mi amor, no crying allowed." Javi wiped his own eyes dry and pulled Camilia closer to them, squishing both Camilia and Lola into a family hug. "My girls, you make me so happy. How did I get so lucky?"

"Remember this feeling when we are waking up at three in the morning to soothe a crying baby and changing messy diapers." Lola laughed.

"I can't wait." The sincerity in Javi's voice made the butterflies return tenfold. The nerves from earlier disappeared. They would come back once she was closer to giving birth and things wouldn't always be easy.

But she learned long ago that sometimes doing the hard things produced the best outcomes. And she wouldn't be doing this alone and neither would Javi this time. They would have each other and Camilia.

It was all she would ever need.

The End

Stay Tuned...

Marisol Roberts deserves her redemption arc and a happily ever after. Coming soon...

To stay up to date with Anastasia, make sure to subscribe to her newsletter here.

Also by Anastasia Dean

<u>**A New Beginnings Romance**</u>

On and Off the Field

Fixed Up Ever After

Marisol's story - Coming soon

About the Author

Anastasia Dean is a pen name for Tati B. Alvarez. She lives in Austin, Texas, where she spends most days lost in her own head, creating stories. When she is not writing, you can find her vacationing at Disney World.

www.ingramcontent.com/pod-product-compliance
Lightning Source LLC
Chambersburg PA
CBHW030110310726
48970CB00004B/1220